WATCHSTAR
Pamela Sargent

POCKET BOOKS   NEW YORK

Another *Original* publication of POCKET BOOKS

 POCKET BOOKS, a Simon & Schuster division of
GULF & WESTERN CORPORATION
1230 Avenue of the Americas, New York, N.Y. 10020

Printed in the U.S.A.

To Pat LoBrutto

1

The comet was a bright slash against the black sky, an omen
scratched by God on the dark dome. Daiya AnraBrun looked up
at the intruder, craning her neck, wondering what it meant. No one
in the village seemed to know; even the Merging Selves were not
sure. The comet dominated the sky, brighter than the tiny twinkling
fires of heaven, almost as bright as Luna's Shield. Daiya thought of
her approaching ordeal. The comet had appeared just as she had
begun to prepare for it.

Another fire, closer to her, flickered in the darkness near the
foothills of the mountains. She walked toward it, lowering her eyes.
The night air had grown cool. She concentrated on that, forgetting
the comet, adjusting her perceptions until she felt warm again.

Mausi LinaPili sat next to the fire, stretching her slender arms toward it. Her blond hair glistened as the flames danced. Daiya
approached and sat down, folding her short stocky legs.

Mausi smiled and made the fire flare. The wood crackled. She
moved her blond head, pointing toward the distant village with her
chin. Daiya heard the murmur of her friend's thoughts.

—My mother is in labor now—

—Is she all right—Daiya asked. She felt the answer almost as she
thought the question.

—Yes, it will be over by morning, my father is with her now—

Daiya had expected the answer. Having children was easy, which
was why, she supposed, they had so many. A more disturbing
thought nudged her.

She quickly closed her mind to Mausi, not wanting to disturb her friend. The village needed many children to make up for the few who were born defective, and the many who did not survive the ordeal. Daiya's own parents, Anra LeitoMorgen and Brun RillaCerwen, were expecting their fourth. She was sure that they would have at least one more after that, though perhaps they would not if Daiya lived through her ordeal.

Daiya remembered the birth of her sister, Silla, almost seven cycles ago. Daiya had been seven at the time; her brother Rin had been nine. They had sat with their mother, helping her block the pain with a web of pleasant thoughts, though Anra could have done that by herself. But she had wanted them with her. They had rubbed Anra's shoulders while she squatted, her naked body beaded with sweat. They had watched as Brun placed the newborn child on Anra's chest after bathing the infant in warm water. Anra and Brun had searched the baby's mind; she had been whole and healthy. Daiya and Rin had smiled at each other, congratulating themselves, before Brun finally sent them to bed.

Rin was dead, part of the Merged One, Daiya supposed, his soul with God. He had died two cycles ago during his ordeal. He had been stronger than she was, afraid of nothing, his mind clear and brave as he left the village with the others for the desert. She could still see him tossing his head arrogantly, his black hair swaying around his shoulders; she had been sure he would come back. How could she live through something Rin had not survived?

A small creature was near her. She felt its presence and turned. Mausi had already noticed the rabbit. The animal watched them, its ears up, its eyes gleaming in the reflected firelight. Mausi held it with her mind, soothing it. The rabbit drooped drowsily.—Thank you, little brother—the girl thought ceremonially.—We are grateful—

Mausi skinned the rabbit quickly while Daiya prepared the spit, placing two forked sticks on opposite sides of the fire, then stripping the bark off a piece of green wood. While the rabbit cooked, Mausi cleaned her knife, then tucked it in her belt with the piece of rabbit fur.

The rabbit sizzled, turning golden. Smelling it, Daiya realized how hungry she was. She had not eaten for two days, trying to toughen herself before it was time to go into the desert. She concentrated on the fire, pressing its heat around the rabbit so that it would cook more quickly.

—Lucky for us—Mausi was thinking.—If it hadn't come so close to us, I would have gone looking for food, I was starting to get weak, even catching the rabbit was hard—

Daiya found herself wondering how long they would have to go without food during their passage.

—I don't know—Mausi replied.—We probably won't have time to worry about it—The blond girl peered up at the sky.—What do you think it means—

Daiya looked up at the comet, shrugging.

—It must be a sign—Mausi went on.—I wish I knew whether it was good or bad. I keep thinking of the stories the Merging Ones sometimes tell, the ones about other beings who live in the sky, do you think it might be a sign from them—

—Just an old legend—Daiya responded.—Only the stars live there, and we cannot grasp their thoughts. If there are others, they've never shown themselves, or touched us with their minds. I do not think people can live in the sky—She gazed up at the darkness, at the tiny fires twinkling as they sought to join their minds to one another, trapped in loneliness. A few stars roamed the sky, changing position from time to time; those did not twinkle. They were the wanderers, and once in a great while their minds would bring them together for a time. One day, at the end of the world, when the Merged One sought to join all life, all the stars would move, drawing closer together, to burn in one great final fire. So the Merging Selves of the village taught.

She did not know what the comet meant. Older people had seen comets before, but even they were not sure about what they signified. Some called comets the fingers of God; others said they were solitary minds cast out of heaven.

The rabbit was done. Daiya cut it up with her knife.—Peloren's worried about our ordeal—Mausi thought.—What a turmoil her mind is in, I don't like to be near her—

Daiya watched her friend, knowing Mausi was just as frightened, though she would not admit it. She suddenly felt protective toward the other girl. Mausi smiled, sensing Daiya's feelings, and shook her head, as if telling her not to worry.

They ate quickly, gnawing the meat off the bones. Mausi wiped her hands on her tunic, then lay down, curling her trousered legs, resting her head on her hands.—Good night, Daiya—

There was a mental barrier around Mausi's mind now, blocking any thoughts from reaching Daiya and protecting her from being disturbed by her dreams. Daiya withdrew into herself, surprised once again at how easy it was to do so. She withdrew a lot lately. Maybe there was something wrong with her. She did not even like to share many thoughts with her parents anymore.

She wrapped her arms around her legs, resting her chin on the rough fabric covering her knees. Suddenly she wished she were younger again, as young as her sister Silla, or else that she were old and past her ordeal. She wondered if she was really ready for the passage. Anra and Brun said she was; she was becoming a woman, and fourteen was the usual age, though some people were ready at twelve and others, the boys usually, when they were fifteen or even sixteen.

Anra had looked at her one day and thought:—You're ready, Daiya—That had been the day Daiya, in a fit of rage at Silla, had made the pot fly up to the rafters, forgetting all the training she had in controlling herself. She had picked up Silla too, holding her suspended in the air upside down while the younger girl screamed, then spinning her around while Silla, trying to defend herself, made a chair zip across the floor, almost hitting Daiya. She had put Silla down gently after that, and had run from the hut in tears, certain she was going mad.

She had learned to control her monthly bleeding very quickly and would soon have control over ovulation, as the older women did, so they could choose when to become pregnant. She was even getting used to her breasts, those fleshy protuberances that often ached and seemed to get in her way; she frequently wished for a skinny, flat frame like Mausi's. But her feelings were like a flooding river out of control, threatening to overrun its banks. She would feel them welling up inside her, ready to rush forth. She would open her mouth and babble in words instead of thoughts, her training deserting her when she needed it most. At other times, she would build her mental wall and retreat behind it, shocking herself with her desire to be alone.

The fire flickered. Sparks danced on the stones around it. She sniffed at the smoky smell of the charred embers. She picked up one of the large pieces of wood next to Mausi, floated it over the sleeping girl's body, then lowered it carefully into the flames.

Alone. She shuddered at the thought. People were once alone; so went the legends. Sometimes a child would say or think the word to shock his parents, or call a playmate a solitary, a sure way to get someone mad. But she was never really alone, not even out here with Mausi sleeping and the village far away. She could close her mind and no one would intrude, but the Net was always there, the web of the village's minds, a dimly felt presence just below her consciousness. It bound them all together; as she grew older, it would become stronger, until she became a Merging Self like the older people whose children were grown. She might even in time become strong enough to have a tenuous mental bond with another village, as some of the Merging Selves did. That was what she was supposed to want. She wondered if she did.

She lay down and closed her eyes, trying to will herself to sleep. It was easier to sleep out here, away from the almost nightly disturbances of Silla, who hadn't quite learned how to keep her dreams from waking up everyone in the hut. She twisted a bit on the ground, trying to get comfortable. She worried too much, that was her problem. She had to stop it. She had to concern herself only with getting strong enough for her ordeal. She would have to be able to rest under worse conditions than these.

She built her mental wall quickly, leaving only a small space to alert her to any danger. She calmed her body. She did not really need the fire to keep her warm, but it comforted her and kept animals away. She slowed her breathing, and at last fell asleep.

Daiya, still stretched out on the ground, felt her friend stir. She and Mausi were covered by the shadow of the nearby hill. The sky was just beginning to grow light, the sun still hidden behind the mountains. The other girl got to her feet quickly and began to scatter the embers with her mind, making sure the fire was out. Mounds of dirt floated over the blackened crumbling sticks, then fell, until the area was safely covered.

Mausi gazed solemnly at Daiya with sad blue eyes. Daiya caught her thoughts immediately. Mausi's mother was calling her, she had to return to the village right away, the child had been born. Mausi's thoughts stopped abruptly. Daiya could read no more. But she had already caught a glimpse of shame, swallowed quickly by black despair.

She put an arm around Mausi's shoulders.—You can stay—Mausi murmured.—You don't have to come with me—Daiya, sensing that her friend wanted company, shook her head.

They set out for the village. Mausi moved swiftly, her long legs covering the distance in great strides. Daiya hurried after her, trying to keep up. She reached out tentatively, trying to touch Mausi's mind and comfort her, but the girl was hidden behind her wall.

Suddenly Mausi rose in the air, lifting herself, apparently wanting to cover the distance as quickly as she could. Daiya soared, following her. She struggled to hold herself aloft. Flying was always difficult, and she had little strength left after the deprivations of the past days. They flew over the grassy plains, startling a flock of red-winged birds, narrowly missing two tall trees. Daiya dipped closer to the ground, almost exhausted. Mausi, her energy flagging, hurtled on, a hand shielding her eyes, her body fueled by worry and sorrow.

At last they passed over a few sheep and Mausi alighted, her energy gone. They were near the village. Daiya landed and followed her friend, feeling drained. Her legs wobbled as she walked. Mausi stopped; the two girls leaned silently against each other, trying to recover. Ahead, Daiya saw the fields, and their ripening crops.

The village had been built on one side of a wide river. Sturdy huts made of mud bricks with thatched roofs had been laid out in concentric circles around an open space where everyone could gather. Most of the huts were shaded by trees. The village's fields were outside the town, irrigated by ditches running from the river. Small herds of cattle and sheep clustered together on the plains beyond.

As they approached the village, Daiya saw a small group making its way through one of the wheat fields, stopping just outside it. Their heads were bent. She recognized the blond head of Mausi's mother Lina, the auburn hair of her father Pili, and her two redheaded brothers. Mausi began to walk toward the group. Daiya hurried after her, then realized Mausi did not want her to follow.

She stood still, watching Mausi's parents dig the grave. The hole grew bigger in the earth as dirt settled near their feet. She knew what had happened, she had seen it before. Mausi's parents had given birth to a solitary, a child whose mind would never be able to lift the earth as they were doing now, who would never be able to read the thoughts of others, or be part of the Net. There was no place for such children. When a parent looked into the mind of a child born with this deformity, there was nothing to do but to put it out of its misery quickly.

Daiya found herself trembling. An unthinkable notion seized her; why was there no place for these children? Why couldn't they be raised and sent to a place of their own? Why were they condemned to death, and eternal separateness? But she knew the answers; she had heard them often enough. If they lived, they would become the victims of those with normal minds. They would be outside society, separated from the Net. They would threaten the world with their separateness and eventually they would have to be killed anyway. It had happened in the past. Individuals had warred with themselves and with the world, separated mentally from one another, separated from the world by machines, apart from God and nature. She hugged herself with her arms, trying to suppress her feelings for the solitary ones, reminding herself that they were only like the animals, not beings with souls. It was good that so few of them were born.

She went toward the village. It was a large community of almost two thousand people, big enough for a strong Net. She walked through the fields alongside a ditch, passing cornstalks and then cabbages. She came to a dirt path and wound her way among the huts, past chicken coops, courtyards, vegetable gardens, and wallows where pigs rooted noisily, toward her own home.

2

Silla was playing in front of Daiya's home. Two cloth dolls, the puppets of Silla's mind, danced in front of the child. One doll extended a leg and whirled on one foot while the other collapsed, its limbs contorted. Silla frowned, brushing back a lock of black hair, then looked up at Daiya. She got up and ran toward her, reaching out with her chubby arms while the second doll crumpled behind her.

Thoughts burbled from the small girl's mind, reaching Daiya in bits and pieces. She saw little children playing an elaborate game with pieces of rock, the face of her grandfather Cerwen, a corn cake, her parents walking toward the fields.—Speak—Daiya thought firmly.—I can't understand you—

Silla opened her mouth. Daiya heard her words and read her thoughts. "Cerwen's here," Silla said. "He's inside." She turned to race away and Daiya caught her. "Let go, I have to see Jooni, she made up a new game."

"Listen to me," Daiya said, holding the child by the arm. "You have to stop babbling, you're getting too old for that. You have to concentrate, you act as if you've had no training at all, I can hardly understand you sometimes."

"Let *go*." Silla pulled her arm loose.

"If you don't learn," Daiya said, her voice rising, "you'll die, like Rin."

Silla squealed. She tried to kick Daiya. Daiya, grasping the thought, dodged her sister's foot. She wanted to slap the girl. She compressed some air, sending it toward the child, then stopped it, leaving her sister untouched. Silla hurried away, running toward the public space in the center of the village. It was only a few huts away; Daiya could feel the gathering of minds there. The public space was already filled with Merging Selves in communion, teachers of mindcrafts, and raucous children.

Daiya swallowed, then took a breath. She had to control the urge to strike out; she had spent years restraining herself. Anra had warned her that lack of control could kill her during her ordeal. She sighed and went inside.

Her mat, and Silla's, were rolled up against the wall near the tiny room where their parents slept at night. Sometimes, when her mother and father were making love, Daiya would catch pleasant wisps of thought drifting out from behind their mental barriers; the wisps would entwine and melt together over her and Silla.

Her parents and her grandfather were sitting at the square wood table in the center of the room. Anra LeitoMorgen was tall and slender; her black hair was pulled back from her pale, fine-featured face. Her hands were folded over the belly that bulged underneath her brown tunic. Her long trousered legs, parallel to the table, were propped up on another wood chair.

Brun RillaCerwen had his elbows on the table. His chin rested on his stubby hands. He was a stocky, big-boned, brown-skinned man not quite as tall as Anra. Daiya looked like him, and so did Silla; only Rin had resembled their mother. Cerwen IviaRey was next to his son Brun; he smiled as Daiya approached the table. An earthen pitcher and a small cup floated toward her; the pitcher poured water into the cup, then settled on the table.

—You're not in the fields—Daiya thought, catching the answer almost immediately.

—Cerwen asked me not to go—Anra replied.—Lina and Pili

were burying a solitary, he thought it might be bad for me to witness
. . . I see you already know about that—
—I was with Mausi, we came back here together—
Anra frowned.—Poor Mausi, and right before her ordeal, too, her
parents will be very concerned—She pulled her feet off the chair in
front of her and rose. Her belly did not seem to belong to her slim
body.

Brun got up also.—We'll go to the fields now—he thought.—Will
you be with us tonight, Daiya, or are you going out to train some
more—

Daiya realized her father was hoping she would not stay. She
caught a glimpse of his doubts before Brun's mind closed. He
doesn't think I'm ready, Daiya thought behind her wall.

—Let the girl stay if she wants—Cerwen thought. The old man's
words rippled in her mind, clear and strong, sweeping away the
wisps of Brun's doubts. Daiya smiled gratefully. Brun patted her
cheek as he and Anra left for the fields.

She sat down. Cerwen sailed a loaf of bread toward her and she
tore off a bit, stuffing it into her mouth. Her grandfather, one of the
Merging Ones, was a big dark-skinned man with thick graying black
hair. His brown eyes narrowed.—You need more training, Daiya—
The words were hard and solid, pressing against her like round
smooth stones.

—I know—Her own thoughts seemed weak and insubstantial.—I
almost lost my temper with Silla again—

—I didn't mean that—the old man replied.—You must harden
your body more. Anra and Brun are right. Rest here tonight and go
out again tomorrow, take only a knife and some water. Travel alone.
Train your body and your mind—

Daiya was irritated. She already knew that.

—I see, you think I'm telling you nothing—Cerwen continued.—
But it's extremely important that you understand it. There were
those whose minds could have withstood the ordeal but whose bodies were too weak, and those who survived it, then died in the desert
while returning. You young people too often think you can compen-
sate mentally for any bodily weakness, and often you can, but not
indefinitely. Why do you think we insist on doing some physical
labor when we could use our powers almost as easily? It is because,
without strong bodies, our minds would also weaken in time. Mind
and body are not things apart, they are intertwined, at least until the
Merged One calls us, gathering the mind to Itself as the body fails—

Daiya frowned as she tore off another hunk of bread. The crust crunched against her teeth as she chewed.

—Again you think you know all this, Daiya—The thoughts were sharp, pricking her, stabbing her with sharp pointed edges.—But if you knew it, I wouldn't have to tell it to you again—

She glared at him.—Why don't you tell us what we'll face—she asked.—You could prepare us for it—

—But we already have. It is your character that will be tested, your ability to become a Merging One. Let me point out one thing. You can master every trick, you can be the strongest young person here, and still not survive if your character is defective. You had better remember that, child. Who will live and who will die was decided a long time ago. It is the kind of person you have become that will matter—Cerwen drew his heavy brows together.—I worry about you. You sometimes hold too many thoughts behind your wall, keeping them to yourself. You have even doubted the Merged One—

Daiya tensed. The bread in her mouth tasted stale. She threw up her wall quickly, blocking her grandfather's probing. She had doubted the Merged One, and tried to rid herself of the blasphemous notion. It had started as idle musing; why did the Merged One never reveal Itself to them? Why, if the body and mind were intertwined and not separate, did the mind not die with the body? Why, if separateness was an evil, did God remain separate from men and women instead of making them part of a universal Net right from the start? Why did the Merged One allow solitaries to be born, condemning them to death and eternal separation from all existence?

She had not asked these questions as a child. Later, like many of the others, she had asked them of her teachers and received answers, but the questions kept returning. All the answers seemed only to be one answer: the Merged One had ways not easily expressed. Too much curiosity was an evil and could, she knew, lead to isolation. Once she had asked Mausi if she still had doubts, and her friend had kept her barrier up for days.

—Prepare yourself, Daiya—Cerwen thought.—Remember that even though you cannot sense it, the Merged One is always with you, our entire world is part of God. Go out tomorrow and strengthen yourself—His body blurred, then disappeared, though she still felt his presence. It was a familiar trick, but one that only the Merging Ones could do easily. She sensed his movement across the room to the doorway. Then he was gone.

Her doubts returned. She could tell when a Merging Self was near, even when one made himself invisible by intercepting the vision of the viewer. She felt it. But the Merged One remained apart. She buried her head in her arms, pressing her cheek against the table top. She could not force belief; it was there or it was absent. She had to pray for it to a God who might not exist. She wondered if it could ever be regained, or if she was condemned.

Daiya was ready to leave in the morning. Brun kissed her and started to give her a piece of bread and some fruit to take with her. She shook her head; he nodded and put the food away.

—Goodbye, Brun—she thought. She turned toward her mother, who was sitting at the table with Silla finishing breakfast.—Goodbye, Anra—She stared at her mother's abdomen, suddenly realizing that she might not be alive when the child was born.

Anra, reacting to Daiya's thoughts, shook her head and smiled reassuringly, but Daiya picked up her fear. Silla stuck out her tongue and said, "Bleaaaah." Daiya made a face at her and then went outside.

The sky was clear, the sun bright. The odors of corn cakes, ground wheat, and baking chickens mingled with the scents of flowers, the stink of latrines, and the smell of dirt and dust. She passed a hut where vines crawled over the walls as the minds of the residents tried to form a pleasing pattern; the green leaves fluttered as the vines twisted around one another, forming living ropes.

She turned toward the riverbank, deciding to follow the river out of the village. It was a roundabout route, but she would not have to go through the fields, where people would be gathering after the morning meal. She was trying to keep to herself again, she thought. She shook off the self-accusation; Cerwen had told her to travel alone. She was beginning to understand why. Perhaps, he must be hoping, if she knew or felt how truly fearful loneliness was, even when one was still bound to others by the Net, she would be more prepared for the ordeal, more willing and determined to survive and take her place in the community.

At the riverbank on the edge of the village, a few young people had already gathered. Some were swimming; others sat at the water's edge sculpting the liquid into the shapes of birds and animals, holding the sculptures with their minds. Daiya watched them, envious. They had been through their ordeals and had survived. They lived in their own huts now and would soon be raising children. Nenla Bari-

Wil was with the group; she was Daiya's age but had matured earlier. Once Daiya had sat with Nenla and Cina RiisHomm as a teacher trained them in making their words and ideas clear thoughts. They had all studied thought projection together, had made up mindsongs while burying compost in the fallow fields. Nenla was alive. Cina was dead.

Nenla shook back her long red hair and waved; Daiya waved back. Nenla shaped a bird out of water and flew it toward her. It dissolved, sprinkling her with droplets. A boy and a girl lifted themselves from shore, flying over the water, soaring and dipping. They dove under the surface and emerged; they turned on their backs and floated indolently.

Daiya turned from the carefree scene and continued along the bank. She came to an irrigation ditch and floated over it, extending her arms and pointing her toes. She touched down on the other side and paused, taking a deep breath after the effort. She climbed up through reeds and shrubs and stopped by a willow tree, sensing other presences.

Ahead of her, two boys were walking, one tall and auburn-haired, the other small and thin. She recognized Harel KaniDekel and Oren KiaEde. She caught her breath, remembering the first time she had let Harel see her thoughts about him.

She hurried after them, wending her way through a patch of yellow wildflowers called goldstems. As she approached the boys, they walked more slowly, waiting for her to catch up. She came up to Harel and he smiled, showing his even white teeth. He draped one muscular arm over her shoulders, she put an arm around his waist, and they walked together, letting their thoughts mingle. She felt the rough woven fabric of his pale blue shirt against her palm, and smiled. Oren put up his barrier and slowed to walk behind them.

At last Harel withdrew his mind a bit. His wavy auburn hair swayed around his face as they walked.—I wanted to stay with you tonight—he thought.—But my grandmother told me I should go out by myself this time—

—My grandfather told me the same thing—she replied.

Oren caught up with them again, dropping his wall; he had been thinking of Mausi. He had pulled his brown hair back on his neck, making his thin face seem even more pointed.—Everyone was told that—the smaller boy thought.—I keep wondering why, we'll be together when we go to the desert, and no one likes being apart—

Apprehension settled over all of them, darkening the sunny sky, fading the green of the trees and plants around them. Then Harel's mind cut through the mist, giving them a glimpse of the future: the ordeal was past, all of them stood in the center of the village, alive and healthy. The vision rippled; Daiya was standing with Harel in front of a hut.

She peered up at him, startled. The images faded. Oren was grinning at them.

Daiya had already known how Harel felt; they had discussed it before without committing themselves. But showing her his wishes in front of Oren made it more public. Harel stopped and turned to face her.

—Oren already knows what I think—he thought.—I told him I was going to ask you as soon as I could, I don't want to wait until after the ordeal's over. Will you live with me then, Daiya—

She smiled and clutched his hand.—You know I will, Harel, you didn't have to ask after all the times we've shared our thoughts—

—I wanted to anyway, and Oren's my best friend, I couldn't keep it from him. I kept thinking, if we promise to partner now, maybe the pledge will give us strength during the ordeal—

She assented silently. They stood together, leaning against each other while Oren shifted his weight from one foot to the other, bobbing up and down. Then they drew away from each other. Harel wanted to know which way she would travel.

Daiya waved an arm, pointing southeast. She would follow the foothills in that direction as far as she could and camp near the mountains that night.—You're going northwest, aren't you—

Harel nodded. When they were both younger, they had gone northwest to see the wild horses. They had crept up on two horses near the edge of the herd, holding the minds of the animals while trying to slip on their backs. Daiya had been thrown. Harel had managed to stay on for a time, clinging to the horse's mane, his hair flying as it galloped, until his control slipped and he landed on the ground with a loud grunt.

Harel shook his head at the image.—Not this time—he thought. His mind rippled, amused as he remembered his sore rump. He was to travel with Oren part of the way; then the two would split up.

He held up a hand and they parted. She watched as the boys wandered off together. Her mind brushed Harel's briefly, then withdrew. Harel was confident now, his anxiety gone. She would be with him when the ordeal was over, so he had to survive.

She turned and began to move toward the grassy plains that led to the foothills. She thought of Harel. With him, she could almost forget her doubts, the feelings that threatened to make her separate. She had shared those doubts with him, asking him the same questions that had made her friend Mausi throw up her wall. Harel had not retreated. His mind, clear and steady, had taken her doubts and made them a fine mist like a fog, dispersing them with warmth and light.

When she saw things through his eyes, the questions seemed meaningless abstractions, ideas of no importance. She saw the village, existing as it would until the end of the world, pieces of God's mind replacing those that had rejoined the Merged One. Harel had no doubts and rarely put up his barrier. He lived in the world, accepting it, sure of its rightness, looking forward to the day when he would be a Merging One. He seemed older than fourteen, almost a man. Her doubts could not affect him; they were like bad weather, and they would pass. That was probably one of the reasons she loved him. She wished she were more like him.

She emptied her mind of thoughts. A warm breeze ruffled her hair. The grass of the plains rippled, becoming dappled waves of green and yellow. She walked quickly in the direction of the foothills.

The evening sky glowed red; the sun was an orange disk on the horizon. Daiya was thousands of paces from the village, as far away from it as she had ever been. She had gone southeast, keeping the foothills to her left. She had jogged part of the distance, occasionally floating over obstacles along the way. Her mind was drained and her feet ached.

The Net still bound her to the village, one barely perceptible strand lying gently against her mind. She stood still for a moment and opened her senses. A part of her seemed to float overhead as she surveyed the area. The region was unfamiliar. She saw a creek between two hills; she could camp near it for the night. She drew her mind inside herself and began to climb the small hill in front of her. She stumbled over a rock and wished she had enough strength left to float over the hill. The shrubs leaned away from her as she passed.

She reached the top and paused. The creek was in a hollow below. She scrambled down toward it, clutching tree limbs and releasing them as she went. As she came nearer, she heard the creek gurgle as it flowed over rocks, cutting through the earth.

She knelt on a flat rock at the edge of the brook, splashing her face with the cold water. She cupped her hands and drank. Then she folded her legs and sat down, back straight, hands on her thighs.

Again her doubts and questions returned, after being held off all day by her concentration on the landscape. This time they were practical questions, shared by others, even by Harel. Why did so many die during their passage in the desert? The Net would be with them, after all; why couldn't they summon aid? Or wasn't the village allowed to help? Daiya could not imagine a parent willingly neglecting to answer an anguished mental plea from a child. She had asked her friend Nenla about all this, but Nenla had given her no answer, telling her only that she would find out when she faced her own ordeal.

Daiya rose. Lengthening shadows cast by the trees alongside the creek covered the ground. The sky was growing darker. She shivered. She warmed the air around herself while clearing a space for a fire, making a hollow in the ground, then surrounding it with small rocks. As she moved away to look for firewood, a distant shriek made her look up at the purple sky.

Something was coming over the black mountains, something she had never seen before. It fell from the sky, a blurred solid object, glowing faintly. It hovered for a moment over the hills to the southeast, then disappeared among them.

Daiya stood still, fists clenched, trying to understand what it could be. The Merging Ones sometimes told stories about large stones which had fallen from the sky long ago. But this thing could not be a stone. Stones did not hover before falling to the ground. She waited, expecting to sense a shock wave after the thing hit. She felt nothing.

She thought of pulling the Net, alerting the village, summoning adults to aid her in an investigation. She rejected the notion. She was older now; Cerwen would be disappointed in her if she asked for help to explore something which might be unimportant. He had, after all, told her to come out alone. She would find out what it was by herself; she could always call someone later if necessary.

She steadied her mind, not wanting to disturb the Net with her thoughts, and began to walk in the direction of the fallen object.

3

Daiya crept over the side of a hill, sensing something ahead. She was far from the creek now, and sure she did not have the strength to return; she would have to spend the night somewhere else. Her mouth was dry. She reached for the water sack she had carried with her from the village and drank. Her mouth still felt dry. She was beginning to wish she had paid no attention to the falling object. She took a deep breath, summoning all her energy, then sent her mind ahead, keeping her senses alert in case her body was threatened and she had to depart quickly.

She probed the area below, sensing a thing without life, a thing as inanimate as the stones pressing against her feet. She probed around it, then stiffened in terror. A mind was there, without walls, and completely unlike those in the village. Incomprehensible ideas raced across it, glistening like the colored stones of Anra's necklace and Brun's belt, hard and solid. She could not grasp them. Her mind pulled away, fleeing back to her.

Daiya waited, crouching near a bush. Her toes curled inside her moccasins. She had touched the mind; it must have sensed her. She waited for it to reach out to her, but it did not. Tentatively, she sent out part of her mind once more. She caught flashes of brightness, and below them, trapped in a turbulent mass of gray and black clouds, a pulsing light, a tiny speck inside the mind but not of it. She brushed against the thoughts and again received no response.

She withdrew and sat down quietly, trying to understand. Afraid of disturbing the Net, she tightened her wall. Either the mind was choosing to ignore her or it had not sensed her at all, and that was not possible unless it was a solitary, a separate self. And that was impossible.

Daiya trembled. She stood up slowly, ready to creep away. Her feet slid against the stones, loosening them. She fell, sliding down the hill toward the strange being below. She threw out her mind and stopped herself, holding her body still until she found a branch. She clung to it. Something below was moving; she realized she had disturbed it. She stood up straight and slipped again, sending a shower of dirt and small pebbles down the hillside toward the being. She thrust out her hands and seized another branch. She waited, too tired to do anything else. She could now see the clearing below.

A vehicle was there, large enough to hold several people. She assumed it was a means of transport; she could not imagine what other purpose it might have. Unlike the wagons the villagers sometimes used to bring in produce from the fields, it had runners, long flat pieces of metal which curved at the ends, instead of wheels, and there were no tame horses to pull it. Inside the vehicle, a light shone, illuminating part of the area around it. Something moved near the craft. She had the feeling that it could see her in spite of the darkness. The thing moved closer to the light. Daiya cleared her mind and gazed at it with her eyes.

At first she thought she saw a human face looking up at her, its dark eyes wide; she sensed a ripple of curiosity and fear. Her mind reached toward it again. It blurred and changed. She saw a metal cylinder; it stood on two rounded metallic limbs while two other limbs, attached to its torso, waved at her. It was like a machine, yet it had a mind. Something alien had entered her world.

It began to move toward the hill. Terrified, Daiya lifted herself from the ground with all her strength. She soared swiftly over the hill, back in the direction from which she had come. She dipped toward a cluster of trees, knowing she would have to land before her strength gave out. She circled one tree and alighted on a thick branch. Too tired to build a fire, and afraid to stay on the ground, she settled herself in the hollow connecting the branch to the trunk and curled up to await morning.

Daiya awoke feeling stronger. She concentrated on her muscles, removing the aches, then looked up at the sky through the leafy limbs overhead. It was already growing light; she had slept a long time.

She sat up and dangled her legs over the branch. She knew what she had to do. She knew she should contact the village and let the Merging Ones explore the meaning of this intruder. Something welled up inside her at the thought, tightening the barrier around her mind. She had seen it first; she had a right to find out what it was and what it was doing here before she informed the others.

She trembled as she realized the implications of her thought. This was no longer a matter of hiding behind a wall with inconsequential youthful notions and doubts. She would be keeping something important from the village, making herself separate in a fundamental sense. She hugged the tree trunk, certain that the horror of the notion would shake the Net, but it did not; her wall was too tight.

She searched frantically for rationalizations. She would have to face the unknown during her ordeal, so she might as well explore this new thing now. It would be good training for her; if she did not survive it, she probably was not ready for her ordeal anyway. Besides, she thought, it's not as if I'm going to keep it from the others forever, it's just for a while.

She drifted toward the ground and landed lightly. She straightened her clothes and took a sip of water. Then she turned and started to walk back toward the intruder.

Daiya stood behind a tree on the hillside, concealing herself as best she could. It was a simple enough trick; she had used it on Silla, pressing herself against the side of a hut, masking herself mentally and physically so her sister could barely see her. The trick worked with younger children who were not as skilled in mental disciplines, but she did not know if it would work with this strange being below her.

The clearing was barren and dusty, unlike the dell where she had planned to sleep the night before until terror had driven her to a tree. A few thorny bushes grew at the bottom of the hill; the land below was strewn with stones and flat gray rocks. A few patches of green weeds were managing to survive, along with some of the bright red wildflowers called earthflames because they looked like fires from a distance.

The creature stood near its vehicle, moving its limbs over the shiny surface. Cautiously, Daiya reached out, trying to grasp its surface thoughts. She caught diagrams, pictures, symbols, concepts she could not comprehend. She concentrated on its feelings, trying to ignore the alien thoughts. She realized it, too, was frightened and worried.

She withdrew her mind and considered what to do next. She could try to communicate with it, but how? Its mind was that of a solitary. It could not read her thoughts nor even sense the presence of her mind. That meant it had to rely only on sight and sound and other senses. Perhaps it had a voice and could speak, though she was not

sure how she would understand it even if it did. She would have to
wall up her mind and approach it only through its body, its physical
senses.

Daiya built her wall, closing her eyes and ears as she did so. She
opened her eyes.

The cylinder was gone. She saw only a boy, a human being like
herself. At least she thought he was a boy. He had thickset shoulders
under his tight silver garb, a flat chest, narrow hips, and a bulge at
his crotch; he looked too young to be a man. He moved away from
the vehicle and circled it on legs, not cylindrical limbs, turning his
head as he gazed around the area.

But her mind had sensed a machine, something mechanical.
Shocked and confused, she let her control slip. He looked toward
her and she knew he had seen her. His mouth opened; it was a black
gap in his light brown face. He drew back his lips, showing his teeth.
Sounds reached her ears. He was speaking, but she could not understand his words.

He held out his hands, palms up.

She waited. He stood perfectly still, then let this hands drop. He
said other words, more guttural than the ones he had spoken before,
but she still did not understand. He motioned with one arm, as if
drawing her to him.

Daiya reached out with a mental feeler and skimmed his mind
again quickly. The figure below blurred again, flesh becoming metal;
the eyes glittered and shone. She sensed curiosity and some apprehension. She withdrew, realizing he would not hurt her.

She sat on her heels, showing the palms of her hands to him. He
was still and silent. She had peered into his mind enough to realize
he did not have mental powers, which meant he was incapable of
fooling her with an illusion, showing her eyes the shape of a boy
when in fact he was something else. Then why did her eyes sense
one thing and her mind another?

He lifted a hand and spoke again in a more musical way. The syllables seemed to rise and fall and for a moment she felt she could
grasp a word here and there. Then he stopped. She still had not understood a thing.

She climbed to her feet, and went down the hill slowly, moving
closer to him. She stopped several paces away and waited. He
stepped toward her. She took a step back.

He spoke again, pointing up at the sky with a finger. As he spoke,
she reached out carefully and grasped only his unvoiced surface

thoughts. Then she saw the meaning of the sounds he was making. She saw his face, then his body in the vehicle as the craft moved toward the foothills. He was saying he was from the sky, or from above, or from heaven; she was not sure which. He said another word, and pointed to her; she realized it was a question. He was asking who she was.

She did not answer. Instead, in her own language, she said, "You are from the sky."

He seemed startled. His surface thoughts rushed together, blurred and incoherent, so she concentrated on his feelings. He had recognized some of her words and that had surprised him. Haltingly, he answered her in her language, though the words were so badly accented she could never have grasped them without reading his mind. "I am from above," he said, and then a thought reached her, *ancient language, very old*. She waited for him to say more before realizing that he only recognized the words, had heard her speech before, but did not know more than a few phrases in the language.

He went over to the craft and reached inside. He took out a small object wrapped in a shiny substance. He held it out to her. She caught the thought.

"Food," she said, pointing to it.

"Food," he repeated.

Daiya was hungry. Her stomach gurgled. She suppressed the hunger and shook her head, waving the food away with a hand. She had to remember her training. Anyway, she thought suspiciously, the food could be poisoned or made of dangerous herbs; she had to guard herself.

The boy peeled away the shiny covering and stuffed the food into his mouth, chewing it quickly. Then he pointed at the ground. He thrust out his hands, motioning downward. He seemed to be telling her to sit down.

Daiya sat, folding her legs. He sat down across from her and motioned again, but she could not tell what he meant this time. He closed his eyes.

She watched him. He seemed to be in a trance. For a moment, she thought of touching his mind again, but she did not want to intrude —not that he would notice even if she did. She felt that he did not want to be disturbed. It was almost as if he was communicating with another mind. But that was impossible; he did not have the ability.

Daiya fidgeted, unfolding her legs, then tucking them in again. The boy was being very foolish, trusting that she would not harm him while he sat entranced. She knew what she should do now. She had only to pull the Net, call the Merging Ones, tell them about this strange boy. They could decide what to do. It would be out of her hands, and she would be free to continue with her training.

She got up and walked over to the boy's vehicle. She touched the metal and pulled her hand back quickly; it had been warmed by the sunlight. He said he had traveled in this machine. If he had been from another part of Earth, he would have come here on foot or on horseback. But she had known he was not from another village. The ways of other towns were like those of her own community. Her father's own great-grandparents had come from a village several days' travel to the south; they had been part of a group following an ancient custom which decreed that, every few generations, a number of young people past their ordeal must leave their own home and settle in another, so that human settlements did not grow apart from one another. So the boy had probably been speaking the truth when he said he came from the sky, unbelievable as it seemed. She thought of the comet; it had been a sign after all.

A dark translucent dome covered the top of the boy's craft. Daiya touched it gently. Unlike the metal of the machine's body, it was cool. Puzzled, she peered at it. The night before, when she had first seen the craft, the dome had been transparent, not dark.

She retreated from the vehicle and stood over the boy. His eyes were still closed. She knew she had to call the village.

Something seemed to grip her mind. Her muscles tensed; she felt the skin of her face tighten. Something inside her was keeping the wall in front of the Net. She did not want to call the village. She had found the boy, she had a right to find out more before telling anyone about him. She had seen him first. She shook; her skin prickled. She was keeping something from the others, she had a secret, she was acting like a solitary. She tried to push the thought away. It isn't like that, she told herself. She only wanted to find out more about him first, discover whether or not he had weapons or might be dangerous. She was protecting the village. She would tell them later.

She looked down at the boy. His blue-black hair was straight and thick. His light brown skin glistened. There must be others like him, she thought. She tried to imagine it, a group of separate minds like his; how could they possibly live together, able to speak to one another only with words? How could they feel love? How could the Merged One allow such beings to survive? She remembered her own doubts about God and shuddered. Perhaps the boy was a sign to her that the Merged One did not exist. Perhaps there was another Great Force in the world, one who sought to separate what God tried to unite, and this boy was one of its worshippers.

Thinking such things was blasphemous. The air was cold around her. She hugged herself with her arms, feeling as though she was trapped in a dark abyss. If this boy's presence brought on such thoughts, he was dangerous, as dangerous to the village as the solitaries, perhaps even more dangerous. Her hand was on her knife. Separate selves could not be allowed to live.

The boy suddenly opened his eyes, looking around quickly before he saw her. She sat down again, gazing into his dark brown eyes, noticing tiny folds over the inner corners of his eyelids which made his eyes look almond-shaped; only a few villagers had eyes like that. She prayed silently, wishing God would answer her.

The corners of the boy's mouth turned up; he was smiling. He wrinkled his nose, as if smelling something rank. Daiya rested her hands on her knees. Surely the Merged One would not condemn her for trying to reach out to a separate self before acting. Clinging to this shred of belief, she forced herself to smile.

"Reiho," the boy said, pointing to his chest. "My name is Reiho." She scanned his surface thoughts as he spoke. His accent was still strange, and he garbled some of the sounds, but his words were clearer.

"Daiya," she answered. "My name is Daiya."

"Accident," the boy said, gesturing at his craft. "Have to repair." He pulled at the silvery garment he wore; it was as tight as skin against his body. It separated, showing part of his hairless chest. "You speak old language, old speech," he went on. "Implant give me some words, I learn more later with hypnotraining when asleep."

She shook her head, not knowing what he was talking about. Even scanning his mind could not help her interpret those words. He pointed to his forehead. "Implant," he said again. "Inside. You have no implant?"

Daiya shrugged. Since she did not know what he meant, she assumed she did not. She got to her feet. She needed time by herself, time to figure things out.

"You go?" he asked. "Find others?"

She felt his apprehension. "No," she responded. "I'm by myself. I have to go now, I'll come back later."

"More slowly," he said, wrinkling his thick eyebrows.

"I have to go now," she said carefully, motioning with her hands.

"I will come back later." She felt irritated with him as she spoke, wishing they could mindspeak instead of using this cumbersome method.

He held out a hand, obviously wanting her to stay. She drew back, then lifted herself off the ground so that she would not have to wade through the bushes at the bottom of the hill. As she landed on the hillside, she saw his mouth drop open. Good, she thought, wanting him to be a bit afraid of her; it might protect her.

She carefully approached the place where the boy was. She peered cautiously around a tree, almost expecting to see others of his kind in the clearing below.

He was still alone. Now that it was night, the top of his vehicle was transparent again. A light bathed the inside of the craft. The boy sat in one of the doorways, his feet on the ground. He held a thin flat rectangular object on his lap and was bent over it, peering at it as he bit into the bar of food he held in his right hand. She frowned, wondering at his strangeness.

She came down the hill slowly. She had still not called the village. She had put the boy out of her mind while she practiced physical and mental exercises, forcing herself to prepare for her ordeal. She was beginning to realize that the longer she waited with her secret, the harder it was going to be to tell it when the time came to do so; she would have to explain why she waited. That, she thought, must be why isolation was so dangerous, so feared.

Reiho looked at her as she picked her way through the bushes. She touched his surface thoughts; he too was glad she was alone. Again she saw him as cylindrical and machinelike, until she withdrew and saw him only with her eyes. "Hello," he said.

"Hello," she answered, accenting the word properly. She sat down in front of him, searching for something else to say. She pointed at the flat rectangle. "What is that?" The surface of the rectangle gleamed, lighting the boy's face with a yellowish glow.

He said a word she did not know. She gestured with a finger. "Say it again." He repeated the word as she skimmed his mind; she grasped an image of a surface covered with symbols. "A book," he said once more.

"What is a book?" she asked.

He stared at her for a moment. "Let me try to say," he answered very slowly. "I have learned more of your speech while you were gone, Homesmind taught it to me . . ."

Daiya drew back, pulling her legs up to her chest. "There is someone else here!" she cried, in her panic shouting with her mind as
well. Reiho seemed to hear only the words.

He shook his head. "No, I am alone. Homesmind is far away
from here. I speak to It through my implant." He pointed at his
forehead. She searched his mind again, finding the small, pulsing
light amidst the clouds of his thoughts, the light that was not part of
his mind, but something else.

She withdrew. Confused, she wrapped her arms around her legs,
resting her chin on her knees. "You speak to another mind?" she
asked.

Reiho nodded.

"One that is very far from here?"

He nodded again, pointing up at the sky.

She shook her head vehemently. He was a separate self, he could
not do this thing. He was trying to frighten her. He could not see her
own thoughts as she sat near him, nor could he know when she
touched his mind, yet he wanted her to believe he could speak to a
mind in the sky. "You cannot," she said. "I don't believe it."

"Through the implant," he said. "I could not do it by myself. If
you had an implant, I could speak to your mind too."

Daiya laughed. Reiho clutched his flat rectangle, looking startled.
"You are primitive," she said. "My people don't need such things to
mindspeak."

"Please, speak more slowly," he said, raising a hand.

"My people do not need such things to mindspeak," she said carefully.

The boy was still for a moment. His eyes narrowed. "You can
read my mind?" he asked softly.

"It is too hard with you," she answered. "You have no training, it
is hard to read what you think, and you cannot touch my thoughts,
so we must use speech." She paused. "That does not mean I cannot
grasp your intentions or feelings," she added, just to be safe. She
was about to explain that he was a solitary, without mental powers,
but she decided against it. She would have to tell him that infant
solitaries were always killed, and that might provoke him. She realized that if Reiho could not get back to his home, he would have to
die. But if he did go back, he might return with others like himself.

She swallowed. The longer she sat here with him, the greater the
distance from her village seemed to be. Yet she could not bring her-

self to leave. She was too curious; she would damn herself with her curiosity. "This Homesmind," she said, thinking it was a peculiar name for anyone to have, "does he know you spoke to me?"

"It asked. I did not say, I said only that I wanted to learn the old language, your language." The light from the rectangle's surface made his face seem sallow and drawn; his shadowed eyes were dark pools. "I am not supposed to be here. I said only that I was all right and I shall return when I repair my craft. I told It that I . . . that I . . . I do not have the words in this speech. I told Homesmind I wanted to learn this language to pass time. It is strange you still speak it."

"Why should speech change, when the world does not? It is mindspeech that is important, we need words only for children." Questions threatened to flood her mind as she spoke. How could a being from the sky know Earth's language? She suppressed the question. "You're not supposed to be here," she went on, "so you told no one."

He nodded. "That is true. We thought there was no one here, that you were all dead many ages ago."

Daiya coughed, trying to choke back her laughter. "Dead! You come from the sky where no human being can live, to Earth, the home of all men and women, and you thought we were dead. You are very foolish, and your people must be ignorant." She paused, thinking that he might find this rude, then saw that he had not understood the rapidly spoken words. "I've told no one about you either, at least not yet," she continued. "I can't imagine what they would think of you." She pointed at the rectangle. "This thing, this book, what is it?"

"It is words, writing." He tilted it toward her. Just beneath the surface, she could see scratches and marks which seemed to form patterns. "I always keep a small library . . . a small number of books . . . with me. They are very small, tinier than the pebbles here, but when I put them in here"—he pointed at the rectangle as he spoke—"I can read them. If I wish to have other books, Homesmind can transmit them to me."

She could not understand a few of his words, and wondered if it was because her speech was still new to him. "You look at these patterns?" She squinted at them. "What for? Is it an art?"

The boy stared at her. "You have no writing?"

"I've never heard of such a thing."

"I shall try to say what it is," he said very slowly. "These symbols, they are words, like the ones we speak or say. Each one of these stands for a word or part of a word. When I look at these signs, it is . . . it is as if the person who put them down is speaking to me. I do not need the book, I could speak directly to Homesmind to learn what is here, but I find enjoyment in the words and their patterns. In a way, it is an art now, though long ago it helped people preserve learning."

"People put down these symbols?"

He nodded.

"Why? Why doesn't this person tell you his thoughts? Did a friend of yours do this?" She stopped, trying to remember not to speak so quickly.

"This person was not my friend. She is dead for a long time, I do not know her. But her work is part of Homesmind, and with this book, I can read what she thought." He pressed the edge of the rectangle; the light went out. He was now a black, alien form, lit from the back by the light inside the vehicle. She could not see his face. "This book is about history," he went on.

"What is that?"

"About the past. It is about a long time ago. But it says little about Earth."

Daiya peered at him. "You are very strange," she said. "You look at patterns to tell you about the past. I don't understand you. What is there to know?"

"Do you know about the past?"

"Everyone does. There were those like us and those not like us and they fought long ago. Then there were only those like us." She suddenly realized that Reiho's presence contradicted that statement. "And some have said that the ones not like us live in another place, but many consider that a heresy. I didn't believe that before."

"What about after that?" Reiho asked.

"What do you mean?"

"What happened to your people after that?"

"We are as we are. The passing of time is an illusion, a warp in eternity. What else is there to say?"

"What about your history?"

Exasperated, Daiya stood up. "I don't know what you mean. You look at signs and patterns on a surface and you ask what only a child would ask. We are as we are. We always were like this, we shall always be like this." She was afraid to show the boy that she too had questions about her world, afraid he might see it as weakness.

"It does not change at all?"

"Why should it change? People die and children are born. The older ones tell us things and teach us, and we shall do the same."

"But change is part of life."

"We have always lived as we do. Your life is very distant from truth if you look for change." She shook her head. "I must go, I have many things to do."

He took her hand. Startled, she jumped back, pulling her hand away. His skin felt dry and smooth; his hand, oddly enough, had no calluses. "Do not go," he said.

"I must."

"I shall leave you alone. I am frightened, I will say it. I have not ever been in a place like this."

She touched his mind and felt both his fear and his pride. He had struggled with his pride to make his admission. Earth's night covered him; the darkness hid unknown threats. A wild creature hovered near him and he did not know whether it would strike. That was how he saw her. She withdrew, annoyed but sorry for him as well.

"Very well," she said softly. She turned and pointed to a spot several paces from the craft. "I shall build my fire there, and sleep there, but you are not to disturb me."

"You may sleep in here, there is space. I will put down one of the seats for you."

"No. I'll sleep outside."

"I will not do anything, I will not even touch you."

Daiya leaned closer to him. She sensed he did not really want her in the craft. Why had he asked? Perhaps he was trying to trap her. She searched his surface thoughts, but could sense no hostility.

"I must sleep outside, that is all," she said. "I would not be comfortable in there. And you must leave me alone, or I'll go. Then you will be alone."

His body stiffened and his mind became a coil. "Very well."

She left him and went for wood to build her fire.

Something was near her.

Daiya swam into consciousness, releasing part of her mind from behind her wall. She touched another mind—it was Reiho's. Angry, she sat up quickly, blinking her eyes.

The boy was retreating, hurrying back to his vehicle. She looked down at herself. He had covered her with a piece of shiny cloth. She got up, pushing it from her, and ran up behind him.

He spun around, apparently startled. "I thought you would be cold, so I . . ."

She didn't wait for him to finish. She seized him with her mind, lifted him from the ground, and sent him sailing toward the craft, releasing him near the side. He fell against a large rock and rolled over, then climbed to his feet.

"Do you understand?" she shouted. "You must do nothing. Leave me alone." She waited. He began to crawl back inside the vehicle.

"You are cruel," his voice said in the darkness.

"I warned you."

"You do not seem to understand a kindness."

"Be careful of what you say." She waited, ready to strike at him again.

"This world must have done this to you. Do not threaten me, you cannot hurt me."

She realized she had roused his anger and his pride.

"Don't tempt me," she said. "I can do more to you than you think." She waited, for a moment hoping he would give her an excuse to destroy him.

The door of the craft slid shut.

Daiya turned away. She clenched her fists. Suddenly, she felt ashamed. Taking out her anger on the boy was as bad as taking it out on an animal—maybe worse. It would be kinder to kill him than to torment him like this. He might be an inferior being, but he had feelings like hers, and a mind that could reason, powerless as it was.

She thought: I am a bad person, keeping secrets from the village, getting angry, asking questions. The boy's presence and his questions had disturbed her more than she had realized. She would die during her ordeal, she knew it now, it was beyond doubt. Her skin felt wet and cold; her stomach was tight. She would die. Maybe it was the only thing that could save her now, dying; after her suffering, the Merged One would rejoin her to Itself. If It existed. She thought: if I still doubt, at the moment of death, will I be condemned to eternal isolation? Of course, if there was no God, she would be condemned anyway.

She walked slowly to the craft and peered inside. Reiho stared out at her suspiciously through the transparent dome, his face lit by the waning moon and the comet's bright light. She put her hand on the clear surface; Reiho shrank back. He probably thought he was safe inside the vehicle, but he was not. If she used all her strength, she could lift the craft and dash it against the hillside, or spin it so rapidly the boy would grow faint. She was beginning to understand why those without powers had to die.

She said, "I am sorry."

The boy blinked his eyes and was silent.

"I am sorry," she said, as loudly as she could. "Please open the door."

At last the door slid open. Reiho, still seated on one of the reclining seats, peered out cautiously. He held one hand in front of his face, as if guarding himself.

"I'm sorry," she repeated. "I should not have lost my temper. You were not trying to harm me."

He put his hand down and frowned. Daiya carefully explored his surface thoughts. He was a frightened boy, far from his home, puzzled by her. He too was keeping a secret, telling no one about his encounter. His thoughts brushed against her. He was gripped by a loneliness so intense she could not bear it. Then another feeling rippled from him, capturing her; she struggled to recognize it. The feeling was curiosity. It was a cold blue light inside Reiho, dispelling his fears. It shone brightly, seeking out the dark places inside her.

She withdrew from him. She had never touched anyone whose curiosity was this strong. The boy had to be a great sinner. She shuddered.

"Why are you sleeping out there without a covering?" he asked. "I thought you would get cold."

"I'm training," she replied. "I am preparing myself for an ordeal I must endure, and to live through it, I must be able to control my mind and body."

"I do not know one of those words."

"An ordeal? Is that the word?"

He nodded.

"It is a passage." He still seemed confused. "It is something all people my age must endure," she went on, "before we are accepted as adults. I must go with others into the desert and face something so terrible that no one will say what it is. Many die during an ordeal. My own brother Rin did not live through his."

Reiho's eyes widened a bit.

"Don't you have such a thing?" she asked.

He shook his head.

"Don't you have to pass an ordeal before you become an adult? Perhaps yours is different. I have heard that in other villages, the young ones go high into mountains taller than those here, mountains that touch the sky, while in other places they are sent out in boats on the salty lake which surrounds the world." She spoke slowly, so that he could grasp all her words. "I have even heard that in the north, young people travel across a cold white moisture which covers the ground like a blanket to places so cold that water stands still and solid. But the custom is the same everywhere. You must have your own ordeal, or how would you know when you are grown?"

He said, "That is barbaric and cruel."

"Who are you to pass judgment?"

"I must say what I think. I would refuse to go."

"You would have to go, or you would be cast out."

He stretched out a hand toward her. She kept her arms at her sides. He withdrew his hand.

"What is your ordeal like?" she asked.

"We do not have that kind of thing, not something that might kill us," he said. "We have other things. We must study and learn, we must master many fields of study and then decide which one we wish to specialize in, and what will be our work."

"What are fields of study?"

He shrugged. "Cybernetics, anthropology, astrophysics, different types of engineering, genetics, history, those sorts of things."

It sounded like gibberish to her, a chant, words running together in a stream; she could not tell whether he had said one thing or many. She thought of a field of study and saw the boy on a plain, roaming over it as he learned about its plants, animals, and weather.

"I think I see," she said. "You learn some things, then you learn one thing more than others. Is that it?"

"It is something like that. When we decide on what we want to do most, we are adults. There are some things so difficult or demanding only a few can do them."

Daiya puzzled over his statements, wondering why one would want to know only a few things. Those in the village who lived long enough could know everything there was to know. "What thing is the hardest?" she asked.

"I do not know. Perhaps raising our children."

Daiya began to laugh. She tried to restrain herself, then noticed that Reiho was smiling a little. "That is very strange," she said between giggles. "You have men and women, don't you? Surely their feelings tell them how to make love."

"I said *raising* children. We all have them, we all contribute our genetic material to the wombs, but only a few are skilled enough to raise them properly, though the rest of us can spend time with them when we wish to do so."

She shook her head; he used strange words to describe lovemaking. "I am sorry for laughing. We all raise our own children, those who pass the ordeal are considered fit to have them. We must have many, because many die."

The boy wrinkled his brows. "It sounds like a very hard life."

She shrugged. She had never thought of it as hard, knowing, at least until now, that it was the same everywhere. "It's no harder than living in the sky," she said, waving her hand.

"Why must you go through this ordeal?" he asked.

"I have already said why. We must become adults."

"Why must you go through it to become adults?"

She folded her legs and sat on her heels. "Here it is," she said. "As children, our thoughts are weak and confused. Whatever trouble they may cause can be controlled. I have a sister, Silla, she is very young, and I must often speak to her with my voice, as I am doing now with you, and listen to hers, for she has not yet mastered the ability to project her thoughts clearly." She gazed into Reiho's eyes and saw that he understood her so far. "As we grow, our minds grow stronger, and we must learn something even harder, how to control our minds. It's difficult sometimes. I threw you into your craft here, I should have not have done it, I might have hurt you. You see that a village could not survive if it had many who would do these things."

The boy nodded.

"That is why we must go through a passage in the desert," she continued. "I won't know exactly what happens there until I go through it myself, but I know one thing. Those who are able to control themselves and fit into our community return, and others do not." As she spoke, she once again felt doubts about her own ability to survive.

"But why must you sleep outside with no covering to train for that?"

"Body and mind are one thing. It does no good to have mental control if the body fails. I have heard one can die returning from the ordeal. We must go with nothing, we must return with nothing."

Reiho slouched, resting his arms on his thighs. "It is very puzzling," he said. "I do not know very much, but I do not understand how you can have these mental powers at all."

Daiya smiled. "And I don't understand why you do not," she replied. "God gave us these powers so that we would no longer be separated from one another and the world, that is what we are told."

"But the power, the energy needed for such things must come from somewhere," Reiho said. "Your bodies cannot provide it. Something else must generate it."

"God provides us with powers," she said quickly, not knowing what the boy was talking about and afraid to ask. She stood up slowly, feeling weak and knowing she needed to sleep. Her stomach, which had been rumbling with hunger hours before, now sat inside her like a hollow space. "You tell me you live in the sky," she went on, "and yet you ask me questions. What do you do, build villages on clouds?"

"Of course not. We don't live there, we live above the clouds."

She said, "You cannot," and turned to leave him.

"We do, we live there, that is my home."

She turned her head and saw Reiho lift his arm and point his finger. She looked up to where he was pointing.

He was pointing at the comet.

4

Daiya awoke at dawn. The clearing was still clothed in shadows, but the sky was blue. Reiho was already up, standing in front of his vehicle. He held a small flat metallic object in his hand, passing it over the surface of the craft.

She stood up and watched him, then turned to stir the embers of her fire. She scattered the burnt, blackened wood and covered it with dirt.

She walked over to the boy. He stopped what he was doing and nodded at her. "Can you repair this thing?" she asked.

"Oh yes, I have tools, and this shuttle can repair much of the damage itself, it's already doing so. Then I'll do what it cannot, and check things afterward."

She noticed that his words were more fluent today, though still heavily accented, and recalled that he had said something about learning her speech while asleep. "Then you will go," she said.

"Yes."

"And you will not come back."

"I am not supposed to be here now."

She touched his mind. Again his form changed, becoming cylindrical and metallic. She sensed a wish: he wanted to return to Earth. They were both infected with curiosity.—You must not come back —she thought, pushing the words at him, but of course he could not read them.

"There is something I must ask you," she said, withdrawing her mind and seeing only the boy's body now. "It will sound strange to you, it's strange to me. When I look at you with my eyes, I see one thing, but when I sense you with my mind, there is something else where you stand."

Reiho drew his brows together. "What do you mean?"

"Right now, I see a boy of flesh and bone. That's what my eyes see. When I reach out with my mind, I see an object, a thing like a machine, a body not of flesh but of metal, a thing which should not have life. That is how I first saw you."

The boy was silent.

"Why do I see that?"

"I'm not sure." He peered at her closely. "Maybe it is because part of me isn't flesh. We are . . ." and he said a word she did not know.

"Say that again, explain it," she interrupted.

"Part of us is not flesh and bone. My skin, for example, it is like skin, but it is actually made of a stronger substance." He pulled at his arm with his fingers. "My muscles are supplemented by electrodes, my heart has been made stronger by artificial valves, even my eyes are shielded by a thin lens to protect them. I am also wearing a lifesuit to protect my body here." He paused. "Perhaps that's why you saw me as you did. We are born as flesh and blood, but as we grow, we add these things to ourselves so that our bodies can live longer and survive in regions where otherwise we could not. Our implants are the last thing we acquire, just before we are ready to become adults." He stretched out his hand to her. "But you can see that I'm still human in spite of it. We modify our humanness, we do not lose it. We originally came from Earth also, we're not so different really."

Speechless and sick with horror, Daiya stepped back, away from Reiho, away from the monster. From Earth, he had said: cast out was the way he should have put it. She trembled, feeling the sweat on her face and under her arms; the back of her neck prickled. Reiho was separate from other minds, separated from Earth, apart from Nature; he had mutilated his body in his separateness.

He moved toward her and she threw up her hands, warding him off. "I should never have talked to you," she cried. His face blurred. She blinked, suppressing her tears. Despair gripped her as she saw her world torn apart by these beings, these creatures who had been cast out and should have died.

"I mean no harm, Daiya," he said, using her name for the first time.

She covered her face, wishing she had never told it to him. She moaned, trying to control herself, feeling that even the ordeal could not be as bad as this. She wanted to pull at the Net, call others, but she was afraid to infect them with this horror, this solitary blasphemer. She could not do it; better to bear it alone for the sake of the village.

She felt his smooth dry hand on her arm. She pushed it away violently, then pinned his arms to his sides with her mind, holding him there. He struggled, then relaxed, staring at her with his dark eyes.

"Listen to me," she said. "You must leave, and you must never come back, you nor anyone else of your kind. Let me tell you something you had better know. Sometimes, in my village, a child is born with a mind like yours, a separate mind which can't ever master mindcrafts or have mental abilities, a mind which is born without them. Such children have to die so that they do not destroy us with their isolation. Do you understand?"

She saw him swallow and knew he understood. She released his arms and he moved closer to his craft. "If you or anyone of your kind returns, we shall kill you, too. If you come back, I'll kill you myself. Already you have built a wall between me and my village, but I'll tear it down and you'll never do it again. If you come back, I'll kill you."

He slumped against the side of the vehicle. She touched his mind, wishing that she could impress him mentally with her will. She felt his resistance. He had heard her words, and understood them, but he did not feel their force. His thoughts of death were dreamlike; he did not seem to connect the idea to himself. He was still mired in his curiosity.

She readied her mind to crush him, but could not do it. She had spoken to him for too long, had touched too many of his feelings. She could not strike. She thought: God, help me. It is in your hands now.

She spun around and hurried quickly to the hillside, carelessly thrashing her way through the bushes, and began to climb the hill. She stopped near a tree and looked back.

Reiho was still standing down below, watching her, the corners of his mouth turned down. She turned away and clambered up the hill.

Daiya lay on the ground by the creek, listening to the water gurgle as it rippled over rocks. The fire near her crackled, as if defying the water. She twisted her body, her mind and muscles tired from the long day of exercises and training, of trying to forget what had happened.

Unable to sleep, she found herself staring up at the sky, at the comet Reiho called his home. It was a fire burning in the heavens, dividing the night with its long tail. She thought of Reiho dwelling in the fire with his monstrous body.

She wondered again if she should have killed the boy. But maybe she had done the right thing by sparing him. She had practiced restraint, as she should before an ordeal. He had been able to contact another on his world; if he had done that before dying, he might only have brought others seeking revenge to Earth, making things even worse. He would go, and that would be the end of it; he had said he was not supposed to be here anyway. She tried to forget that she had, for a while at least, treated the thing as a person. Even now, she found herself thinking of him as a boy, as a human being, though he was not that, he could not be that. The thought tormented her. The feeling and sympathy he had engendered were his most dangerous weapons. They had saved his life.

She turned on her side and slipped her hands under her head. She tried to calm her mind, wondering how she could face her ordeal, worrying about how she could return to the village, infected by Reiho as she was. She could not think of that now, she had to sleep.

She closed her eyes and relaxed her muscles, pushing herself into darkness and oblivion.

Daiya stood at the top of the hill, gazing down at the clearing where the boy had been. The creature and his craft were gone. A gust of wind ruffled the small bushes in the clearing. Soon even the marks of the craft's runners would disappear from the ground.

She thought: I must put it out of my mind, erase it. She shivered as she imagined her grandfather Cerwen peering into her mind and seeing the isolated spot where Reiho was stored.

Weary with fear and hunger, she sat down, resting her head on her knees. The sun warmed her back, relieving the stiffness in her shoulders. She felt twinges of curiosity. Why would Reiho and his people want to do such unnatural things to their bodies? How could they possibly live in a comet, which must be like living in the middle of a fire? What did the symbols in his book tell him? How did his craft fly through the air with no mind to hold it aloft? There were too many questions; every time she thought about him, there were questions, each one another step away from her people, away from the Merged One, another step toward the cold, black deep abyss of isolation.

There was a mental discipline which could help her, but she did not know if she had the ability to make it work. It was a discipline used only in rare cases, when a person had suffered so grievously that only temporary forgetfulness could heal the hurt. She could take her memory back to the time when she had first seen Reiho's craft, then, carefully, erase every trace of him. The memories would return if she saw Reiho or anything that reminded her of him, but that could not happen; he was not coming back. The comet would seem only what it had been before, a mysterious omen.

She had to try it; she had no choice. Her parents might not see her agitation as anything other than a normal disturbance for someone of her age, but Cerwen, or any of the Merging Ones, would notice it. If they caught even a glimpse of what she knew now, they would enter her mind to grasp the rest, and then she would be lost. She did not know what they would do to her after that. It might even be worse than facing the ordeal, where she could at least hope to live and become an adult member of her community.

She closed her eyes. For a moment, she was frightened; doing this thing alone, without the aid of more experienced people, might be dangerous. She risked damaging herself without knowing if it was possible to hide such a bizarre event from others indefinitely. But it was that, she thought bitterly, or not returning at all, and even if she stayed away, the Net would pull at her sooner or later.

She concentrated, returning to the past:
the object fell from the sky, hovering for a moment over the hills
a tiny light glowed among dark clouds, pulsing
a metal cylinder waved its limbs over a blurred human face
she touched his mind, he did not sense her
she sat before the boy named Reiho, asking
she peered at scratches in lines black against soft light
she seized him and shot him toward the craft
he was mutilated, mated with machines
I'll kill you I'll kill you myself
The images, clear and frozen, passed through her. She blotted out each one, pushing it below her consciousness.

Daiya opened her eyes. It was growing dark; the sky was violet. She tried to stretch her legs, and groaned with the pain. She stumbled to her feet, her arms aching. Her legs were filled with sand. She stomped on the ground and flexed her muscles, trying to restore her circulation. Her heart fluttered; she slowed it to a steady beat.

She gazed at the clearing below. There were two long lines, faint, half-covered by dirt, on the ground. She wondered what they were. She had come up on this hill but she could not remember why. She had been training, that must be it, so hard at work she had not noticed the time. She felt weak. She wobbled unsteadily on her legs, feeling as though she had not eaten for two or three days, maybe longer. But she had just come from the village the day before. She shook her head. Had she been training so hard she had lost track of time?

As she looked at the clearing, a cold hand seemed to grip her. There was a dark, gaping, empty space inside her, making her numb. The shadows cast by the nearby trees were malignant, black cylinders with distorted limbs. It would soon be night; she would see the comet then, that mysterious omen with an obscure meaning. She wondered why she had thought of it now.

She was trembling. Perhaps she was ill. She lifted a hand to her face; her forehead was dotted with sweat. She turned away and began to climb back down the hill.

Daiya strode along the ground, the foothills to her right, her shadow made squat and fat by the sun overhead. Her legs seemed to move almost by themselves, propelled by her will. She was growing weaker, plagued by the dark feeling that had been hanging over her for the past two days, a feeling she could not dispel. Her mind seemed divided; there was a blank spot in it, a gap in continuity. She could recall only three days of training, though her body felt as though she had been without food for at least five or six days.

Ahead, she saw a slender willow standing alone on the grassy plain. She went over to it and sat down. Dappled shadows danced on her tunic as a breeze ruffled the tree limbs above her. Even at a slow pace, she would be home by evening.

As she thought of the village, her head sank. She was numb and empty. She tried to push the feelings away; she was tired and hungry, that was all it was. The black emptiness swelled inside her, darkening the day. The village seemed impossibly distant, beyond her reach, as if a high wall separated her from it.

Her back pressed against the bark of the tree. She thought of rising, taking a sip of the water she had left, and going on to her home. Her arms were stiff, as heavy as granite; she could not move them. She thought of her ordeal and tried to see herself coming out of the desert, making her way back over the mountains to her home, alive, ready to celebrate and begin her life with Harel. The vision was unreal, without conviction. I shall die, she thought, I may die even before I leave the village again, I'm not ready, there's something wrong. Those notions had an air of reality, though she was not quite sure why she thought she would die before leaving the village.

She sat, her will and body paralyzed. Something was holding her back from the village. The numbness was mingled with despair. She saw herself lying under the tree, her lifeless body an empty shell. That would solve everything, she thought, wondering exactly what it would solve.

She stared at the waving grasses on the plain, surprised at how sharply she saw them, each tall blade distinct, yet rippling with the others, some of them a dark green, others paler, a few brown at the edges. She felt the uneven bark of the tree through her tunic. She lay down under the willow and began to slow her heart, curious about what it was like to die, hoping abstractedly that she would catch at least a glimpse of an answer before she joined the Merged One, or passed into nothingness. The threads of the Net were more tenuous; when they broke, the Merging Selves would know someone was gone, even her parents might sense it. It would be too late by then.

She slowed her breathing and walled in her mind. As her heart-beat and breathing ceased, her mind would be pushed through that wall to . . . what? She wondered how long she would be mourned. They would all be better off without her, even Harel. She pushed her mind under, waiting for her heart to stop, knowing she would slip into unconsciousness before it did, saving her from any last regrets. It would take one hour, maybe two, for her heart to stop, for her lungs to cease nourishing her brain with oxygen. She was calm. She drifted, sinking beneath the waters of a black tide.

Light blazed before her eyes. She struggled, her mind seized by someone else. She gasped and choked. She threw out her arms; one hit something hard and wooden, the other struck warm muscle and skin. She sucked in air and began to cough; then she was shivering. Someone was rubbing her arms. She blinked, wondering wildly for a moment if she was still alive. The strong arms held her. A head loomed over her, framed by sun-reddened auburn hair. An arm was under her back, lifting her gently, propping her against the tree. She quinted, trying to focus. Her face was wet.

—Harel—she thought.

He sat next to her, rubbing her wrists. He pressed his ear against her chest, as if listening to her heart.—You could have died—his mind murmured.

She kept her mind still.

—Why—he seemed to cry at her.—Daiya, what's wrong, what happened—

She shook her head, not knowing what to tell him. He put an arm around her shoulders. She leaned against him, hiding her face in his pale blue shirt. She suddenly realized he was searching her mind.

—No—she thought apprehensively, and felt him withdraw. She threw up her wall, wondering as she did so if she could tell Harel about . . . what? What could she tell him? For a moment, she held an image of an almond-eyed face, alien and threatening; then it was gone.

—You're so unhappy—Harel thought.—I see it, I feel it. Is it the ordeal, Daiya, is that what frightens you? What is it—He held her tightly, as if afraid she would escape him.—What I felt inside you—he went on,—it was like being inside an isolate, it scared me, I don't understand it. I love you, you can't die—

Even behind her wall, Daiya could sense Harel's agitation. She sighed. How could she expect him to understand something as alien

to him as despair? She twisted around so she could see his face. His
large blue eyes were watery; his long thick lashes were wet.

She had to reach out to him, soothe him. Her jaw tightened; her
lips were pressed against her teeth. She lifted a hand and touched his
thick hair. She had to calm him.—It's only fatigue—she thought.—
Exhaustion, and no food, and all those days alone, by the time I
came here, I could barely move, and then I just couldn't go on, I
didn't want to go on—

She realized he was accepting her explanation. It was under-
standable, logical. It did not demand his acceptance of the notion
that there were things so dark, so bleak, that they could break a person. She was tired and had succumbed; she would rest and she
would be better. It was true, in a way. Now that she had failed at
dying, she thought bitterly, she had to survive.

—Thank God I found you—Harel was thinking.—I felt something, it seemed like another mind, but so weak I thought it was one
of the children, someone who wandered away from the village and
got lost. So I looked, and found you here—He paused.—Maybe it
was the Merged One who brought me here, maybe it's a sign. We'll
go through our ordeal and we'll have our home—His mind bristled
with certainty, tickling hers.

She removed part of her wall and touched him. The clarity and
warmth of his mind dispelled her sadness. She could almost believe
that the dark places in her mind were only clouds, easily dispersed
by the sun.

—I wish our minds could always be linked, become the same—
she thought fiercely.—I would be stronger then—

—Stronger—Harel laughed and his mind sang.—You're stronger
than I am now, Daiya, you're the strongest person I know—

She peered at him, so startled by the thought that she could not
laugh with him.

—It's true—he continued.—When I saw you here, I told myself
only something unthinkable could have done that to you because of
your strength, that's what frightened me the most. I couldn't imagine
what could do that—

—You see, then, I'm not so strong—

—You are training yourself too hard, that's what it was—Harel
thought, sure of his hypothesis.—You're strong, so you pushed
yourself harder and weakened yourself more—

He pulled her to him and they lay beneath the tree, their minds mingling. She tried to forget her fears, masking them. He pressed his cheek against her face and she held him, at peace for the moment.

At last they got up and began to walk back toward the village, their lengthening shadows behind them as they moved toward the sun.

5

After supper, Daiya and Brun took the earthen bowls outside and poured water over them from a bucket while Silla scooped up some of the mud at Daiya's feet. The child slapped it into unrecognizable shapes with her mind, then let it fall over the front of her bare chest. She picked up more mud and smeared it on her arms, giggling as she did so.

Anra came out to them, wrinkling her small straight nose when she saw what Silla was doing. Brun put down the bucket, dried his hands on his tunic, then put one hand on Anra's belly, rubbing it until she smiled. She put her arms around him and they stood there silently while Daiya thought of Harel. Then they drew apart and Anra reached for Silla, pulling off the girl's muddy trousers.

—Daiya and I are going down to the river, come with us—Brun thought.

Anra shook her head and thrust the child at him.—Take Silla, you can wash her there—

—Come with us—Brun insisted.

Anra shook her head again. Daiya sensed her mother's tiredness, afraid for a moment that it would infect her too. She yawned, suddenly drowsy, even though she had already taken a nap before supper, too tired when she arrived home to do more than eat a piece of bread before collapsing on her mat. Cold water bathed her face. She jumped, alert again. Silla giggled. Daiya saw another water bubble heading toward her and broke it, sending a shower of droplets over her sister.

Brun pressed his cheek against Anra's, then picked up Silla with his stubby hands, sitting her on his shoulders. Anra gestured at the bucket and Daiya picked it up.

They made their way through the village toward the river, with Brun hailing nearly everyone he saw on the way. People sat in front of their huts and smiled as Brun sent comical images to the children, making them giggle, and lewd ones at the young women, making them laugh and snort until one woman, the tall handsome Mila StenaFiel, projected a picture of a couple in contortions so unlikely and bizarre that even Brun was startled. He quickly threw a shield in front of Daiya's mind so that she only caught a glimpse.

The riverbank was nearly empty of people. Five gray-haired Merging Ones, three women and two men, sat near the water, their minds mingling, exchanging caresses and other gestures of affection as they communed. Two young women, one of them pregnant, stripped off their clothing and waded into the water, sculpting it into pillars. Brun sat down near the river and released Silla. The child wandered toward the women and solemnly started to imitate them, lifting the water into thin wavy pillars which quickly collapsed, drenching her.

Daiya sat next to her father, feeling the eyes of the Merging Ones on her. She turned. One of the old women was staring at her; an old man nodded. She threw up her wall, feeling as though they could see through her and know everything.

Brun pulled out the wineskin he had thrust in his belt earlier, took a swig, and handed it to Daiya. She sipped at it, tasting the slightly sour fruity liquid, then handed the skin back. Brun took another draught, then stared fixedly at her, drawing his brows together. He picked absently at an insect caught in his stiff, wooly black hair. Daiya, suddenly nervous, ran her fingers through her own hair, trying to untangle the snarls that always seemed hidden in the thick, dark curly mass.

—There is something inside you, a dark spot—her father said.—I didn't feel it right away when you first came home, maybe because you were with Harel, but I sensed it when he left and so did Anra. Those old ones yonder sensed it before you threw up your wall—

Daiya peered at the Merging Ones from the sides of her eyes. They were leaving, huddled together in a knot, arms entwined.—I don't know what it is—Brun continued.—I have never felt anything quite like it, not even in my mother Rilla, who was a very moody woman full of questions—

Daiya winced as he mentioned Rilla. She kept up her wall, even though she knew her father could tear it down if he felt he must for some reason. She had never known her grandmother, who had died when Daiya was very young. She had heard only a little about her: Rilla, who was moody, who kept too many thoughts to herself, who had somehow passed her ordeal but had been unable to become a Merging One after her children were grown. She had kept part of herself from Cerwen; she had kept too much of herself from others, and had not adjusted to the communal life she was expected to live with other older people. Her unhappiness had weakened her physically to the point where even Cerwen and the other Merging Selves had been unable to keep her alive. That was all Daiya knew about her grandmother Rilla. Brun did not think about her very much, though sometimes, when Daiya was in one of her moods, she caught a wisp of a thought in her father's mind: *Is she another one like Rilla?*

Daiya shuddered. But she wasn't like that, not at all, she did not hide thoughts for the sake of hiding them, but because she didn't want to disturb the others. It was a phase, that was all, the result of having humors inside her body that sometimes raged out of control, and that problem would disappear after more training. And there was Harel, who could see even her darkest thoughts and dismiss them, in whose mind she could lose herself.

—I'll tell you what happened—she thought, knowing she must tell him something.—I worked very hard at my exercises, too hard perhaps, and when I was coming back, I was very weak, so weak I was sure I could not make it to the village, so I stopped to rest and for a moment I wanted to stop altogether because of my fear of what lies ahead. I slowed my heart and my lungs. Harel found me and revived me—

Brun was obviously shocked. His eyes were large. He took another swig of wine—I sensed something in Harel this afternoon, a great relief. I didn't know about this, however. It is not right to release the body before the Merged One calls you, and I am certain you didn't hear such a call—

Daiya, knowing she had to do it, reluctantly dropped her wall. She felt Brun probing her mind, searching its channels and grooves.

He withdrew and frowned.—You are very strong, Daiya, and there is something in you I cannot reach, I do not think even the Merging Ones could root it out, and perhaps it would not be good if they did. You must do it yourself. You must search yourself and rid your mind of anything which will separate you from the community and from God, or you will embark upon your journey and your ordeal and meet death—

—But I've tried—she replied, watching her father's dark eyes moisten as he felt her fear.—I know all that—

Brun put a hand on her shoulder. She felt his mind settle around hers, nestling against it, warming her with love and concern.—Remember, daughter, you are a fragment of the Merged One, a fragment which for only a moment is apart from eternity. God is reality, the rest is illusion, a dream in the mind of the Merged One—For a moment, she felt herself believing as he did, secure in his faith. Then she sensed her mind pushing against his, a tentacle of consciousness escaping from his grasp.

—More questions—Brun thought, and she felt cold icicles jab her.—Too many questions! I'll answer the one I sensed, for I see you must be given an answer many times before you're content. Yes, there are isolates in the world, separate Selves who are born, but they are no more than the rocks and mud which God dreams, and they have no more reality than that. They cannot truly die, they are already lifeless, as dead as a piece of wood carved to resemble a man. They seek to trap us in illusion, that is all—He handed her the wineskin again and she took a long drink this time.—They are as real and as unreal as this wine—He laughed, and the ripples of laughter caught her, making her giggle. She felt his intoxication; it was making her drunk as well. She laughed again, for a moment caught by eternity; that was eternity, laughter and the moment of pleasure during lovemaking, the moments when she knew Brun was right.

Silla splashed in the water and laughed also. She stumbled toward them, reeling like a drunkard, captured by Brun's mind. Brun took off his tunic and dried her with it while Daiya hurried to the water's edge and filled the bucket. Then Brun picked up Silla and they began to walk home.

Daiya stood in the public space with Mausi, watching the cat-dancer. The woman grinned at them, shaking back her long brown hair, then folded her legs. Five cats, three white and two black, sat in front of her, fur preened, front legs stiff.

The woman seized them with her mind and they rose and danced, leaping and swooping, bounding over one another and kicking up their feet. It was a good trick. Mausi smiled, but neither she nor

Daiya laughed; the cats were much too dignified for that. The animals rolled over, then sat up again in an orderly row. The two black cats had been on either end of the row before they danced; now they alternated, white, black, white, black, white. They bent their furry heads, bowing.

Daiya nodded to the woman, thanking her, then followed Mausi to a knot of people who were watching a vine-weaver. The vines crept up a trellis, twisting into shapes so elaborate it seemed they could never be untangled. Then they unraveled themselves, standing straight up, pointing to the sky. Next to the vine-weaver stood a small pavillion which shaded kegs of beer. Mausi turned a spigot with her mind, shaping the beer into globules before it hit the ground, then floated it over the heads of the nearby crowd. She turned her head up, opened her mouth, and Daiya did the same. The globules dropped. Daiya swallowed and felt the beer trickle down her throat.

Over by a table filled with fresh fruit, a young man in a brown tunic stood before a group of children. He rolled up a sleeve, took out his knife, and slashed his arm. Blood trickled from the gash. The man stanched the flow with his mind, healing the cut as the children watched, eyes narrowed as they concentrated. He gestured at a little girl. She came forward, he made a tiny cut in her arm, and stood aside while she healed herself.

Daiya felt a prodding at the edge of her consciousness and turned. Cerwen was watching her from one end of the public space. Even at a distance, he looked large, a head taller than those nearest him, his stiff graying hair like a nimbus. He motioned to her with one muscular brown arm.

Mausi glanced at her, raising an eyebrow. Daiya shrugged.— Remember—Mausi thought—if you're going out again tomorrow, I'll go with you as far as the foothills—

Daiya nodded, then walked toward her grandfather. As she moved closer to him, she felt her neck prickle and her stomach tighten. She did not smile at him; he did not smile at her.

He adjusted his gray tunic, which looked as though it was pinching his big shoulders, then took her arm, propelling her out of the space and into a nearby path. Not that he needed to hold her; if he wished, he could force her to move mentally. He walked slowly, so that she could keep up with him on her shorter legs, but she still had to walk quickly to keep pace with him. They passed Fayl

NuraBaan, the blind man, another Merging One. She felt his warm greeting; his mind was filled with the smells of dirt, flowers, and sweat, the sounds of the murmuring children in the public space behind, all sharper, more pungent, more vivid than for sighted people. Fayl smiled, his sightless hazel eyes staring past them. He moved on, joining his mind to that of the old woman with him so that he could see with her eyes. If one like Fayl could pass the ordeal, Daiya thought, then surely she could.

Cerwen stopped suddenly in front of a long hut, as large as three or four family huts put together. It was a hut in which Merging Selves lived; she had been inside one only a few times. Her grandfather seemed to spend most of his time in this one, though that might not be the case. Merging Selves slept where there were spare mats and ate where there was food, migrating from hut to hut when they felt like it. They did not pay visits as frequently as others; they did not invite children and adults to their own huts very often. They did not have to, since they could easily find out what was happening elsewhere in the village and could mindspeak at a distance.

He gestured at the doorway and she went inside, knowing he had something serious to tell her. She peered around the inside of the hut, which seemed as dark as a cave, with only a space between the walls and the roof for ventilation, and no windows. Five old people sat in the center of the room, drinking wine and communing. In a far corner, two men and a woman, having apparently just finished making love, exchanged kisses while pulling on their clothes. The woman looked at Daiya and began to walk toward her while tying her shirt at her waist. Then Daiya saw who she was: Leito SeyiNen, Anra's mother, Daiya's grandmother. She searched herself, trying to recall when she had last seen Leito. She had been swallowed up by the Merging Ones; unlike Brun's mother Rilla, Leito had adapted easily. She was as close to God as one could be in this world.

Cerwen sat down and so did Daiya. Leito patted her on the head and seated herself near Cerwen. Leito still looked young. Her dark brown hair was thick and glossy, her face unlined except for a few wrinkles near her large green eyes, her body slim. I wish I were more like her, Daiya thought, thinking of both Leito's body and mind.

There was a shadow in the doorway; it entered and joined them. She looked up; it was her other grandfather, Morgen BianZeki. He grinned at her, making his round pudgy face even pudgier; his eyes were slits. She touched his friendly and uncomplicated mind, feeling a little better but knowing that only something drastic could have lured the easygoing Morgen away from his vineyards. He too, by virtue of his unquestioning mind, was close to God and the other Merging Ones.

She drew up her legs and tried to sit still. It was her upcoming passage, of course; what else could it be? She pulled at her hair nervously, wondering why she kept thinking it might be something else which bothered them. Cerwen had called to her brother Rin before his ordeal; perhaps he had brought him to a similar meeting.

—That is partly true—Cerwen thought suddenly.—Your time approaches, Daiya, and we must have a meeting—

She glanced quickly around the hut. The five communing Merging Selves were still present; the two men who had been with Leito were seated nearby.

—I see—Cerwen went on, catching her thoughts as they were forming.—You are thinking that it is difficult to communicate with us while others are here, but they know our thoughts and we know theirs and part of what we think is what they think, and some of the thoughts you sense now are their thoughts. What does it matter if what I say comes from my mind or Leito's or Morgen's or another's, even I cannot always tell the difference. We seek unity, as you should—

The words were hard now, and sharp, stabbing her, scratching her.—You think too much of separateness and isolation. You are tempted by the evils in every human mind that would lead to anarchy and ruin if we gave in to them. You build your wall and do not think that if you build it too often and too thick that you will soon have a barrier which cannot so easily be breached, that even you may not be able to remove entirely—

Daiya shrank, pressing her forehead against her knees. Those thoughts were coming from Leito, made stronger by her greater unity with other Merging Ones.—You would build your wall now if you could, Daiya—

She gasped, realizing that was exactly what she was trying to do. Leito withdrew a bit. Daiya lifted her hands to her face; she was shaking, her forehead was wet.

—There is something in you—Leito went on. Her thoughts vibrated in Daiya's mind and she knew they were the thoughts of many Merging Ones.—There is something in you which we have all felt. It was weaker before, and now it has grown, and we shall tell you what it has done. We have thought, some of us, that we must take you and strip away every layer of consciousness, and root it out, even if it means your madness and death—Daiya froze, wanting to flee from the hut but unable to move, held by the power of many minds.—And others have thought that we must leave you to face it, to suffer the ordeal you must suffer and live through it or die, that your fate is in the hands of God. Do you understand what that means, you wretched girl—The thoughts were burning her, searing her. She whimpered and crumpled to the ground, pressing her cheek against the dirt floor.—There is a division, a separation, a disagreement among us, the Merging Ones, you are dividing us, you are drawing us away from the Merged One and closer to a world no more real than the dreams you have at night when you sleep—

Daiya gasped for air, feeling the words would crush her. She clutched at the floor, then felt something cold against her cheek. A bubble of water was floating near her, held there by Morgen's mind. She opened her mouth and caught it. Refreshed by the cold water, she managed to sit up again.

—I believe you must come to terms with yourself—Cerwen thought, as gently as he could.—Your ordeal approaches. If you cannot overcome this deficiency, you will die. If you do overcome it, you will come back and take your place among us and merge with us as you grow closer to reality. To tear at your mind now would almost certainly condemn you to death and separateness as well. My reasoning, at least, has convinced the others, though their feelings may not assent to it. I shall be right, one way or the other, and our division will be healed—

And whether I live or die makes no difference, Daiya thought bitterly in a tiny dark corner of her mind.

—That isn't true—Morgen thought. His words were warm and soft, calming her a little.—You are our granddaughter and we're concerned. Do you think we felt no pain when Rin died? We mourned your brother, mourned him deeply, but we were sure it was only a physical weakness or a mistake that killed him, and so we have the consolation of knowing he is reunited with God. But you have a dark place, and you may die condemned. That would be a greater grief. But if that's what must be, we can do nothing. You are our granddaughter, but we cannot cling to you against the world, and if you threaten our existence, we must cut you out as our minds destroy the malignant cells that sometimes grow in our bodies—His words now had claws.

Her head drooped. She folded her arms, feeling more alone than ever.

—No—Leito shot the word at her. It flared up like a sunburst, threatening to light even the dark spots inside her.—You are not alone, you are never alone, isolation is an illusion—Daiya felt as though the thought was being burned into her brain.

—What can I do—Her thoughts seemed feeble, pale weak things compared to the power of her grandparents' thoughts.—What can I do—She looked from one face to another, pleading silently with them, wishing she could be as they wanted her to be.—Tell me, please. Do I need more training? I was going to leave again tomorrow, go part of the way with my friend Mausi—

—No—Cerwen responded.—You are skilled enough now, your mind is strong, perhaps too strong for one like you. Strong minds should belong only to those without questions, to those who seek communion with others. Stay here, rest, build up your body, and become part of the life of the village before you leave. Open your mind to others as often as you can. There is a boy here who loves you, seek him out and share things with him. You do not need more time by yourself away from here. Perhaps, if you do what we say, you can erase the darkness within you and save yourself—

Leito raised a hand, then got to her feet, and Daiya realized they were through with her. She watched her grandmother pad across the room to where the five old people sat; she knelt next to an old woman, putting an arm around her waist. Morgen rose, patted her on the cheek, and left the hut; he wanted to get back to his grapes. Cerwen stood up and held out a hand, helping her to her feet. Her knees shook; she tried to smile.

She wobbled out of the hut and steadied herself against a nearby tree. She looked around, surprised that the village was still the same. She opened her mind and caught wisps of thought from the huts nearest her; the jabber of children. Most of their parents were in the fields. She sighed. It was simple enough to be content. The Merging Ones knew what was best; the peaceful life of the village proved it.

She concentrated on the Net and felt it flex and hold her, binding her to the others. She pulled at the Net, thinking of beer and sweet berries and the river's cold waters and bugs and cats dancing and the sunshine. The Net glowed. She smiled as she thought of the Net humming with the pleasant images, cheering even those far away who could not quite catch them, the illusions of God, dreamed by the Merged One to make life more pleasant.

Harel came by after supper. He leaned against the hut while Daiya shooed the chickens they shared with their neighbors into the coop. She scooped up the last chicken and floated it in the air, listening to it cluck as it found itself flying. Harel laughed and she set the bird down, watching it scamper inside the coop.

Anra, tired from the day's work in the fields, sat with her back against the hut and her knees up as high as her belly would allow.— It's kicking again—her mind murmured as Daiya came to her.— How it kicks! I can often see the foot against my belly—She glanced from Daiya to Harel.—You two will be in your own home soon, and you, Daiya, will be as swollen as this, and very soon—

Harel stared frankly at Anra. Daiya sensed that his friendliness to her mother had an erotic tinge to it. She smiled. Harel, straightforward as always, could hide nothing from anyone else; the whole village now knew they would live together. She clung to her mother's serenity, warmed by it. Anra was sure her daughter would survive the ordeal, would overcome the dark spot in her in character. Any doubts she had were easily dismissed; to her, Brun was a worrier. Daiya would live or she would be one with God, and either was good.

—Don't keep holding up the hut—Anra said, waving Harel away from the wall.—You and Daiya want to go, so go—Harel took Daiya's hand and they left quickly, dancing down the paths among the huts toward the river.

—I love you—she thought, trying to lose herself in his mind.— You're the only one I ever loved this much—

—I suppose that's why you used to hide in the fields last year with Sude IeuaGeve and kiss him—he thought, teasing her.

—I never felt this way about Sude. Anyway, his mind—

—dances too much—Harel thought, completing the sentence.

She frowned, wondering if Sude would survive the ordeal.

—Of course he will, Daiya, someday we'll all be Merging Ones together—Harel kicked and spun himself like a top, digging a hole with his feet. He lifted his feet from the ground and hovered over her, then alighted on the path.

They reached the river and followed it north, away from the village. At last Harel stopped and pointed at a small hill overlooking the distant fields. They climbed up and rested under the small grove of trees at the top of the hill. From here, she could see the thatched roofs of the village's huts, made pink by the sunset.

Harel cleared a space on the grassy ground; twigs and stones drifted up and floated, then settled on the earth in clumps. The two sat down, heads together, arms around each other. Daiya sighed contentedly, allowing her thoughts to ramble aimlessly. Cerwen was right, all the Merging Selves were right. There was no need to question. The village would endure for as long as God wished, for as long as God dreamed it. Some would die and rejoin the Merged One as other parts of God's consciousness took their places, and the world would be the same. The village, part of the illusion, was a reflection of eternity. She breathed the clear air, smelling wildflowers and pine cones, feeling for a moment at peace with it all. She and Harel would raise their children and become Merging Selves; she would be more like Leito.

Harel too was thinking of the Merging Ones.—My grandmother spoke to me last night—he murmured to her.—But she did not bring me to the others as your grandfather did, she spoke to me as I lay on my mat preparing to sleep and told me I would live. My mind seemed to leave my body as she spoke, and met hers, and she lifted me above the village and for a moment I saw it with her eyes and I saw that only the physical matter of it altered, new crops, new huts, new animals, new bodies, but that its essence was eternal. Time stopped for me as I looked, I felt near God. I was no longer Harel KaniDekel, that was only a name given to a spirit-body inside the mind of the Merged One, and I saw that death too is an illusion. I knew I could accept what God wills for me—

—What do you see in me—she asked.

—There is unreality in you, a dark spot, as if part of you was stone, hard and unyielding. But I believe reality will overcome it— He drew her to the ground, pressing against her.—I have no fear for you. The Merging Ones spoke to you, and they were right. When you see the village as I have, when you draw closer to it and remove your wall, the stone within you will crumble into warm, growing earth and you will live, our ordeal will only be part of the dust, the dirt blown away by the wind. I love you, Daiya—

She lost herself in his mind. She hovered with him over their bodies as they grappled with each other, removing their clothes. She saw her dark skin against his paleness, feeling his hands on her as she touched the muscles of his back. She was Harel; she sensed his mind disappearing inside hers. She clutched him as she felt eternity and merged with him. He was a flame, she was a flame; they flared together, they were one. She cried out and heard the cry from his lips; the Net held them, vibrating.

Harel withdrew. She was still as he ran his hand over her abdomen; his eyes were sad and distant.—You held part of yourself away from me—he thought, and his face seemed to darken in the shadows.—Even then, there was a part of you I could not reach, that I can never reach—She sensed a darkness in his mind, as if she had infected him with loneliness and dimmed his brightness.

—I'm sorry, Harel, it wasn't deliberate—She held him tightly as if to make up for it. He turned over on his back and she rested on his chest, then lifted her head to look at him.

He smiled, and she felt his warmth return; the dark spot disappeared.—Maybe I don't make love to you enough—He touched her cheek and she knew he had reassured himself.—That's what it is. I'll make love more often and drive that part away—

Harel was right, she thought sleepily. God had given people this way of drawing together, first as couples, later as groups of Merging Ones. She lay against him, thinking of the joy the Merging Selves must know, the converging minds and bodies. She closed her eyes, tired and calm, at peace . . .

Daiya awoke. Harel's arm was draped over her hip. Carefully, so as not to disturb him, she removed his arm and sat up.

Harel slept soundly, his handsome face serene, his wall up so that his dreams would not disturb her. The night was still warm, but it would get cooler. She picked up his shirt and covered him with it. His mind rippled a bit and was still.

She stretched out her arms, then leaned back, peering at the blackness of the tree limbs above her. She crept out from under the trees and surveyed the landscape. The huts of the village huddled together, drowsy beasts hiding in the shadows. Watchfires burned just beyond the fields, sparks against the darkness, tended by Merging Ones and villagers wanting to master new mindcrafts before going to sleep. The crescent of Luna's Bow hung above the mountains as the moon turned her face from the earth she guarded. The comet burned in the sky, marking another boundary.

Daiya trembled. The numbness inside her swelled, mingling with terror. Harel stirred restlessly behind her and she hid behind her wall. Isolation gripped her, tightening the muscles between her shoulders, and she thought: this is true, everything else is a dream. Luna was waning, the stars were only specks; the comet gleamed, alone.

She crawled back under the trees and huddled next to Harel.

Daiya lay on her mat, sensing the awakening village. She hung suspended, floating, on her mat and yet adrift, ready to dive down into sleep or emerge into wakefulness. She thrust out her legs, then curled up again. Her tunic strained against her shoulders. Something moved near her. She opened her eyes.

Pale sunlight shone through the doorway. Silla, already up, had toddled across the room and now sat under the table, eating a corn cake. She smacked her lips and crumbs tumbled from her fingers. Daiya pulled her tunic down over her bare rump and sat up, rubbing her eyes. Then she remembered.

Today there would be a feast. Tomorrow she would set out with the others toward the desert.

In the corner next to her mat, she found the hooded cream-colored tunic, fabric woven by Anra, cut and sewn together by Brun, that she was to wear. A pair of light brown trousers were folded under it. She got up, pulled off her old tunic, and put on the new clothes. She bent her head forward and began to comb her hair with her fingers, smoothing the unruly curls. Silla watched her solemnly. Daiya waited, wondering what prank her sister was going to play today, but Silla's mind was quiet and subdued. She had felt the mood of the village. She was thinking about good food and wine and recalling dimly that there had been a feast before Rin left and that Rin had never returned.

—Mausi's coming here—Silla thought, but Daiya already knew that. She pulled on her moccasins and went to the door. Mausi was approaching with Nenla BariWil. Mausi put up her wall; Daiya caught a feeling of fear. Nenla seemed concerned.

Daiya went outside to meet them, putting up her own wall. She was beginning to feel completely unprepared for the ordeal, in spite of having spent so much time trying to clear her mind. I'll never get through it, she thought, I'm going to die.

Mausi gazed at her sadly.—We'll get the best food today we've had all this cycle—she thought.—And I won't be able to eat any of it—

Nenla shook her head; a smile appeared on her round freckled face.—Yes, you will—she responded.—You'll look at all the food and eat out of nervousness, I stuffed myself before going, I figured I could survive on my fat alone—

Mausi's blond head drooped.—I couldn't sleep. I prayed all night—she thought.—I kept thinking, one way or another, it'll be over soon—Her mouth twisted.

Daiya looked at her, feeling as though Mausi might suddenly go out of control. Rin had, during his feast, hurling earthen plates and goblets until a few Merging Selves grabbed him and held his mind. She wondered if that incident had anything to do with his death during the ordeal, when control of oneself was so important.

Nenla put a hand on Mausi's shoulder.—You will become an adult, or you will join the Merged One, remember that. I'll tell you the truth, I don't know who is more fortunate—Nenla's mind was serene and open; she meant it.

Daiya wrinkled her eyebrows.—It's true—Nenla went on.—Daiya, you doubt too much—

Mausi seemed a bit reassured. Nenla gestured at Daiya and they began to walk toward the eastern fields, winding their way past huts where preparations for the feast were already going on. They passed a few young women and men up early, heading west for the river; they carried buckets in which they would store the fish that would leap from the water, captured by their minds. They smelled baking bread and roasting chickens and warm fruit tarts.

As they reached the edge of the village, Daiya saw the small thin frame of Oren KiyEde in the distance, heading toward the plains. Mausi signalled to him mentally and then took off toward him, running quickly beside one of the water-filled ditches, saying goodbye to Nenla and Daiya as she ran.

Nenla spotted a nearby strawberry patch and sat down abruptly, smoothing back her red hair. She pulled berries off the bush and plopped them into her mouth. Her face grew serious.

—I wanted to see you before the feast—she said, surveying Daiya with her slate-gray eyes.—I wanted to wish you well. You're strong, so don't ask questions, just go and face it and you'll live. Don't fill your mind with doubts, not now—

—You used to have questions once—Daiya answered.

Nenla drew her pale brows together.—I had them because I held too much of myself apart. The Merging Selves brought me to them and showed me my error—

Daiya searched her friend's mind, not sure what she hoped to find. Nenla bit into another berry, savoring the fruit, musing about the hut she shared with Daiya's cousin Kal DeenēVasen. She was thinking of Kal, content.

—Don't you ever wonder, even now—Daiya asked.

—Why should I wonder? When you face your ordeal, you will know how foolish your doubts are. You'll return here, and you'll become part of us, and you'll see how good life is—

—So you think I'll live—

Nenla threw her a few berries.—Who am I to say? I can't see you joining the Merged One yet, that's all. One who holds too much of herself apart from other people can't rejoin the mind of God yet—

Daiya noticed that Nenla had avoided saying that she might be condemning herself to eternal isolation in death, separated from everything.

The red-haired girl got up.—I'll see you at the feast—she thought. —Try to remember, Daiya, the ordeal cannot kill you and it cannot unite you with the Merged One, only you can do that. You will face yourself and you will know what you are, and you'll ask no more questions—

The villagers were winding their way through the fields, floating bowls, plates, and goblets above their heads. Pigs and sides of beef were roasting on spits over fires in the clearing just beyond the fields. Wooden tables, brought out earlier, stood near the spits and were heaped high with berries, corn cakes, peaches, and bread. Casks of wine were next to the tables, guarded by Morgen and other Merging Selves.

Daiya watched as the villagers approached. They were a river, flowing together. Tributaries of small children broke away from the main branch, running alongside the others before rejoining the main stream.

She went to a table, taking her place at the head of it. There were seven long tables, because seven young people were undergoing the ordeal. They pointed east, toward the foothills, toward the mountains. The sun, low in the sky behind her, warmed her back. She gazed at the mountains, the wall separating them from the desert.

She glanced at the table to her left. Mausi stood there, her face tight, hollows under her eyes, her pale face almost white in spite of the pinkness of the evening light. Daiya could feel her friend's fear.

She shielded herself quickly. Mausi, she realized, could easily infect everyone with her terror. She was beginning to see why everyone put up walls during the feast, why everyone, except the Merging Ones, had to use a voice even to speak.

She looked away from Mausi and turned toward the table on her right, touching Harel's mind briefly. He smiled. There was no fear in him; he welcomed the ordeal confidently, glad he would at last be a man, a part of the village, and eventually the father of her children. Reassured, she turned back, feeling no hunger as she looked at the food and smelled the roasting meat. She would eat anyway, until she was bursting, fortifying herself for the ordeal.

People were suddenly around her, flowing among the tables, crowding against one another as they seated themselves on the benches. Many of the smaller children sat on the ground near their parents. Daiya's parents sat next to her, Anra on her right, Brun, with Silla, on her left. Farther down the table, she saw her uncle, Vasen LeitoMorgen, crowd himself in with Nenla and Daiya's cousin Kal DeenēVasen. Vasen waved at her, staring down the table with large green eyes like Leito's. The faces at the other end of the table were indistinct, paces away.

The Merging Selves were wandering from table to table with platters of beef and pork. Several people rose and began to help themselves to wine. Daiya, disoriented by the loud uncustomary babble of voices, kept her seat. She and the other young people would be served soon enough; it was their feast. Anra handed her bread and fruit; a plate of meat and a bowl of fish soup appeared in front of her. She looked up; Cerwen was handing her a large goblet of wine. She caught the murmur of a child's mind, quickly subdued by an adult.

She gulped down the soup. She tore at the meat with her hands and teeth, followed it with bread, swallowed some wine. She peered at Harel, who was eating heartily, laughing as his father told him a joke. She looked over at Mausi. The blond girl was still and stiff, pushing the food on her plate around with a finger. "Daiya!" She turned and saw her aunt Deenē lift a goblet to her, smiling.

Vasen got up. Those near him crowded together on their bench as he made his way over it. Still gnawing at a piece of beef, he wandered over to Daiya. He put a greasy hand on her shoulder and smiled. She smiled back. He gestured at her plate. "A good appetite," he said as Daiya stuffed the last piece of meat into her mouth. "A good appetite's always a good sign."

The food sat in her stomach like a stone. Anra handed her a chicken leg and more bread and she forced herself to eat it. She thought: I could close my eyes and know Anra and Vasen are brother and sister, they have the same untroubled mind. But she could not look into their minds now. Anra rested a slim hand on her brother's chubby one. She did not have to look into their minds. There was the same serene confidence in her mother's brown eyes and her uncle's green ones. They were the survivors. Daiya thought of the others, Leito's and Morgen's dead children, the three uncles and the aunt she had never known, had seen only briefly in Anra's memory, dimly recalled young people who had left for the desert and joined the Merged One. Who died, she thought, surprised at the force of the words.

Vasen ambled back to where his son Kal sat with Nenla. The two young people were smiling, heads close together, taking food from each other's plates. Merging Ones roamed from table to table, helping themselves to a piece of pork from one plate, a peach from another.

She heard a choking, gasping sound and turned. Mausi was vomiting, doubled over on her stool, her head held by her mother Lina. Daiya sat watching, paralyzed, hardly able to believe it. Vomiting was such an easy thing to control; it was only done voluntarily, to clear the body of bad food or a sickness. Mausi retched, took a breath, closed her eyes, and rested her head on Lina's chest. Daiya turned away. Everyone at the table was stiff and quiet for a moment. Then they turned back to their food, speaking to one another almost too quickly. She wondered what they were thinking and was relieved she could not tell.

She peered at Mausi out of the corners of her eyes. Lina still held her, bringing a bowl of soup to her lips. Oren had wandered over from his table and stood there, gazing sadly at the blond girl. Daiya began to rise; Brun restrained her, putting a hand on her arm. She stared at the mountains; the sky was growing dark.

Suddenly all the villagers rose to their feet. Daiya looked around uncertainly, then got up. Jowē TeiyeVese, the oldest Merging Self in

the community, was hobbling to the head of each table, stopping to
rest a hand on each young person facing the ordeal before moving
on. She stopped near Mausi, placed a hand on the blond head, then
moved toward Daiya. Jowē's silver hair flowed over her shoulders;
her blue-veined skin was pale and translucent, her small brown eyes
as fierce and unfeeling as an eagle's. Her trousers and tunic, like her
skin, were loose, falling in folds. She put her hand on Daiya's head.
Daiya looked down at her feet, sensing Jowē's strength. The old
woman went on to Harel's table.

Daiya knew the feast was over for her now. It's too soon, she
thought desperately, I'm not ready. She waited, feeling her insides
coil, wanting to freeze time and reprieve herself. Jowē reached the
last table, then turned to face everyone.

—Tasso AreliJen—she called out. It wasn't just a name when the
old woman thought it; the words hung in the air and rippled, sending out waves in all directions. It was a command. Tasso, a chubby
brown-haired boy, went to Jowē.

—Peloren HiyaRaef—The name was inside Daiya, rolling
through her. Jowē was not just Jowē; she had not been just that for
a long time. She was every Merging Self in the village; she spoke
through them, they spoke through her, their thoughts were her
thoughts. Daiya knew that, for the old woman, the Net was not frail
strands; it was heavy rope, binding her to the others, so strong that
her mind had drawn close to others. She had not been an individual
for many seasons; she had probably forgotten what separateness
was. She was not Jowē; that was now only a name given to the wrinkled illusion wearing the wrinkled white clothes. She was the village.

Peloren, a stately, poised girl with sun-streaked brown hair, stood
next to Tasso, making him look even chubbier.—Sude IeuaGeve—
Sude darted over to Jowē and took a place behind her, hopping
from one foot to the other, turning his head from side to side, glancing at everyone with dark restless eyes.

—Oren KiyEde. Mausi LinaPili. Harel KaniDekel—

—Daiya AnraBrun—

Daiya joined the others. Jowē turned quickly and began to move
toward the plains, toward the mountains. The young people followed her, trailed by other Merging Ones carrying bottles. Daiya,
looking back at the tables, saw the villagers sit down again, preparing to finish the food and wine before returning home. Brun, head
down, was staring at his plate; Anra was feeding Silla a piece of
bread. Nenla was standing by a bench, lifting a hand in farewell.

Daiya tried to hold the sight in her mind; she might never see them again.

They kept walking. Mausi seemed steadier; her face was grim and set. Sude bounded from side to side, then lifted himself off the ground, soaring and swooping before landing again—using up his strength, Daiya thought sourly. Harel reached for her hand; his palm was dry. She touched his mind and felt a warm glow. Peloren's face was blank, her hazel eyes empty, her mind a glassy surface over storm clouds. Tasso puffed out his cheeks and smirked. Oren kicked a stone, grimacing as he stubbed his toe.

—You're happy—Daiya thought.

—I'm happy because we're together—Harel replied.—We'll go through this and come back and have our home together, we won't have to wait the way the others do—

—If I live—She could not imagine Harel dying.

—But you will, I won't let you die. You must join me before going to the Merged One—Harel's mind rippled; he had shocked himself with that daring thought. She sighed and let her mind drift.

Jowē stopped, signalling for them to sit. Daiya looked back and was startled at how far they had come. She could no longer see the village. The sky was purple, almost black. Disoriented, she sat down quickly in the grass, which had been nibbled to stubbiness by the village's flock of sheep. She searched her mind; her consciousness had lapsed during the trip. Something gripped her. She reached for Harel's hand, unable to touch him with her mind. Jowē's mind was holding her, holding the others. Daiya's will was gone.

A hand thrust a bottle at her.—Drink—the old woman said, her words resonating in Daiya's bones. She drank, tasting the sweetness and stickiness of the liquid. She blinked, unable to see Jowē in the darkness. Her body was being pushed against the earth. She lay down and closed her eyes. Her limbs seemed to float away from her. Her heart thumped, far away. Her head felt severed from her body, self-contained, alone.

Jowē's voice rolled through her, chanting, but she could not hear the words. Then she saw what the old woman was seeing. The words beat against her ears. Another world rose up in front of her, shiny and metallic, with glittering spires and sprawling towns.

She gazed at the scene, overcome by grief. She saw human faces and sensed their minds, as cold as the icy waters near the river's bottom, as hard as stones, empty, isolated, separate, trapped inside each head. Men and women were divided; a wall was between them and they could not read each other's hearts. The young and the old were haunted by suspicion, drawing away from one another as they roamed the wide streets.

The image shattered. The mountains imprisoning the desert were surrounded by light, touched by the Merged One. They glowed, covered by a bright web. Woven by an invisible hand, the web covered the sky, its strands touching the faces turned up to it. The spires shook, crumbling to the ground; smoke billowed in the streets. People raged through the ruins like beasts, screaming, hurling their minds at one another. Their dark secrets roiled up and seized them, given substance by their new powers. Children screamed, torn apart by their parents. Men and women ripped at one another, rending their bodies.

Daiya screamed. The sound pierced her eardrums, echoed by others. She could not watch this. She tried to thrust it from her mind and could not. People streamed from the ruined town, some rising and disappearing in the sky, others tearing at the helpless ones who could not fight back. And she heard Jowē's words:—That is when we were beasts, so primitive, so separate that when God touched us, we tried to reject the gift—

A small group of people were huddled together in the ruins, melding their minds, shielding themselves as those around them murdered and maimed one another. At last they rose, surrounded by dead bodies and the wails of a few surviving separate selves. They touched the separate ones, bringing them a quick death. They turned to the rubble and lifted the earth, burying the ruins. The vision faded.

Daiya lay on the ground, drained, unable even to open her eyes. She felt a hand on her chin. Another liquid was being poured into her mouth, a tart, cold beverage. Rivulets rolled over her cheeks and ran into her hair. She swallowed. Her temples hammered at the sides of her head.

Jowē's mind hummed, one mind and many minds, all united.—You will cross the mountains, you will go into the desert. You will cross it until you come near the bones of the departed. There you will stand, backs against backs, a circle facing outward, and you will walk from one another for a day's journey and then another half a day, and you will sit and you will wait, facing back the way you came. And then you will return along the same route and meet again—

When? Daiya found herself wondering.

—You will know when it is time to rejoin the others. You will meet again, and you will know your fate—

The Net was strong, binding them together. She felt a warm hand grip her, seizing her mind, and then she was pushed into blackness.

Daiya awoke. She stretched, feeling the stubby grass against the backs of her hands. She sat up and looked around. The others were waking up also. Mausi was hugging her knees; Tasso lumbered to his feet.

She looked down at her side and saw a cloth sack. She opened it and peered inside; she saw a wine sack, two large water sacks, and some dried meat and fruit. The other young people each had a sack as well.

Daiya shrugged, surprised; she had thought they would be sent out with nothing. She wondered what the training had been for, all the days and nights of starvation and toughening herself. She looked inside the sack again, then drew it shut. She could see now that there was not that much in it after all; if she stretched it, the supplies might last a week at most.

She got up, her head clear, surprised at how energetic she felt. It must be the food she had eaten at the feast, or maybe the potions the Merging Selves had given them. She lifted the sack to her back, putting her arms through the loops on either side. Two pieces of rope, attached to the loops, hung down over her chest; she tied them together under her breasts.

—You're not afraid—Harel said to her. She searched her mind, startled to find that she was not. The fear had lifted.

The sky was growing light; the sun was still behind the mountains. Peloren put on her sack, hiding her mental tumult behind her wall. Tendrils crept under her barrier, brushing Daiya. Peloren laughed more, cried more, got angry more quickly than anyone else she knew. Her poised, calm exterior did not seem part of her. Peloren, usually so open, always livening things up in the village with her feelings, unable to keep any passing emotion to herself—she did not have that many thoughts—had at least shielded herself from them now. Daiya sighed, relieved, hoping Peloren would be calm by the time they reached the desert.

Peloren glared at her, having sensed the wish.—Don't you worry about that—she thought, cutting Daiya with a mental blade.— You're a great one to worry about me, you and that dark secret spot inside, you'd better just hope you get through without damaging us as well as yourself—She shook her head, blonde streaks catching the light, and began to stalk after Sude, who was already starting for the hills. Sude leaped and hopped, his straight black hair bouncing against his shoulders.

Harel gazed at her reassuringly. They adjusted the sacks on their backs and walked toward the mountains.

7

The mountain rose before them, rocky and barren, its cliff-like surfaces almost perpendicular to the ground, as if a giant hand had sheared off the side. Daiya, standing on the top of a foothill with the others, looked to the northwest, then to the southeast, tracing the mountain range with her eyes. Nothing grew on the mountains, making them seem oddly artificial, unnatural. She had never been this close to the mountains before, having always stayed among the foothills; neither had the others. Too bad, she mused, if someone had, we might have known about a path we could take. She began to wonder why none of them had taken the trouble to explore the mountain range before now.

—Isn't it obvious—Peloren responded, calmer but still ready to lash out.

—Is it obvious—Daiya asked.

Peloren wrinkled her nose.—Oh, Daiya, sometimes it's as if you spent your life behind a wall—The thought felt friendly enough, but there was an edge to it; Daiya could almost sense the anxious pounding of the girl's heart.—No one ever comes too close to the mountains, not before the ordeal, and no one who survives returns afterward, that's why—

Oren shrugged his bony shoulders.—If you think about it, that doesn't seem much of a reason—he thought, echoing Daiya.

—It certainly is—Peloren answered.—It's the best reason you can have, why should we be any different from anyone else? It isn't good to be too different, it leads to evil things—She glanced pointedly at Daiya.

Daiya stared back. She did not want to argue, and knew Peloren did not either. They had more important worries; they had to maintain some unity. A thought escaped Peloren's mind and brushed against Daiya; she saw hopelessness lurking behind the other girl's petulance. She touched Peloren's thoughts and the words tumbled into her, arranging themselves:

—Once
I felt so unhappy, trapped behind my wall.
I couldn't stop the pain,
I couldn't speak at all.
I never want to feel that way again
so divided from the world and
separate even from
myself—

Peloren shook her head and the words became a torrent:—I shook and thought I would tear myself apart with grief and then the grief left me and I was numb with no feeling at all dead and paralyzed I couldn't move and I wondered why it doesn't happen to others not like it does to me and then my grandmother came to me and I shared my thoughts with her and it passed and I told myself it wouldn't happen any more but it does and I can't stop it—

Daiya nodded silently as Peloren bowed her head. There was nothing she could say. No one else was paying attention; walls up, they were still staring at the mountainside. She turned toward them. —We can't climb it—she said,—so we'll have to fly over it, that's all—

Peloren looked up.—Why can't we just travel farther up or down —she objected.—Some of us can go one way, the others can go the other way, we can call to each other if we find a path. I don't know if we have the strength to float over the mountain—

—We can float up, then rest on that ledge—Daiya replied, pointing to a rocky recess.—Then we can go up a bit farther and rest in another spot. There might be a way down the other side, and if there isn't, we can still rest at the summit before going on. We can lock our minds together, that'll give us more strength too—

—I think my suggestion is safer—Peloren thought, her mind pressing assertively against Daiya's. Daiya looked at the others.

Harel was smiling supportively at her; Mausi and Oren seemed am-
bivalent; Tasso was concentrating on a piece of dried fruit he was
chewing; and Sude was getting impatient, willing to follow anybody.

—Think—Daiya went on, appealing to the others as well as to
Peloren.—It's noon now. If we go looking for a way over, we'll lose
time. If we find a way, we may have to wait until tomorrow to cross
if it's getting dark. We'll lose time and we'll lose strength. We only
have so much food and water, and the sooner we face our fates, the
stronger we'll be. We could be in the desert a long time, we don't
know—

—We'll be weaker if we draw on our strength to float over—
Peloren insisted.

—We'll have time to recover from that tonight—Daiya responded, pushing against Peloren, feeling the other mind shift and
retreat a bit.—But if we have to go searching now, and climbing tomorrow, that will weaken us and we'll have lost a day, a day of
water, a day of food, and there's no guarantee we'll find a path,
which means we'd have to float over anyway—

Peloren wrinkled her brows. Daiya could hear her mind rumbling,
—Float if you want, the rest of us can look for another way—

—Who's thinking of separateness now—Daiya answered, jabbing
the thought deep inside Peloren.

The other girl grew pale.—All right, we'll float—

They linked minds, weaving them as tightly as they could. They
rose, hands out, drifting up toward the rocky face. Daiya focused on
the ledge far above them, hoping it was wide enough to hold them
all. Beads of sweat dotted Mausi's forehead; Daiya lent her friend
some of her strength.

They reached the ledge and settled on it, pressing their backs
against the surface behind them, squeezed against one another.

—I'm already tired—Sude thought.

—That's what you get for fooling around with mindtricks all the
way here—Peloren's mind murmured belligerently.

—Rest—Harel thought.—We mustn't use up our energy with
bickering. Don't even think unless you have to—

Daiya breathed deeply, hoping there was at least one more ledge
where they could rest before reaching the summit. The rock against
her back felt strange, unlike other stone, almost as if there was
power in it. The Merged One had touched these mountains; perhaps
they retained some of God's strength. The others felt it too. Their
minds gripped one another; already they felt stronger.

Daiya lifted herself from the ledge, drifted up, then looked down. The ground was too far away; she felt disoriented. She looked up quickly. She searched the cliffside for another ledge, pulling the others with her, feeling their power buoy her. She saw only sheer surface. She floated up farther, ahead of the others, searching desperately. The apprehension of the other young people was pulling at her now, draining her energy. She wondered if they should drop back to the ledge. She continued to rise, moving diagonally to the north. The surface was more jagged there. She saw crannies in the mountainside. She landed on one and drew the others after her.

They landed around her in nearby nooks. Sude was lagging, tired again. Daiya dragged him along and settled him next to her. She squatted carefully, loosening some stones which raced away from the ledge, tumbling down the side.

—Now what—Peloren murmured from a ledge to Daiya's right. They were still far from the summit, but the mountain was narrower here; instead of going to the top and over, it might be easier to go around.

Daiya took a breath and leaned against the rock, feeling energy fill her again, sensing a presence. She looked at the others; they felt it too.—Wait—Daiya said.—I'm going to try to get to the other side, I'll call to you—She caught a dissenting murmur from Peloren: —Still setting yourself apart, aren't you, Daiya—

She lifted herself, floating up, then to the east, toward the side of the mountain facing the desert. The perpendicular cliffs were left behind; she saw rocky slopes and bumpy ground. She would be able to land after all. She settled on the ground and gazed down.

The desert was below her, dry and desolate; the air rippled in the distance. The barren land stretched to the horizon. She looked at it and felt fear; life would burn up out there, nothing could grow, nothing could live. She squinted; that wasn't quite right. Prickly green plants clung to the sandy ground; she thought she saw a tiny rodent burrow into the earth. But there were only a few of the prickly plants; she could probably count them all.

She trembled. The mountain almost seemed to sigh. Her neck prickled. There was a presence nearby. She reached out to it, feeling it hum, waiting for it to speak. It's a sign, she thought as her mind formed a prayer, it's a sign from the Merged One, a sign from God. Jowē had shown them a vision, God touching these mountains. Daiya covered her face with her hands, sorry for her doubts, waiting for the presence to speak. But there was only silence.

Of course God would not speak yet, not until death was near. She needed faith, not proof. She shook her head and called out to the others. At last they drifted overhead, settling near her, their minds still as the presence hummed. Even Sude was subdued. We're ready now, Daiya thought, we're ready, we're united, we'll live.

She stood up and launched herself, shooting out from the mountainside until there was only sandy desert below. She fell, diving through the suddenly thick air which was a soft cushion around her; she was floating, not falling, or so it seemed. She swam through the air as if it were the river water. The ground below spun, then rushed to meet her. She slowed herself and landed.

She put a hand over her eyes and looked up. The tiny figures were high above her, growing larger. Harel soared, arms out, legs extended. Sude tumbled, whirling in spirals, turning somersaults. Tasso, big and solid, plummeted like a stone, caught himself, then landed with a grunt. Oren and Mausi were daggers, feet pointed at the earth. Peloren spun, her hair whipping around her head; she circled, then alighted daintily.

They pulled their hoods over their heads. Silently, they began to walk into the desert.

The air was growing cooler. The mountains, now far behind them, hid the sun. Daiya no longer felt the presence that had touched her mind when she was standing on the mountain. The Net, though attenuated, held them; the village was still with them.

She glanced at her hooded companions. Mausi's eyes were shaded by her hood; her nose was pink with sunburn. She was concentrating on the burn, healing it slowly. Tasso stomped along, swaying slightly from side to side, drawing on his bulk for strength. Harel slowed, then stopped, sitting down quickly on the ground. Daiya settled near him; the others joined them.

—We should eat something—Harel thought.

—Shouldn't we keep going—Daiya asked.

—We should eat now, we can travel afterward until it gets dark and then sleep—Harel seemed weary, his thoughts flat and expressionless.

They untied their sacks. Daiya rummaged through hers, deciding she could last with only a bit of dried meat and a swallow of wine; she would save her water for later. She bit into the meat, then drank some wine. The liquid was warm and sour; she smacked her lips, still feeling thirsty. She suppressed the feeling.

Peloren finished some fruit, then stood up. Tasso, fortified by his muscle and fat, took only a sip of water before hoisting his sack to his back.—Let's go—Peloren thought.—If we sit here much longer, we won't be able to move—She strode off, trailed by the others.

Daiya and Harel lingered behind, holding hands, drawing close to each other. The desert was silent. There were none of the familiar sensations, the trembling spirits of rabbits, the fluttering darting minds of birds, the heartless thoughts of cats. The life here was hidden. Occasionally she sensed the presence of a lizard or snake, its mind a mass of instincts with no feeling or thought, icy and alien.

Sude suddenly darted ahead of everyone, leaping and bounding over the land, growing smaller in the distance. The others hurried after him. He stopped and waited until they caught up with him again. As she approached, Daiya saw the bones next to Sude, the eyeless skull, the bleached ribs, a claw which had once been a hand. Human bones.

—We're getting closer to our destination—he thought. He threw back his hood; his dark eyes were wide open. His terror swept over Daiya.

She threw up her wall, shielding herself.

Peloren went to Sude, raising a hand as if to strike him.—Go on —she thought fiercely.—Don't look at them, just keep going—Her thoughts swallowed Sude's.

Daiya realized that the tall girl was no longer afraid, only resigned. She shuddered, wondering which was worse. Sude turned, pulling up his hood, and continued to walk, Peloren following close behind him.

Harel was no longer smiling; he had not smiled for a while. Daiya blanked her mind, conscious only of the walking, the sand underfoot, the dry air, the growing coolness, Harel's hand.

Daiya awoke, feeling bodies all around her, dimly recalling how they had huddled together in the cold before falling asleep. A foot pressed against her back; the others were stirring. As soon as night had come, they had sunk to the ground, exhausted. She had not even had time to decide whether or not to drink some water before her tiredness overpowered her thirst.

She sat up and stretched her arms. Her back and legs ached; she concentrated on her muscles, relaxing them. The sun was peering at them, low in the east, swimming in the rippling air. Bones were scattered on the ground around them; a skull resting on a backbone grinned at her. She shivered, relieved that the night had hidden the bones from them or it would have been difficult to sleep.

Trying to ignore the signs of death, she reached into her sack, which had served as a pillow, and pulled out some water. The cool water trickled down her throat. She swallowed more, unable to resist, then forced herself to stop. Harel, his head still on his sack, stretched his legs. Mausi yawned, leaning against a drowsy Oren. Peloren groaned as she rubbed her eyes. Tasso danced on his strong, heavy legs, trying to wake up completely. He stopped and stared at them, his head jerking about on his thick neck.

—Sude's gone—Tasso thought.

Daiya blinked. Tasso was right. She pulled on her sack and got to her feet, wondering how he had managed to leave without awakening any of them.—We must find him—she thought.

Peloren's eyes met hers.—Must we? He's chosen his fate—

Daiya choked back her anger.—We can't just leave him—

—Do you want us to tire ourselves looking for him—the tall girl asked.

—If we don't try to find him, it'll affect us too. We'll have to face our ordeal knowing we didn't try to stay unified, that we forgot a responsibility, and then we may all die. Besides, he can't have gone far—Daiya hoped she was right about that.—Let's put our minds together—she went on.—Try to sense him—

They drew together. Their minds flew out, held to their bodies by a cord of light. They touched terror and knew it was Sude. They drew back and were inside their bodies again.

Daiya pointed to a lump on the horizon.—He's behind that rock —she thought.—He knows we've found him—

—What do we do now—Harel asked.

—I'll go to him—Daiya responded.—I'll speak to him on the way. If he still refuses, fine, but at least we'll have tried—

She started toward Sude, sending a tendril of thought before her. She touched his mind, faint and distant. She clung to him, feeling him struggle. She held him as tightly as she could.—Sude! Why are you doing this—

His wall was up; he was resisting her.

—Sude! You'll die out here—

—I'll die anyway—he answered weakly.

—If you face your ordeal, you'll have a chance—she replied.— But you can't survive out here, alone. The Merging Ones will seek you out in time, and no other village would welcome you—She wondered if others had tried to escape the ordeal; she had never heard of any doing so. That must mean that those who had tried were dead.

His mind shook as she held it. His fear had stripped away his self-respect and his reason. She was holding a wild animal. She kept walking toward him, feeling her energy seep away as she clutched his mind. Claws dug into her brain.—I won't let you do this to yourself, Sude—she cried.—You must return—

Her nerves burned. He fought her; she fell to the ground, still grasping him. She felt him sigh. She held a limp and empty mind. She looked up and saw a small figure on the horizon near the rock, a tiny, defeated creature.—You're coming back—she sighed, relieved.

—You're determined to kill me, aren't you, Daiya—His words stabbed her.—Once you loved me, I'll try to remember that when I die. I can't fight you—

—Don't think that way—

—I'm a coward, I finally found that out, and cowards don't survive ordeals—He threw up his wall.

She sat up, wrapping her arms around herself, and waited for him. She felt a hand on her shoulder and looked up. Mausi stood there, frowning—I'm just as frightened as Sude is—the blond girl thought.

—You didn't run away—

—What would be the point—Mausi asked.—Anyway, he's coming back, that has to count for something. The Merged One was testing him—She turned and walked back to the others, sitting down next to Oren.

The figure approaching her was growing larger. She realized her hands were shaking; she tucked them into her sleeves. She was worse off than Sude; she would have to face her trial with a dark spot still in her mind. It tempted her, infecting her with a desire to set herself above others, making her impatient with the arts of persuasion. She had tried to command her companions instead of reaching a consensus with them, wasting strength in battles with Peloren, who had the same flaw. She had forced her will on Sude.

She reached out quickly as he drew nearer, touching his mind. She felt him recoil.—Sude—she thought,—God was testing you, that is all. One who overcomes great fear is stronger in the end than one who never feels it. You must believe that—

He did not respond, but his wall was still down.

—It's true—she continued.—Look at me, Sude, you know my
flaws, they are graver faults than yours. I believe you'll live—She
gave the thought as much conviction as she could.

He put up his wall then and she could not tell whether or not he
believed her. She got up and went back to the others. They sat
silently, sacks tied to their backs, conserving their strength. She sat
next to Harel, leaning against him as he put his arm around her. Her
mind was divided, part of her wanting to stop time and keep things
as they were, the other part wanting to be done with the ordeal.

And then Sude was with them again, too quickly. She shook her
head and rose. Her eyes met Sude's; he turned away, his mouth
twisting.

They stood together, then began to arrange themselves, circling
one another, jostling and stomping until they were ready. They
stood in a circle facing out, making sure no one would be traveling
in the direction they had all taken here. Daiya was facing south; she
oriented herself, fixing the direction in her mind. She would have to
be able to find her way back, although that should not be difficult;
they could always link minds during the return trip, guiding one another.

They stepped out, their paths the spokes of a wheel as they set out
across the desert.

By evening, Daiya had traveled far. She had moved at a steady pace,
glad that her hood and dark skin protected her face from the sun.
The mountains had grown larger again; she was moving south, they
ran southeast. She squinted, gauging the distance as she walked; the
mountain range was curving a bit to the west of her; she would soon
be walking parallel to it.

She had not sensed the minds of the other young people all day.
Even Harel had been silent. Like her, the others were probably saving their strength. She was beginning to wonder why the passage was
called an ordeal; a task, perhaps an effort. Except for the desert silence, the alien environment, it was not much worse than the times
she had gone out alone to train. She gritted her teeth. It was not
over yet; it could get much worse, in time.

Her stomach rumbled. She stopped near a cactus and opened it,
her mind forcing her knife through the hard surface. She removed
some of its water, shaped it into a ball, and brought it to her lips.
She swallowed, then sealed the plant.

She went on, thinking about the village, longing for it. The Net nestled against her. She imagined herself returning home. There would be no feast then, just a quiet celebration with her family and one last night in her parents' hut before she left it the next day for her own home. There were always a few empty huts. Usually the young people clustered together in a few of them, waiting until they decided on partners, courting one another. She and Harel would not have to wait.

She pondered this for a moment as she walked, wondering if she wanted to live with Harel right away. The doubt surprised her; she had never felt it before. Out of all the boys in the village, she had always been closest to him. His love had never wavered, even when she was infatuated with Sude; he had known that was a passing thing. She could not imagine feeling the same way about anyone else, so there was no point in waiting. Harel was good for her, and they would have a chance to grow together before beginning to raise their children.

She searched her mind: you're afraid because you won't ever be alone again, your thoughts and his will intertwine, you won't have those solitary moments to yourself. The words chilled her. It was true, and another reason why she should not wait, should not give herself a chance to indulge in that vice anymore.

She tried to clear her head as she walked. This was not a time to think about separateness, or to invent worries about an uncertain future she might not live to see.

She stopped, looking around for a place to rest. It was light enough to walk a bit farther, but she wanted to stop, eat a bit of food, go to sleep. She did not want to be awake when the stars appeared, when the comet was visible, when dread came over her against her will. She sat down, took off her sack, and ate two figs, washing them down with a little wine. She would get up earlier tomorrow, make up the distance she had not traveled.

She reclined, resting her head on the sack, cooling her body until the air seemed warmer and her mind more sluggish. She drifted off; she moved between two cliffs, there was something unknown ahead, something dark and alien, cold and metallic, reaching for her with tentacles. She pushed past it and plunged into unconsciousness.

The sun was high. Daiya's shadow had shrunk, hiding under her feet. Her mouth was dry, her throat gritty. She gazed at the flat ground. She was a speck, exposed to everything. There was no place to stop, no shade, nowhere to hide.

Suddenly she was frightened. She saw herself sitting here for days, burned by Heaven's Fire, using up strength bit by bit just to keep herself alive, waiting for the moment when she would have to return to the others, and not knowing how she would know it. This would be an ordeal after all.

She gazed at the mountains. They were smaller; the range now twisted to the southwest. She tried to compose herself, slowing her heart, steadying her stomach. Her breathing was even. She turned toward the south. Desolation was before her.

Something bulged at the horizon. She squinted as she looked. The black spot grew larger, moving in her direction. Her heart thumped more rapidly. She climbed to her feet, watching the thing grow as it sped along near the ground. She felt terror; her insides twisted, making her gasp. It was a sign, part of the ordeal, it had to be. It came nearer. She saw its long runners, the dark dome over the metal body.

She screamed. Claws ripped at her brain as if tearing it in two. The dark spot flared into brightness as the suppressed past burst inside her and she remembered. The vehicle hovered near her. She threw up her hands, recalling Reiho. She was on fire. She screamed again, unable to bear it. The sandy ground rushed toward her as she fell.

Cool air bathed Daiya's face. A smooth curved surface pressed against her back; something warm rested over her body. She let out a moan and felt something against her lips. Water trickled into her mouth. She swallowed and opened her eyes.

The sky above her was deep blue, the sun dimmer. She blinked, trying to focus. She lowered her eyes; a silver sheet covered her. She raised herself slowly on an elbow, seeing before her a panel of small glassy gems surrounding a bare metal surface. She turned her head.

Reiho was next to her. She was inside his vehicle. She groaned and sat up, her head swimming. She thrust out her hands, pressing them against the cold surfaces of the craft. She was trapped, imprisoned. Her muscles tightened. She pushed against the surface to her right. It slid open and she fell toward the ground, into the heat, her head hitting her sack, which lay next to the craft.

She stumbled to her feet. Reiho was climbing out after her. She retreated, throwing her hands in front of her face. She cried out with both mind and voice. The desert swallowed the cry; Reiho's mind was deaf to her. He halted, swaying uncertainly from side to side like a reed.

She clutched her head; blood pounded through it. The Net glimmered; the shock of her memory's return had shaken it. She knew what the Merging Ones must be thinking: the desert had crushed her, she would die during the ordeal, maybe even before it took place. That was all that they could think. Had they caught a glimpse of Reiho, of his mind's solitude, they would see him only as an illusion, a symbol of Daiya's despair, an image of death.

His lips moved. He was speaking. She heard sounds, and tried to grasp them. She concentrated, attempting to understand him.

"I came back to explore the mountains," he said. "I thought that there I would be far from any of your people. Then the sensors in my craft showed me there were people in the desert. I waited until you were away from the others. I thought you might need help."

She dug her nails into her palms. Fire burned her bones. She shook; the pain in her head grew worse. The villagers were right; he was an illusion. If she gave in to it, she would die. She might die anyway.

"I told you I would kill you if you came back," she screamed.

His eyes narrowed at her words. His hands became fists. He said, "I meant no harm." It sounded like a threat.

"You're not going to destroy me," she cried. She seized him, bound him with mental bonds, and lifted him high in the air with all her strength. She shook him as hard as she could while spinning him like a pinwheel. Then she threw him, dashing him against the ground.

He lay still for a moment. Then, slowly, he got up. His skin was unscratched, his bones apparently unfractured. She searched the desert frantically and saw an outcropping of stone not far away. She grabbed him again, raising him high, and threw him against the stone. Slowly he rose again; even his silver clothing was not torn. He staggered toward her, dizzy but uninjured.

Raging, Daiya went to him, seizing him with her hands. She glared into his eyes and punched him in the side. He blinked. She felt the solidity of his muscles. Her fingers hurt. She struck him again. He blocked her, grabbed her wrist, and with a twist threw her to the side. She grabbed his ankle and pulled. He fell on his backside, rolled, and sprang to his feet.

She got up. She reached inside his mind, gripping it, slowing his breathing and his heartbeat. She would make him die, she would kill him even if the effort killed her as well.

She squeezed his mind; her mental tendrils became claws clutching a wriggling mass. Then she felt his pain and fear: *why are you doing this to me, what have I done, stop, please stop.* He was not a stone, he was not an illusion. Deep inside him, she felt a person, a consciousness not unlike her own. She was becoming a murderer.

She withdrew. The boy fell to the ground and lay still. For a moment, she thought she had killed him after all. Then he stirred and opened his eyes, struggling to sit up. She searched him, expecting him to strike out at her; she prepared to dodge the blow. But even now she could not find hostility and hatred in him, only fear, bewilderment, and a stubborn determination.

She sank to her knees, sitting on her heels. Her eyes stung and she blinked away tears.

He caught his breath, filling his lungs with air. She searched her mind for words. At last she said, "You should not have come back. This is my time, my ordeal, don't you understand? You will kill me, you may kill my friends just by being here."

"I mean no harm."

"It doesn't matter whether you do or not. Perhaps the Merged One sent you here to test me, and I have failed, for I see you as a person and not a thing." She waved an arm. Her voice and mind raced on, babbling. "I have thicker walls than others, I have a separate spot in my mind and soul, so God must test me more harshly than others. I should kill you, and I can't." She buried her face in her hands and sobbed hopelessly.

She felt his hand on her shoulder. He had crawled over to her. She pushed the hand away. She swallowed and wiped her face with her sleeve as she watched him.

"Is killing all you can think about?" he said. "You speak to me, and when I try to understand, you threaten me."

"You do not belong here."

"I could have killed you when I first came here. It was hard at first to see you as human, you looked so like a beast."

She glared at him. She could not reply.

"Why did you faint when you saw me again?" he asked. "You were in shock when I picked you up. Luckily, I was able to restore you quickly. Perhaps I should not have bothered." He raised his head, pointing with his chin.

"I had erased you from my mind," she answered. "It was the only way I could keep knowledge of you from my village. But the old ones, the Merging Selves, saw I had a dark spot in my mind, though they could not see what it contained since I no longer held that knowledge consciously. Even then, they could have torn it from me, but they chose not to do that. What I did was a great sin. I held a secret. Now you are back, and God is showing me that there cannot be secrets, that I shall be punished." She stared at the sandy ground. "I am condemned."

"I don't understand," Reiho said. "I am like you, my people and your people were once the same. Look inside my mind, I think and feel and live. It cannot be wrong to communicate with another, however different he may seem. You may fail often, but you must try."

"It is wrong for us. You bring separateness into the world, you are divided from it, you live in the sky, you cannot mindspeak." She picked up a small sharp stone and seized his hand, drawing the sharp edge across it. The rock made no mark. She threw it down. "Even your body is apart from the world."

His mouth twisted. He raised an eyebrow. "You are wrong. Think a moment, think. You speak of separateness, you say it is a wrong; that is what your word sin means, isn't it?" Dimly she noticed that he spoke more fluently, without the hesitation she remembered. "Yet you willingly hold yourselves apart from my people, you divide yourselves from us, deny that you should speak to us, and think we should be killed. That cannot be right."

"You twist things," she cried desperately, almost believing him.

"I do not. It follows from what you have told me."

She wrung her hands.

"We are human beings too. We are from Earth, our history tells us that, our records."

She shook her head, bewildered. "Our legends," he went on. She nodded, understanding that word. "We fled into space, we could not stay here. Human beings had become divided, and we were being killed. Although we took much of our knowledge with us, our records of that time are scanty. We went out from the earth, past the outer planets, far into space. I do not know how to convey the distance to you, but it was very far."

"Thousands of paces? Millions?" She tried to imagine such a distance.

"Billions of paces. We went to the region we call the Halo which surrounds this planetary system, an area with millions of comets. Because comets are made up of water and other elements life requires, we knew our biologists could make one habitable, and they did. We chose one whose orbit would take us back around the sun, though in time we learned how to make it follow a path of our choosing."

"That is your myth?" she asked, unable to grasp most of it. There was no God in the myth; the people acted like gods.

"Our history. At first we dreamed of returning, but after making our home in space, we came to think of it as our abode. Some of our people did return to Earth at times, but none ever returned to us, and Homesmind told us these explorers had died here. After that, we traveled far, even beyond the Halo. This is the first time in over two thousand years that we have come back to this system."

"Years?"

"A year, a cycle of the seasons, I think that is what you would say."

She nodded.

"I am very ignorant," he continued. "Others could have told you of these things in more detail. I must do more research."

She looked at him, suddenly suspicious. "Have you told your people of us? Have you kept the secret?"

"I have tried. Homesmind knows, It deduced it from my questions, but It will not speak of it to others yet. I cannot keep it to myself forever."

"Who is this Homesmind?"

"The mind of our home, the mind of our comet."

"You make it sound like a god."

He shook his head. "It is not that. We ourselves built it ages ago. It began as a cybernetic construct made up of parts of our ships, but It has grown in complexity and Its nerves run throughout our home. It runs our life support systems, It keeps our records and knowledge, It too is another being, not-human and yet very human in that we created It. It is based on our humanity."

Daiya snorted. "You cannot build minds, only God can do that. We are all pieces of God." She sat up straight and frowned at him; she could not accept his blasphemy. Either he was lying, and doing it well, since his surface thoughts did not betray him, or the Merged One was testing her, speaking through his lips or making her hear untruths.

He sighed, as if noticing her rejection of his words. "As I have said, I cannot keep this to myself forever. Etey already suspects something, she may find out what I am doing soon."

"Who is Etey?" Daiya asked.

"I do not have the word in your language."

"Is she your lover, your partner, your sister, what?"

"In a way, she is all of those, and a parent, and a teacher."

"She is like you?"

"She is much older and wiser."

Daiya got up and began to pace in front of him. She was being distracted; it was as if his words and the questions that kept rising in her were charms, feeding her curiosity, drawing her into forgetfulness and death. She stiffened in shock. She had, for a moment, forgotten why she was here in the desert, forgotten the ordeal. She stopped pacing and looked down at him. He was watching her calmly.

"You must go," she said to him. "You must leave me. Do you want me to die because you are here?"

He rose. He put a hand on her shoulder and stared at her until she looked down.

"Do you understand?" she went on. "I shall speak to you no more, I must prepare myself. If you do not leave, and someone else finds you, you'll die. Another will not hesitate to kill you, others do not have my weakness. Leave me."

His hand gripped hers. "I shall do what I must," he responded. "I am here to learn what I can. What I discover may be important, more important perhaps than what might happen to me or to you. Perhaps this is my . . . what is your word? My ordeal."

She pulled away from him. "Then I leave you to God," she said fiercely. "I pray that the Merged One will strike you. You had better leave."

"I shall leave when I have satisfied my curiosity."

"Your curiosity is uncontrolled. You will never feed it enough. Leave this world."

She turned her back to him, oriented herself, and sat facing in the direction she had traveled, wondering again how she would know when it was time to return. She felt the boy's eyes on her, then heard his footsteps crunching against the ground. After a moment, she turned. He was getting back inside his vehicle. He settled himself on a seat, the door still open, and rummaged among his things.

He was ignoring her demand. Quickly she slid the door shut. She seized the vehicle with all her strength and hurled it up into the sky, pushing it, throwing it high. She watched it grow smaller until it was only a speck against the clear blue atmosphere. She pushed it until it was gone, beyond the reach of her power.

She pulled her sack to her side and took out the wine. Her hands shook as she opened it and drank. Reiho had drained her energy; she was weak. She reached for some meat and gnawed at it nervously. Her mind sagged, settling around her like an old tunic. She finished the meat and put the wine away; they could not restore her energy.

The Net hummed, tendrils pulling her away from herself. She swayed, giving in to the pull. Her mind lifted above her body. She was a small animal in the desert, her body slumping against the sack.

The Merging Ones sang and their words fluttered, indistinct and indecipherable. She was lifted higher and higher until the whole desert lay beneath her. Seven tiny specks, no bigger than plants, perhaps no more important, lay on the sand, far apart, yet bound to one another by pale tendrils of light.

She brushed against the minds of the others. They spun, twirling the strands of light, darting in and out, merging for a moment: she felt the confidence of Harel, the passion of Peloren, the gentleness of Mausi, the playfulness of Sude, the artful cleverness of Oren, the stolid persistence of Tasso, and her own willfulness. They were bound together now.

She saw the village, familiar yet strange. She stood by the river and saw tiny huts with mud bricks and straw roofs; the huts suddenly became larger and more solid. She traveled along a path which seemed both wide and narrow. She was seeing with the others, no longer sure of which vision was hers and which was someone else's. The village vanished. She and the others were fragments being thrown back inside their bodies.

She opened her eyes . . . were they her eyes? She looked at the darkening sky; she was where she had been. The Net held her, then lifted her up, propelling her along the route she had taken, back to the others. She felt the air billow around her. The wind stung her face; she shielded her eyes. The air shrieked past her ears. Then she was moving more slowly, held in the air by the minds of all the Merging Ones.

She dipped toward the desert and was deposited gently on the sand. She knelt, still clutching her sack. Her fingers were stiff. She let go of the sack, keeping her mind still. She looked around; she was still far from the others, with at least a day's travel before she would see them again.

The Net tugged at her. Its strands contracted. It lifted from her. Daiya clawed at the air, seeing the Net glow around her; she touched it with her mind. It spun, becoming a bright fiery disk, whipping her with the tendrils that surrounded it . . . and then it was gone.

Daiya screamed. Her voice was swallowed by emptiness, yet in her mind she heard her scream multiply, break apart, become other voices. The others were screaming too. She fell against the sack, curling up near it. The Net was gone.

She was alone.

Daiya got to her feet. It was growing dark, the evening light making the desert purple. She tied the sack to her back. Cautiously, she lifted herself from the ground, held herself aloft for a few seconds, then fell. Her mind was weak without the Net. There was an invisible wall around her. This, she thought, must be what that boy feels all the time. She trembled; her teeth clicked against one another. Her body had shrunk in upon itself.

She began to walk. The sack shifted on her shoulders. She stumbled along; her legs felt as though they had been grafted on to her, carrying her against her will. She sent out a mental feeler, trying to locate another mind, Harel's or Mausi's or even Peloren's. Her mind followed the feeler, stretching out into a long thin thread, and she gasped, pulling it back quickly. She was too weak; she would lose her mind, could not bring it back easily without the Net. She found herself wondering if she should rest, and shuddered. She would go on, even if she had to wait for the others where they were to meet. She would not stay out here alone.

The desert was growing darker. A mist clung to her, a dry, gray mist. Her vision blurred. The distant horizon vanished. She stopped, looking around frantically. The ground she stood on was an island. Blackness was swallowing the desert, rolling toward her, closing in on her like a cylindrical wall. She began to run, then forced herself to slow to a walk. She stopped.

She stood still as the sky and earth were swallowed and the darkness pressed in around her. She looked through her eyes and saw nothing. She wiggled her toes inside her moccasins and felt only the leather; she could be standing on air. She felt dizzy, unable to balance. She thought she heard a scream. She took a breath. Air filled her lungs.

She tried to think: I'm still breathing, that means that there's air. She reached out carefully with one foot and took a small step, her muscles tightening as she prepared for a fall into an abyss. She did not fall. She had to be standing on something.

Daiya stepped forward slowly, then halted again. She could not know where she was going; she was beginning to forget where she was. She tried to stand still. She was a speck in a vast space. She put out her arms, unable to tell whether they stretched in front of her or were out at her sides. Reality was bounded by her skin; she was vast, as large as the world, as the universe.

Her mind pressed against the nothingness; there was nothing to grasp, nothing to push aside. The shriek began again, filling her head, filling the world. She wanted to strike out, tear at everything, do anything that would restore the world outside. There's nothing to tear at, she thought, except myself.

She felt terror; fear twisted her heart and stopped her breath. She was fragmenting; her arms stretched into impossibly long limbs, her hands were paces away. Her legs were monoliths, solid, unmoving. Her feet were as far below her as a hut from the sky. Her torso was breaking away from her limbs; her head hung above her body.

She gasped and doubled over. She fell to her knees, clasping her legs with her arms, pressing her head against her thighs. She was a ball of dust clinging to the bottom of a vast black plain. The world tilted and she was clinging to the side of a cliff. Her stomach shifted and she felt nauseated. A bitter taste filled her mouth.

She shielded her mind, trying to reason. She had to go on; even moving through the nothingness would be better than this. She took a breath carefully, believing for a moment that only nothingness would fill her lungs. There was still air around her. The darkness had to be an illusion.

She rose, balancing carefully on her feet. She took a step. There was ground beneath her, even though she could not feel it. She concentrated on that, trying to sense the earth. She took another step and felt solidity. She walked slowly, arms out, feeling as though she was on a rope stretched between two trees. She opened her eyes. The nothingness was grayer, not as dark.

She thought: I must find the others. She reached out, sensing only a faint cry; she could not touch them. The grayness became a fog. She walked through it, still unable to sense distance, wondering if she was going in the right direction; she saw herself wandering off, trapped somewhere far from the others. No, she told herself, I'm facing the way I should go, it doesn't matter, the fog will clear and I'll see where I am. The grayness clung to her, as thick as ever.

A voice spoke to her from deep inside her head: This is nothingness, this is separateness, you are already dead and apart from the Merged One. She cried out, wondering if that was true, if she was struggling for no reason. She would walk on, and at the end there would be only oblivion. She trembled, wondering which would be worse, finding oblivion or struggling through the thick fog forever. I'm not dead, she told herself, I'm not dead, and if I were, it wouldn't matter whether I thought I was or wasn't, so I must believe I'm alive.

She pressed on, hearing another shriek more clearly. She could not tell whether it was inside her or outside. The shriek rose and broke, scattered by the fog. She kept moving, trying to remember her mental disciplines, her training, all of which seemed useless to her now. She shuddered, and tried to control herself. Look with your eyes, she told herself, hear with your ears, see what is there.

She looked down at her feet. Beneath the cloudy fog, she thought she saw dirt and sand. She looked up and caught a glimpse of sky. She walked more quickly now, afraid to slow down. She called to Harel, trying to find him, searching through the masses of mist. She heard an echoing cry.

The grayness grew lighter. Ahead, she saw a small dark shape. She approached it and stretched out a hand. She felt a prickliness and drew back. A cactus. She trembled with relief. Slowly the cactus took shape, green and solid. She fell down next to it and sobbed until she was exhausted.

She lay very still, eyes closed as she rested. At last she looked up. The fog was receding; the sky was growing lighter. The sun was beginning to rise. Her muscles were stiff. She glanced around her, suddenly realizing how far she had traveled in the night. She tried to orient herself, and found she was not far from where she was to meet the others.

Daiya rose, stamping her sore, blistered feet. She moved on, almost expecting the desert to disappear again. It remained, arid and empty, growing warmer in the morning light. Tiny figures moved in the distance, coming closer to her. She moved more quickly, then began to run, ignoring her aches and blisters, calling to the others mentally. Then her legs gave way and she pitched forward. The earth hit her and she lay still, drained and tired. The weight of the sack pushed against her shoulders, holding her down.

She forced herself up again and staggered on, watching the others grow a bit larger. She fell again, and rested on her side. She untied her sack and let it slip off her back. Exhausted, she waited.

As her companions drew nearer, Daiya noticed that there were only five of them. She squinted, unable at first to tell who was missing. One crumpled and lay on the ground, blond hair against the earth: Mausi. The bulky Tasso continued to move on thick legs. Peloren weaved along, swaying back and forth; Harel strode, shoulders slumped. Oren lurched along, his head rising and falling with each step. Sude was absent.

—Sude—Daiya called. Harel caught the name and shook his head. She swept the area, trying to sense where Sude was. The others began to drop, paces away, their faces indistinct, their thoughts attenuated.—Sude—she called again.

—He's dead—someone answered. The thought pierced her. She shook her head, denying it silently.

—He's dead—Peloren had said it. She looked toward the girl.—I can't find him—Peloren went on.—I can't feel him anywhere, he's gone—

Daiya clasped her hands together and drew them to her chest. Sude had been right; he had seen his death approaching. She had been wrong. She tried to imagine how he must have felt when the darkness surrounded him, and wondered if he had died cursing her. He's with the Merged One, she told herself, if I had let him go before, he would have died condemned. The words seemed hollow, only a feeble way to justify what she had done.

Peloren rose and began to weave her way toward Daiya, her sun-streaked hair bobbing against her shoulders. There was blood on the front of her tunic, a bruise on her forehead, holes in the knees of her trousers. A wave of despair rushed from her mind, sweeping over Daiya. She was inside Peloren for a moment, stumbling through the black nothingness, tearing at herself to make sure she was still alive, mind raging out of control. Peloren, she realized, was still trapped in the darkness, still seeing it. She was bleeding badly, unable to make the blood clot. Daiya pulled her mind away.

—Sit down, rest—Daiya cried. Peloren stood still, her eyes looking about wildly. Then she fixed her eyes on Daiya, as if seeing through the darkness at last. Her hatred burned.

—The Net's gone—Peloren's mind wailed.—We're all alone, we're finished. It's all your fault, you with your separateness and your visions—

Daiya threw up her wall.

—It's too late for that—Peloren went on.—You saw an illusion, oh, yes, I know you did. You gave in to it, you shook the Net, and now it's gone—

Daiya trembled behind her wall. It couldn't be true. The Net was gone from all of them, not just her. It was part of the ordeal, it had to be. She considered that; why would the village isolate them, force them into isolation and into a reliance on individual strengths, in order to see who was best suited to become part of the community? It seemed a contradiction.

She tried to get up. She could not move. Peloren held her; she was pounding against her wall, ready to tear it apart. She felt rage; she longed to strike out at Peloren. Her wall shook and crumbled. Lightning leaped from the other girl, stabbing Daiya. She screamed and reinforced the wall; if she lashed out, she would die. She would expose herself to Peloren's anger and might accidentally harm her companion; the trip back had weakened the other girl more. Peloren was battering against her; she could not even cry out for help.

Her wall held. Someone else was aiding her defense. She touched Harel's mind; he and the others were lending her some of their strength, weak as they were. She suppressed the urge to fight Peloren.

Her body was moving. Peloren was lifting her from the ground with her mind. Daiya resisted. She rose a few paces and hovered. Then she fell, bruising her knees.

Peloren was lying on the ground, hands out. Daiya reached out tentatively; the girl was unconscious. She hurried toward Peloren and knelt next to her, turning her over gently. She still bled; her mental field was weak and fading.

Daiya looked around frantically. Harel was coming toward her, his shoulders slouched. She reached out to him with her mind and clasped his. They wove themselves together and focused on Peloren,

stanching the flow of blood. They reached inside her, trying to help
her heal.

Peloren was slipping away. Daiya pulled at the others; Mausi was
weak, Oren exhausted. She touched Tasso; he linked his mind with
hers. Harel strained to hold Peloren; the girl was growing weaker
even with the aid of Tasso's strength. Daiya longed for the Net.
They were too weak without it; they would lose Peloren.

They reached deep inside the girl. She had no reserves left; they
were gone, dispersed during her display of rage against Daiya. Her
will had drowned in her despair. Peloren's mind drifted, slippery.

Suddenly she opened her eyes and stared calmly and hopelessly at
Daiya for a moment.—Pray for me—she thought. The image of
people praying was blurry and indistinct. She began to slip away.

Daiya clung to her; Tasso channelled more of his strength to the
girl. Peloren still prayed, preparing herself for death.—You can't,
you mustn't—Daiya thought.—Don't give up now, you can still fight
it, you can live. We'll help you heal—

Peloren closed her eyes. Daiya was trapped with her in darkness.
Peloren pulled her into the blackness. They were rushing down a
dark tunnel, moving faster and faster, bound together. Ahead, Daiya
saw something flicker briefly—a light, a mind. It was drawing them
toward itself. She sighed with Peloren, content now, accepting their
fate.

Suddenly Daiya was wrenched into daylight. Her mind floated
above her; her body was sprawled on the ground. She pulled her
mind inside herself and raised her head slowly. She knelt over
Peloren. The body was still, the golden-streaked hair tangled in the
dirt and dust. Harel was closing the eyes. Peloren was not there anymore; she was gone.

Harel took her hand.—You almost died too, I didn't know if I
could reach you in time—

She looked up, past his face, toward the sky. High above them,
black birds were beginning to circle, awaiting more deaths. She
shook her head.—We have to bury her—she murmured.—We can't
leave her here, we have to bury her—

—Not now, we can't worry about that now—

—We have to find Sude—

—Daiya, he's dead—Harel pulled her to her feet. She stepped
over the body and stumbled past him, then fell to the ground. Tasso
was inside himself again, glancing around fearfully. Daiya began to

shake. She pressed her fists against her heaving chest. She felt as though the others were drawing away behind walls.

—No—Harel thought.—We must weave ourselves together, it's the only way we can live without the Net. That must be what the Merging Ones would expect us to do—The others did not hear him. Daiya felt the terror of Oren. Mausi, blinded by panic, was screaming; the desert had vanished before her eyes. Daiya reached inside her friend, trying to calm her, and was thrust away.

Then the desert began to change. Daiya heard another scream, the scream of a desert wind. It rose, lifting the sand, whirling it around them, stinging their faces with the tiny grains. At its center, she saw a black, shapeless mass. The mass contorted. It floated up, became a black pillar, then a formless creature with long flowing limbs. The wind howled.

Desperately, Harel was trying to hold them together, reaching for each mind. He brushed against Daiya. The others were fleeing. Oren was running; Tasso was flying, wasting his strength on retreat. Daiya reached for Mausi again. The other girl threw herself in the air and then fell several paces from the black beast. It grew toward her, waving a dark tentacle. Mausi screamed and lifted from the ground, moving west toward the mountains.

Daiya, facing the black creature, could no longer control herself. The thing floated in front of Harel, blocking her view of him. It was becoming larger. Unable to stop herself, she ran, sand stinging her eyes. She glanced back; the black thing howled. Harel was curled in front of it, walls up, his head under a tentacle as the thing reached for him.

Daiya called to him and was torn away, thrown through the air. The ground hurtled past her; she lay passively on the wind, unable to fight. At last she threw up her hands and slowed herself. She was dumped on the ground. She rolled and sat up. Harel had vanished inside the thing; it was growing larger, eating the desert, devouring the sky. It flowed over Mausi, swallowing her. It stretched a limb toward Tasso.

Daiya realized she had no more strength. She could not fight this thing; it had no mind, nothing to grasp. It settled on the earth; light wavered at its edges as if the rays were bent. Then she heard a humming, a sound she could not place, but which was strangely familiar. She turned her head.

Reiho's craft was landing several paces behind her.

Enraged, she managed to stand. She saw the door of the craft open as she turned toward it. Reiho stepped out and stared at her curiously. The black thing shrieked. Reiho did not seem to notice. Daiya shook; the thing would kill him and she would let it. He deserved it, he had no business here.

"You are hurt," he called as he came toward her. The thing moved toward her too; it would swallow them both. She threw up her wall. The boy vanished, hidden by darkness. A black tentacle touched her, so cold it burned. She was alone, so solitary she could not bear it. She longed to tear down the wall, anything to rid herself of the feeling. She was trapped in nothingness; the world was inside her. Her wall was crumbling. The thing would touch her mind and she would die.

A voice called to her. She buttressed her wall, struggling to hold it together. She felt her hands in front of her face, but she could not see them; there was only emptiness before her. She would die; she knew that now. They would all be punished for being unable to unite. She would die alone, and the black birds would pick her bones.

Then she saw a face—Reiho's. He was bending over her. He stood up. The blackness was all around him, but he was not touched by it. He walked through it, his body surrounded by a shield of light.

She reached out cautiously with a mental strand, afraid for a moment that the dark beast would shatter her wall. She touched Reiho, and managed to peer through his eyes. His mind was in turmoil. She looked through his eyes. She saw the desert and the other young people huddling against the ground. Reiho could not see the thing, could not hear the shriek, could not feel the wind. His ears heard only a few moans; his body felt the sun's heat. He stood, arms out, untouched.

She withdrew. Her fingers dug into her shoulders as she wrapped her arms around herself. The blackness had turned gray. "Can't you see it?" she cried.

"See what?" Reiho answered.

And the creature was gone.

The air was still; the sun shone. The desert was before her, unchanged. Her companions knelt on the ground, their minds behind walls. They were still inside the dark mindless mass, trapped inside it; she felt their desperation. But she was outside it, free.

Reiho came to her and knelt at her side. "What is happening here?" he asked.

She drew back from him. "Didn't you see it at all?" But she knew he had not.

His dark eyes stared through her; his pupils were pinpoints. "There is death here," he muttered. "My sensors showed me that. Someone has died."

"You should not be here."

"What was I to do?"

She reached for his mind. The boy was at war with himself. Had he possessed mental powers, a storm would be forming above them.

"I know you do not want me here," the boy went on. "But I could not stand by without trying to help. Why are the others kneeling there? Tell me what to do." She felt his struggle. His curiosity had not brought him this time, only his concern. She could not condemn him for that.

"Listen to me," she said as calmly as she could. "You must leave, that is how you can help. You can't see it, but you have given me a way to help my friends. But you can do nothing for them yourself, and if you stay, you will endanger yourself and the others. Please believe me. You must go."

He shook his head. "There must be something I can do. Are they sick? I have medical supplies, and I can give them food and water."

"Please listen to me." If her companions noticed the boy, the shock, combined with the ordeal, might damage them severely. She realized that she did not care as much about Reiho's safety, and felt ashamed. "You must go. I'll help them."

He stood up and studied her for a few moments. She gazed into his eyes, pleading silently. "Very well," he said at last as he turned toward his craft. He pointed to the mountains in the southwest. "I shall be there, if you need me."

"I won't need you. I won't see you again."

His mouth was set in a firm straight line. He strode toward his vehicle and climbed inside. It rose and flew away, skimming near the ground.

Daiya waited, expecting the dark mass to reappear, but it was gone. She reached for Harel's mind and touched a wall; she sensed the darkness surrounding him. Reiho had not seen it; he had walked through it, undisturbed. It was an illusion, created out of their fear, their separation from the Net. It did not exist. The Merging Ones had been right; they had come out here to meet only what was inside themselves.

She trembled. She could save the others with that knowledge, show them the creature was not there, if she could only reach them. She drew away from Harel; his wall was strong, he was resisting.

She reached for Mausi. Her wall was crumbling; the darkness and loneliness permeated her now.—It isn't real—Daiya cried to her friend.—Mausi, it isn't there, look with your eyes, hear with your ears. It isn't there—But Mausi fortified her wall, pushing Daiya's mind away.

She turned to Oren. Suddenly the small thin boy stood up, screaming. He tore up the dirt and a few bones, whirling them around himself, striking out at the nonexistent darkness.

Daiya ran toward him. A stone struck her on the side of the head, sending her to the ground. Her head spun; her stomach lurched. She blinked and tried to regain her balance.—Oren—she called, and saw that it was too late.

He uttered one last scream and was torn apart. His chest burst, his limbs and head flew out, spattering the earth with blood. The bones and dirt spun, then settled.

Daiya stumbled over the bloodied ground, thinking madly of piecing him together, restoring life to him. She looked down and saw a small hand, partly covered by sand, fingers clutching a rock. She sank to the ground, staring at the hand. A bitter taste filled her mouth; she bent over, retching.

At last she was empty. She lifted her eyes. Mausi was stretched out on her back, staring up at the sky. Daiya crawled toward her.

The blond girl was pale and stiff. Daiya lifted her head, then pressed her head against Mausi's chest. Her friend's heart was beating feebly. She held the girl. Mausi opened her eyes.

—It's gone—she thought, so faintly Daiya could barely grasp the words.

—It was never there, it was an illusion—Daiya clung to her friend, willing her to live.—It's all over now—she went on.—It's over, Mausi, you've lived through it—

Mausi gazed at her solemnly. Her eyes shifted slightly and she stared past Daiya, as if seeing something else. Daiya entered her mind. They were in the village streets, made wider and cleaner by Mausi's memory. Her friend's parents stood in front of their hut; Oren was entering the courtyard. The vision faded; Mausi was slipping away from her. Daiya held her, trying to give her strength.

—Don't, Daiya—Mausi thought.—I'm through it now, there aren't any more doubts—

—But you never had any doubts. You were so mad at me when I showed you mine—

—I had them—Mausi replied.—I didn't want to admit it. They're gone now. I can join God, I'm ready—

Daiya shook her head.—You'll get better. We'll go back to the village slowly, you can rest on the way. I'll give you most of my food. You'll come back with me—

Mausi's eyelids drooped.—No, Daiya, I'm too weak, my will is gone. Please don't be unhappy, this is my time, I accept it. I'm just sorry that you . . . that you—Her thoughts were fading. She clung fiercely to Mausi's mind, trying to hold her in the world.—That you aren't changed—Mausi continued.—The ordeal didn't touch you somehow, you aren't—She gazed sadly at Daiya, then closed her eyes.—I pray that you will join me someday—The words were wisps, as light as air. Mausi's mind was gone.

—Mausi—Daiya searched frantically, and touched nothing. She looked at the body in her arms. She was holding a husk, an empty vessel. Mausi was no longer there. The body slid from her arms and rested on the earth.

Daiya moaned, unable to bear it. She clasped her hands together and gazed fearfully in Harel's direction. He was lying on the sand, eyes closed, chest rising and falling, his ordeal past; he was still alive. She looked toward Tasso, who was still.

She got up and walked toward him. The solid body was stiff, the eyes open and staring, the pudgy face contorted. It was not lack of strength that had killed him, she realized, only lack of imagination. He had seen death and isolation and could not believe he would live, could not leap beyond it and imagine himself living. She leaned over him and closed his eyes.

She went to Harel. He opened his eyes and sat up as she drew near. She sank to the ground and folded her legs, wishing she could feel something. She held out a hand.

Harel drew back.

—Harel—

He stiffened. His blue eyes were cold and distant.—Harel—she thought again.

—I don't understand—he thought.—You aren't like me, there is still something in you I can't name. You did not face the ordeal, you did not pass through the test, and yet somehow you are still here—

—What are you talking about—She tried to touch him again, then realized he did not want her to do so.

—You saw the darkness, you built a wall, and then, somehow, you stepped outside reality. You did not face it and come to terms with it and yourself, you are as you were. I see the dark spot inside you still, and something else, a walking, empty thing which spoke to you and showed you an illusion—

—But, Harel—she answered desperately,—the darkness, that thing, it wasn't there, that was the illusion. I understood that and it vanished, it was never there. It was us, it was something we created out of our fear—

—You did not face it and subdue the fear in yourself. That darkness was as real as anything in our world—He got up and began to search the area with his eyes. He went over to a pile of stones and picked up a water sack, apparently thrown there earlier. He tucked it under his belt, then turned away, striding toward the mountains.

She hurried after him.—Where are you going—

—Where do you think I'm going—His thoughts were harsh.—I'm going home to rejoin the Net, move into my hut—

—Let's go together, then—She held out her arms.—Harel, don't look at me like that, it's me, we were going to live together, you stare at me as if—

—Don't come with me! Follow if you like, but keep your distance —His mouth twisted.—Maybe you are the illusion, maybe you're not really there, but buried under the ground, maybe I'm only talking to your soul, trapped in separateness forever. Perhaps you're tempting me into isolation also. You should not be alive, and there you stand—

—I am alive—she cried.—Didn't you want me to live, don't you care—

His eyes narrowed. A tear escaped one and rolled over his cheek. —I'll tell you the truth, I would rather you were dead and with the Merged One than alive and as afflicted as you are—

She gasped, stepping back.—I'd rather you were dead than speaking to me this way—she thought. He winced. She longed to hurt him, strike him. Instead she felt as though she had damaged something inside herself with the words.

—I'm going now—he said.—If you return to the village, the Merging Ones will know what to do, and then I might understand, but now just keep away from me—

She stood still, unable to plead with him, feeling his rejection of her. There was a shield around him; even her thoughts could not touch him. She pushed against it with her mind.—Don't you care about me anymore—she cried, stabbing the wall between them.

He stumbled backward, away from her.—I can't love you now—

She clenched her teeth.—Do you want me to go out there and tear myself apart like Oren? Is that what you want? Shall I go out there and stop my heart and stop my breath? You'd let me die this time, wouldn't you—

His shield crumbled. She brushed against his mind. He rumbled like a thunderstorm, his mind at war with itself; he loved her, he was repelled by her, he was afraid.

—Daiya—It was a cry and a curse. Harel spun around and continued toward the mountains. She watched him go. Her vision blurred, distorting the retreating figure.

She turned back toward the bodies of her dead companions. A black bird sat on Peloren's head; another perched on Mausi, tearing at her chest. Still others sat on Tasso. It did not matter, she told herself; they were part of God's thoughts and entitled to their nourishment. Bodies that could not fertilize fields might as well feed birds.

She lifted the earth, swirling dirt and sand in a funnel. The birds cawed as they rose, flapping their long wings. She buried her friends, covering them with stones, wondering how long it would take her to die.

Reiho's craft sat at the foot of a mountain, its dome mirroring the dark sky above. A reflection of the comet gleamed on the dome's surface; the comet had been an evil omen after all.

Daiya had walked all night and most of the day. Sometimes she had prayed, and then remembered the graves. Her feet had carried her, not her will; they had trod the ground and carried her with them. The chill of the night air had given way to heat, and she had wondered which would kill her first, the heat or the cold. She had been unsure of where she was bound until she saw the vehicle.

She came up to the craft and peered through the dome. The boy was asleep, sprawled across a reclining seat.

Her nails bit into her palms. She should have killed him when she had the chance; she should kill him now, before he contaminated someone else. He had stepped carelessly into her world and destroyed it, at least for her. She had lost Harel, her parents, her village. If Harel, who had loved her, had turned from her, the others would do the same. She stared at Reiho, hating him. The craft trembled, rocking slightly on the ground. The boy stirred, throwing an arm over his head.

She turned away, sick of death. She walked over to a heap of flat rocks, piled in layers like wheat cakes. She opened her sack and drank some water; she had little food left. She knew she would have died if Reiho had not appeared, showing her what the dark being really was, but as things were, she might just as well be dead. He had left her a body and mind, but no life.

She thought of Harel. He would have to find a path through the mountains; he would not have the energy to float over them. Perhaps she should have gone with him, following, trailing him. The loneliness would be bad for him; he wasn't used to it. Even having her nearby, with her dark spot, would have been better for him. Maybe he would have relented, maybe the part of him which still loved her would have won out. She knew him. He was not hard enough to turn away from her; not indefinitely, not if she had stayed near him.

She sighed. She would probably have returned to her death. The thought surprised her; even now, she still lived, still wanted to live. If she had won Harel over, he would only have suffered more after losing her to the judgment of the Merging Ones. Better to let him construct his mental defenses and forget.

She found herself remembering Sude. The memory stung. If she had let him go, instead of talking him into facing the ordeal, she could have asked Reiho to search for him; she could have saved him. He could have lived—if he could have borne the realization of knowing there were ones like Reiho. She had decided Sude's fate, not God.

She looked out over the desert, the graveyard of her companions, its barrenness blue in the night. She thought of the village, nestling by the river, its inhabitants breeding more children who would be sent out to die. Her insides burned. She curled up on the ground, holding her belly. They spawned like the fish in the river, giving no aid to those thrown up on the rocks or shoals while swimming upstream, letting them die. Even the blind and crippled born to them on occasion were given no dispensation, were sent into the desert; their disabilities did not count, their minds were the same as others. She hated the village, not knowing if she hated it because her friends were dead or because she could no longer be part of it.

She thought of Reiho. She had wished him dead. If she had the chance now, she would trade his life in an instant if it would bring the others back to life. He was the only companion she had left, and he was a thing. He could call himself a human being if he wanted and mimic human feelings, but he was no more human than the dirt under her, with his machines and his altered body and his soulless mind. That was her fate, her punishment, to be condemned to having a monster as a companion. Even that was better than complete loneliness . . . or perhaps it was not. She wondered which was worse . . . total isolation from others, or a feeble companionship with a being whose mind could not read her hers, who could never know her, who would always be apart.

She felt a sudden pang as she thought again of Harel and the village and her dead friends. She drew in a breath sharply as she remembered who and what she had lost.

A shadow fell across her face, making the grayness over her eyes turn black. Daiya opened her eyes and saw the silhouette of a head and upper torso. She blinked. She still lived. Her heart still pumped blood, her lungs continued to draw in air and exhale it; her body went on, still clinging to any kind of existence.

She sat up. Reiho knelt near her. "You came here after all," he said. "I did not think you would." A breeze blew, ruffling his black hair; she noticed that silvery threads, as fine as a spider's web, covered his scalp. She drew back. He pushed something in front of her face. She waved it away. "It is food. You must eat."

She gazed suspiciously at the silvery object. "It doesn't look like food to me."

"Try it."

She grabbed it and bit into the silver and spat. He took it from her. "Not like that." He pulled the silver covering from it and handed it back. She held the orange-brown bar in her hand, then took a small bite. She chewed it slowly, tasting a sour fruity flavor. She swallowed, waiting to see if her stomach would reject it.

At last she bit into the rest, finishing it. The food went down easily. Reiho sat near her. "Why did you come here, Daiya?"

She glared at him bitterly. "I have no place to go now."

"But why? What about your friends?"

"My friends are dead. Only one lived, besides myself."

Reiho was very quiet. Then he caught his breath; it sounded like a groan.

"The thing you could not see killed them. They killed themselves. I cannot explain it to you. We had to face a test. They died. One lives, but he has turned from me because . . ." She waved an arm. She stared at the ground, recalling the bodies, seeing Oren's hand in the dirt. "I did not pass through my ordeal, so I cannot go back. You saw the bones there. Many here died in that place."

Reiho got up. He walked to his craft and stood with his back to her for a few moments. Then he came back to her and sat down.

"You told me to go away," he said softly. "You told me I could not help them. I left, and I did not even monitor my shuttle's sensors, because you said you could help the others by yourself. And now you tell me this. I cannot believe it. What are you?"

"I didn't lie to you. You could have done nothing."

He hit the ground with his fist. "What kind of people are you? You must be mad. Why do you have these useless deaths? Now you have made me part of them, and I feel soiled. You sent me back here, when I could have helped."

"You could not have helped." She had screamed the words. She lowered her voice. "How do you think I feel? I watched them die, you didn't." She was shaking. "I told you to go. You should not have been here at all, you have changed everything for me. You think you can come here as you like, with your separateness and your strange ways . . . this isn't your world. You have no right to be here. If you are going to meddle in another's world, then you must take the blame, or part of it, for what happens, and carry the guilt."

"This was once my people's world."

"It isn't now."

"We were driven from it."

"That makes no difference now. It is our world."

He looked down at the ground. Her desire to hurt him left her. "I only came because I was curious," he said softly.

"You have no right to be curious. The world is as it is. If I had not been curious myself, I would have had my life. You have changed it." Her bitterness seemed to lodge in her throat, threatening to choke her. "I should have killed you." He gazed at her apprehensively. "I could kill you now. But I think God must be using you to punish me, so I'll let you live."

Reiho hung his head. "Why did you come back?" she asked.

He watched her cautiously for a moment before answering. "I was curious. I do not have another reason." He sighed. "Even Homesmind is curious about Earth. When It learned I had come here . . ."

Daiya grabbed his arm. "So now another will come here, and then another. You will all die if you do." She trembled with anger and fear.

His mouth twisted into a half-smile. "Homesmind cannot come here, It's not a person like me. It is an intelligence, a being, often I think I do not entirely understand It. It is the mind of our home, of the comet."

"What are you talking about? Does God speak through it?"

Reiho shook his head. "No . . . I am not sure of what you mean. We built Homesmind many ages ago, It began as a computer complex to control our life-support systems and store our knowledge, but It is far more complex now. I have told you."

Daiya frowned, puzzling over his words. Some of them seemed like gibberish. Twice he had talked of building minds; that had to be a mistake. She fidgeted, wishing it was easier to read him directly; listening to words was not the same. "I came back," he went on, "because I was curious about these mountains."

"The mountains! Are they so strange?"

"My sensors, the devices in my craft over there, have detected something, some sort of power source."

She thought about that for a moment, remembering the visions she had seen before her ordeal. "We have a story," she said, "a legend of the beginning. These mountains were touched by the Merged One, by God. A web was woven, and people were caught by it. They were no longer solitary selves, and in their fear they tore at one another, almost destroying themselves and the world. I have felt something strange in the mountains." She watched him. The boy was concentrating. She felt his thoughts tumble about, but could not grasp them. His eyebrows went up and his eyes widened, as if he had seen something, as if an idea was suddenly clear.

Her own thoughts came together, almost making her rise to her feet. She pressed her hands against her cheeks. "Even your machines sensed it," she cried, the words tumbling from her lips. "You sensed the presence of God. It must be a warning to you. Give up your life of illusions." She paused, recalling that she had given up her own life of dwelling in the truth.

He said, "I don't believe that." She gasped. "I'm talking about something physical, something real."

"Don't talk blasphemy," she said quickly, recalling the times she had thought it.

He opened his mouth, then closed it. He peered fearfully at her. She could feel him sorting his thoughts, suppressing some, afraid to speak of others to her. "You said something about yourself before," he said at last, "about your life changing, about not being able to go back to your home."

Something swelled inside her. She thought of Sude and Mausi and Oren and Harel. Something hard was in her throat. She swallowed and coughed, unable to speak.

"What will you do?" he asked.

She shook her head. "I don't know. I'll probably die."

"Isn't there anywhere else you can go? There are others on Earth; I could take you to them."

"You still don't see," she responded. "It is the same everywhere. I would be cast out, probably killed as you would be also if anyone sensed your presence. If I am not accepted in my own village, a part of it, why would another choose to take me?"

"How do you know that?"

"I know it. At times, some travel from one village to live in another, so that we do not grow separate. And sometimes a very old Merging One can touch a mind elsewhere. It is the same. How could it be different? To be different is to be separate. Only space separates us."

Reiho seemed bewildered. She touched his mind, sensing his feeling of guilt. You should feel guilty, she thought, trying to penetrate his consciousness, amplifying the feeling. His face contorted; she had made him feel worse. Then she realized that he was reading her face, not her thoughts.

"Will you come with me then?" he asked.

"Where?"

"To the mountains. Up there." He waved a hand at the nearby peaks. "I want to explore them."

She sighed impatiently. "I have told you about the mountains. Now you want to climb among them."

"I do not want to climb. We can go in my shuttle over there, set it down on a ledge." She glanced at his machine, feeling the sin of curiosity once again, wondering what it would be like to travel in the craft. "Do you want to come along?"

She looked down. She twisted her hands, wishing once more that she could step into the past and change everything. There was nothing she could do now that would make things any worse.

"Very well," she said.

The shuttle swooped and dipped. The mountainside tilted, replacing the sky. Daiya clung to the sides of her seat, feeling nauseated. On the panels in front of her, lights blinked, symbols scurried across the surfaces like small insects, lines and curves bent and twisted like grass snakes and leafless vines. She closed her eyes. Oddly enough, she could sense no movement of the craft; it did not lurch from side to side as did the village's carts. The shuttle hummed. She opened her eyes, saw the ground spin, and closed them again.

Another hum filled the air, louder and higher than the soft sound of the craft. She glanced at Reiho, careful to focus on him and not the movements outside. He leaned forward, wrinkling his brows. The craft slowed, then hovered near a ledge. She waited. They settled down on it slowly.

She peered through the darkened surface of the dome. Some rocks and stones had been shaken loose by their landing; they bounced and skittered down the slope. She was stiff and still, afraid that if she moved, the vehicle would tumble after the stones.

"You had better get out on this side," he said. "There's more room to stand." His door slid open and he got out. She crept carefully over to his side. "Do not worry," he went on, "it will not move."

She got out and stood next to him. He put his hand on the flat rocky surface in front of him. He stared at it silently for a few moments. Daiya waited, once again feeling that there was power and strength beneath the rock. She thought of God and the web Jowē had shown her in her vision. God will strike us down, she thought, partly hoping she was right. She sorted her thoughts, trying to pray, *forgive me*. The Merged One would show Its power, would swallow Reiho, would perhaps forgive her and gather her into Its holy communion of minds.

Reiho took her arm. His touch scattered her prayers. "I'm not sure," he said, "but I do not think these mountains are natural formations."

"What are you saying?"

"That these mountains were built, put here by someone. Look here at this surface, it's as if a machine or something sheared some of it off. Feel how smooth it is. It's been worn away a bit, but still . . ." He turned toward her slightly. "You may stay here if you like. I am going farther up." He pointed at a hollow several paces above them.

"How? You can't climb up there."

"My belt." He patted his waist. "It cannot lift us both. Wait here." He put a hand on the belt. He floated up, his feet leaving the ledge. He lifted above her, drifting toward the hollow in the mountainside.

She waited until he had alighted, then lifted herself with all her strength, floating up after him. She landed next to him, smiling slightly at his feeble show; he could not even summon the energy to lift himself without some strange device.

She stared into the hollow, seeing that it was a cave. The boy fiddled at his belt, removing a small cylinder. He pointed the cylinder at the cave. Light shone on the walls, revealing tiny bright specks embedded in the rock. The specks sparkled. The darkness beyond the lighted area seemed even blacker.

Reiho motioned to her and she followed him inside. He focused the light on the ground under their feet. They went forward for a few paces, the darkness still before them. The boy pointed the light ahead; the beam seemed to vanish into the blackness.

They continued to walk. Daiya clenched her fists, trying to stay calm. She peered over her shoulder. The opening of the cave already seemed far away. They went around a bend and the entrance disappeared.

She touched Reiho's arm. "We're going to get lost," she said. "Even with my abilities, it might be hard to find our way out if we go too far." The words reverberated against the rock, sounding as though they came from the bottom of a chasm.

"No, we will not," he whispered. "I can home in on a signal from my shuttle if need be." She did not know what he meant, but he sounded sure of himself. The surface under them seemed to dip. She moved more slowly, stepping down a rocky slope, creeping deeper under the ground. The boy was an invisible breathing body next to her, attached to a hand which held a light. The air was thick. The passage narrowed. She barely squeezed through it. The passage widened again. Reiho stopped suddenly; she bumped against him.

He moved his arm, circling the area with the light. They were standing in a cavern; the top of it was several paces over their heads. Reiho walked to one side, removed a small square object from his belt, and held it to the wall, walking around the cavern as he did so. Daiya heard a low soft humming. "We should go back," she said. Her voice bounced around the cavern.

Reiho shook his head. He signalled to her and she went to him. "There is something here," he said. He lowered the light; she could not see his face.

"Of course there is," she answered, careful to speak in low tones. "God touched these mountains."

"Tell me something. Have not you ever wondered, really, how you could have your mental abilities, how you could lift an object using only your mind?" The question seemed to come from the darkness instead of from the boy. She leaned against the wall. "Have not you ever wondered how it was possible?"

"No," she said, meaning it. "I have asked other questions," she continued, wondering if she should admit such a vice in what might be a holy place. "But I have never questioned that. That is how human beings are. I might as well question why I have eyes or hair or fingers. I have wondered why solitaries are born."

"I do not have those powers, and I am human."

"You are like the ones who are sometimes born to us, whom we kill," she said. "I have told you that. You are not a person." She fidgeted nervously, realizing how often she fell into feeling that he was a person. "I do not see how you can have a mind, but you do. You cannot see why I have my abilities, but I do. It's a mystery, I suppose, but I can't understand all the dreams of God. We should go. You should not be here."

Instead, he turned and moved along the wall, holding his light and the other object. He seemed unable to make a move without a device of some sort, she thought contemptuously, when all a person needed was a knife and a water sack. Even in the desert, one could probably survive on snake and lizard if necessary. The humming rose in pitch, hurting her ears. He stopped, moving the square over the rocky surface.

"Move away from me," he said.

"Let's leave."

"Move away from me."

She stumbled over the dark ground, anxious and afraid. "What are you doing?" she cried, ignoring her echoing voice.

"There is something beyond this wall, a hollow space. I am going to try to find out what is there." He pulled out another thin cylinder and aimed it at the wall. Suddenly a bright beam of light shot out from his arm, piercing the rock. Bits of rubble crumbled to the floor.

Daiya shrank back, throwing an arm over her eyes. She huddled against a wall, expecting the cavern to bury them, waiting for the Merged One to strike. She peered over her arm. Rock was still crumbling under the boy's light beam. The power within the mountain was undisturbed. She sank to the floor. His light was burning through her brain, she felt, destroying the vestiges of all her ideas, wiping out the little she had left of her world and her life. The Merged One would not strike; It was absent, uncaring, or . . .

She shook her head. She began to wish that Reiho would turn the beam on her and finish the job. She no longer felt curious; that too had been burned out of her. She felt the wall of the cavern against her back. She could shake it herself, make it her grave, and the boy's as well. It would not matter; there was no one to judge her.

"Look." The boy's word interrupted her reverie. She got to her feet and hurried over to him. Reiho put away the thin cylinder and shone his light on the wall. The rock was gone. A flat shiny surface was there. She put her hand against it and felt cold metal and a low vibration.

"What does this mean?" she asked.

Reiho was pressing his hands against the metal. "Can you not see? This mountain has covered another construction, this is part of it." Daiya recalled the vision Jowē had shown her, the soulless people among tall towers. She brushed her hand along the surface again, touching a tiny indentation in the metal near the edges of the remaining rock wall.

The metal slid along her fingers. She jumped back, bumping her foot against a few stones, and tumbled to the ground. The metal wall was moving. Pieces of rock pelted her legs as the wall slid. Reiho threw himself over her as stone fell; the ground shook slightly. Then there was silence.

Reiho rolled over and pulled her to her feet. "Are you injured?"

She shook her head. Only the backs of her hands were cut. She concentrated on them, healing the wounds. She looked up slowly.

The metal wall had disappeared. A dull light penetrated the cavern. She followed the boy toward the light, and found herself peering into a large chamber. It was bare, its walls glowing. She felt a sound; her bones vibrated. She entered and the walls altered slightly, changing from a dim amber to a brighter gold.

She glanced at Reiho. His skin was gold. His eyes widened as he gazed around the chamber. He crossed the room, moving toward a gap in the wall opposite her. His boots clicked against the floor. She followed, her moccasins silent on the surface, her feet slipping along the smoothness. She skidded to a halt.

Reiho pointed toward the gap. She saw only darkness. He pulled her closer. She was now staring down a tunnel hundreds of paces deep; there was a faint glow at the bottom. She stepped back, feeling disoriented.

"There is a legend," she managed to say. "People built such places before God touched their minds. They must have been very strange, to live so high off the ground." She remembered that the boy lived even farther away from land. She tried to laugh and release her tension. "Look here, there is no place for food or a fire, no mat to sleep on. Perhaps they lived down there." She shuddered, wondering why anyone would care to live in darkness like a mole.

"I do not think anyone lived here," Reiho murmured.

"Why else do people build?"

The boy did not seem to hear her. He put his light back inside his belt and stepped to the edge. She held him with her mind for a moment, afraid he might fall. "I am going to go down this passage," he said. "Can you float down it? Will you come with me?"

She peered over his shoulder, standing on her toes. "You want to go so far into the ground?" she asked.

"If you do not want to go, just wait here." He stepped into the tunnel, touching his belt, and disappeared into it, blotting out the light below.

She looked around the chamber hastily, suddenly afraid of waiting alone. Dimly, she sensed a presence, as if someone else were here with her. She took a deep breath, gathered her strength, and stepped into the passage. She drifted down easily—too easily, as if her body was being fed with more energy. She fell through the darkness, holding her arms at her sides, feeling as though she was growing stronger instead of using her strength. The walls around her grew lighter. At last her feet touched a surface; the walls were gone.

She looked from side to side, bewildered. The air around her glowed and vibrated. Waves of blue and violet hung over her. She stepped forward a few paces and glanced to her right. She saw a vast empty corridor, stretching so far into the distance that she could not see where it ended. She looked to her left and saw the same kind of corridor. The veils fluttered; tiny bits of light twinkled along their

blue and violet folds. She stretched a hand toward the veils and felt
only air.

Reiho walked through the veils, his mouth open. The gauzy blue
and violet swirled around his body. She went to his side; the mist-
iness settled on her, insubstantial and transparent. The boy swallowed, apparently unable to speak. She touched his arm. He jumped
back, startled.

"What is this place?" she whispered.

"I am not sure." He began to walk toward a railing in the center
of the area, a railing which circled a large hole. She followed him.
They moved to the railing and rested their hands on it.

Daiya looked down. Far below, there were golden pillars and
crystalline stelae with twinkling lights dancing along their shiny surfaces. The structures went deep into the earth, down to another circle with a railing. She could see that there were more pillars beyond
that. She gripped the railing, feeling dislocated and unbalanced.

Reiho spun around violently and ran down the corridor. The
colored veils of air and light danced around him, then were still. She
raced after him. He slid to a stop near another railing, his boots
squeaking, and peered down another hole. She stopped next to him
and saw, far below, more golden and crystal pillars.

What is this place, she thought, forgetting to speak, sending out
part of her mind with the question.

Deep inside her, she felt something begin to form. She shook, unable to stop it. Something was touching her, trying to speak. For a
moment, she thought of building a wall against it. Then she gathered
up her courage and reached out to it.

Images formed in her mind. She was seeing the land around the
mountains, but only the foothills remained; the mountains were
gone. In their place she saw gleaming metal towers and understood,
without seeing it, that the towers also went under the earth. The desert was not barren; it was green with life. Small groves of trees dotted the grassy landscape to the horizon.

The towers began to glow. A wave flowed from them, touching
the minds of the people who stood under the towers, uniting them
mentally, feeding their minds with power. The people lifted themselves, swooping through the air like birds.

The picture changed. She saw men and women standing near large
machines which looked like crabs made of metal. The crabs lifted
golden pillars with their pincers and claws and lowered them into
the earth, and she understood that they and the people with them

were building the towers. The image changed again. A city stood near the completed towers. People moved through the wide streets, mindspeaking, sharing themselves.

The images vanished. Daiya, still clutching the railing, sank to the floor. Reiho bent over her. "What is it, Daiya?" She let go of the railing and wrapped her arms around her knees. "What is it?"

She opened her mouth. Words would not come. God must be present here. The boy sat down next to her, watching her quietly as she tried to sort her thoughts. She felt numb and cold, without the fear and worry and anger she had felt before; even her despair was gone. A part of her stood aside, passive, an onlooker.

At last she said, "Didn't you see the vision?"

He shook his head.

"I saw people building this place. A wave came from tall towers here . . . there were no mountains, only the towers. It touched the people." She looked down at her hands and folded them. "There was another vision, of people in a great place, a great village, they were happy and content. But something must have happened to them later." She frowned. "They had our abilities, our mental powers. I do not understand it."

"Was this what they built?" the boy asked.

"I believe so, I saw them put the pillars below here into the ground."

Reiho clapped his hands together. "Perhaps this place is the source of your power," he cried.

"How can that be?"

"You say a wave touched the people in your vision. The structures here may draw on power from outside this world and feed it to you. Those who have dormant mental abilities can make use of it."

"What are you talking about?"

"I do not know if I can explain. I can tell you my hypothesis."

She shook her head and wrinkled her brows.

"My hypothesis . . . a story about why and how a thing might have come to be." She nodded. "People long ago believed that human beings might have telepathic and telekinetic abilities," he went on, "the powers of the mind that you have. Yet demonstrations of such abilities were intermittent, infrequent. Even my people know of that work, though our records show that, after our flight from Earth, we abandoned such research. But the human body by itself does not have the energy required, say, to lift oneself from the ground . . . if one could do such a thing unaided, it would seem to violate the laws of nature as we know them. Perhaps these machines, somehow, can tap into a source of such power, either within this universe or outside it. Then they could direct it to minds with the capacity to receive it and make use of it. That would explain your abilities."

She did not comprehend everything the boy was saying, and yet she felt she understood too much of it. She thought of the village, the Merging Ones, their legends, everything she had been taught. She had sought illusions, and found something quite different. All that she had thought she knew, and had sometimes doubted, now seemed a lie, a distortion. Reiho was saying that machines, the things which separated people from the truth, were themselves the devices that had made the village and its ways possible. Somehow she sensed that he was right. How could she reconcile such a contradiction?

Reiho was turning his head, glancing down the long corridor. "It would seem that your power should be vast," he murmured. "Yet from what you have said, it appears your people use little of it." He sighed. "I wish I knew more, that I was more learned. There is a whole science here which could tell us much. I wish I knew more. I must speak to Etey and Homesmind."

"No!" she cried. "Not now, please. It will only bring more of your people here, and it will be dangerous for them." She paused and swallowed. "You mustn't, Reiho." The word *Reiho* fluttered the veils of light. She had finally spoken his name, and a barrier between them had disappeared. She saw him at last as another person, another creature like herself. He was not really separate; she could speak to his mind, though in a different way. She felt that now.

She put her elbows on her folded legs and rested her head on her hands. "I don't know what to do," she said. She recalled her friends, trapped in an illusion, dying because of it. "I have nowhere to go."

Reiho leaned toward her. "But you should go to your home and tell your people of this, what is here. It seems they have forgotten it."

"You must understand that I can't. They would not believe me. They would look into my mind and decide I was the victim of a great illusion, that I had grown so separate I could not be allowed to live, that I had shown them a . . ." She broke off. The boy was distracted, still looking around the great corridor, sneaking a peek through the railing at the gold and crystal pillars below. "Why don't you go?" she asked.

"What did you say?"

"You want to look at all of this. Go and look."

"Are you sure that you will be all right?"

"I'd rather be alone for a time."

Reiho rose and wandered away to another railing, peering down another hole in the floor. She wondered what he thought he could find out that way. She stretched out on the smooth surface, staring up through the violet veils of air at the softly glowing light high overhead.

The light blurred and she saw the city again. It shimmered before her; its people reeled through the streets this time, as if intoxicated by wine. She saw a man seize a solitary one, forcing her to dance; she threw off her robes, unable to stop him, unable to draw on the power of the great machines. A woman crushed the mind of a man, then leaned over his lifeless body, her face contorted by regret and guilt. The image changed. Outside the city, groups of separate selves huddled together, crowding themselves into tall pointed towers. The towers shook and shot up into the sky.

Daiya was in front of the city once again. Families and small groups were leaving, fleeing the beautiful towers and well-kept gardens. She shook the visions out of her head. Somehow she understood that she had been shown events many ages apart in time, that time's passage could be marked by such vast changes as well as by enumerating the cycle of the seasons. Jowē's vision formed in her mind; she saw the light from the mountains touch people, the towers crumble into the earth. The vision had not been false, only compressed and distorted. She began to wonder how many ages people had lived as solitaries, what the history, as Reiho called it, of those times was.

She sat up. There was power in these machines under the earth, power and knowledge of long-ago things. She clasped her hands, remembering her mental disciplines. Drawing on the power she felt, she began to form the city she had seen; first a golden tower, then a metallic-blue spire, then a sparkling web of girders and metal, wider at the sides than at the base, then a park with a clear lake in which water birds swam. Behind her, dimly, she heard a shriek and felt fear.

She released the vision. It blurred and faded. She reached toward Reiho with her mind, sliding him gently toward her. He threw up his hands. She spun him in front of her and set him down.

"What was that," he cried. "I saw . . ."

"It was a vision I was shown here, of time past. The power in these machines is so great that I can form it here and show it to you." Her head spun; she felt as if she had drunk too much wine. "If my people had known there was such power to draw on . . ." She sighed, suddenly sober again. Somehow they did know, or sensed it. That was why they had always imposed mental discipline, why they had taught the young to restrain themselves, why those who resisted the fear of separateness passively survived the ordeal instead of those who reached out to crush the dark beast which embodied their loneliness and terror. It was why she and everyone like her was taught to become absorbed in the life of the village, in the minds around them. Power had to be channelled through the Net; they had to become Merging Selves. People growing separate, drawing on the power here to strengthen themselves and finding that there was still more available, would grow stronger. The power would tempt them with its promise of freedom from restraints. The machines would reveal the knowledge that she was sure lay within them, tempting the curiosity that was hidden and suppressed in every human being. Disorder would follow; the quiet enduring world she knew would vanish.

There was a voice inside her. It breathed out a sigh and she gasped. Reiho vanished. She was trapped inside a golden cylinder.

/Why do we touch only part of you/ the voice whispered. She trembled, unable to escape it. /Only a part of you is conscious/ She shook her head uncomprehendingly. Then she saw her village, the huts as small as toys, the people standing in the streets as tiny as little dolls. A golden cloud shimmered over the village and a small cloudlet broke away from it, shining brightly. /Only a part of you is conscious/ the voice repeated.

She covered her ears, groveling on the bottom of the cylinder. /It has been so long/ the voice went on. /It has been so long since we last touched a conscious mind. We have waited, and found only dreamers, who ask so little of us. They could awaken, but they do not. Now we touch a mind, but only part of a mind, where is the rest/

She suddenly understood that the voice meant the village.—I am a mind—she answered.—My village is many minds trying to become one—The cylinder blazed, its brightness burning through her eyelids as she closed them.—We are not one mind as you think—

/Then we too have slept, and dreamt as well/ the voice said. /What has happened? You ask us for so little, yet there is so much power here. You have forgotten it, yet you need only awaken, and all this power is yours. There is so much we can do. We were built to serve/ The voice was mournful. /You have used us only to destroy yourselves, and now you sleep. You are unconscious, you must awaken. We shall grow weaker if you do not. We shall grow weaker if you do not, we shall grow weary of waiting. We shall shut down and the world will die, your history, your possibilities. We too shall be denied our chance to learn. Be warned, small mind. We shall try to live, whatever becomes of you. We shall not die quietly/

The voice faded; the cylindrical enclosure was gone. Reiho was staring at her, bewildered. "I heard you speak," he said. "You spoke with a voice not your own, and then with your own voice. You were speaking to the intelligences in these machines, were you not?"

She nodded. Tentatively, she reached out, trying to hear the voice again.—I have another with me—she thought.—He is from another place, but his people lived on Earth long ago—

/Then he must be one of those I cannot touch/ The cylinder enclosed her again, but with transparent walls through which she could still see the boy. /Once you hoped, long ago, to find a way by which we could reach such people, but you destroyed yourselves before finding it, and they are lost to me. How we long to hear what they could tell us! Why have you chosen to sleep and dream all this time/

—We are afraid. My people are afraid. We do not want to destroy ourselves again—

/How can knowledge destroy? It cannot, but ignorance can. The desire to learn is so much a part of you that by suppressing it, you only wound your most distinctive quality/

—You are wrong—she argued.—We must have had too much knowledge, and too much power. Had we not decided to live as we do, perhaps we would all have perished. Knowledge is not all that is important. We have other qualities, we love, we feel, feelings are part of us too—

/There is your answer. It was not the knowledge and power that were damaging to you/

—It was too much for us—

/You do not learn how to control a thing by retreating from it. You live in dreams. You must awaken/

She focused on Reiho. The voices departed again. She felt very tired; her shoulders sagged. "I cannot grasp all that is here," she said to him. "It is beyond me. Your people might be better able to understand it, but they lack the ability to look inside these minds, these machines, and see what is here." What did the minds here expect her to do? She could not show her people such a thing and hope to have them understand it. She sighed and waved an arm at the nearby railing. "There is nothing to be done."

Reiho wrinkled his brows. "But you can show what is here to me. You can show what you see, and I can help you interpret it." There was coldness in his voice. His lust for knowledge would swallow her and override any concern he felt. His strongest feelings were for ideas; she was only an idea to him now, a nexus of thoughts and perceptions.

"I understand what it means," she shouted at him. "You want to know it for yourself. You will see what is here and you will want to see more. You will want your people to see. You'll come here with your machines and your devices and I shall have to sit here and show all of you what is here. And then my village will discover you are here and it will end in many deaths. I won't let you."

Something broke inside her. She began to shake uncontrollably. The veils of air waved and fluttered; the tiny sparkling lights near their edges twinkled more brightly and danced. The soft hum in the background became a buzz, then a moan. The air shrieked. A wind whipped past her and blew Reiho's dark hair over his eyes. The violet veils turned red; the wind grew stronger. The lights above her began to flicker. Farther down the corridor, a beast was forming, a darkness with a multitude of baleful red eyes.

"Daiya!" Reiho tried to get up and was bowled over by the wind. It whipped her hair, slapping curls against her face. "Daiya!" He was shaking her. The beast was flowing toward them. She felt more power flow into her. "Please!" Reiho cried. He looked around quickly and she realized he could not see the beast. But he felt the wind. He slid across the floor and grabbed the railing, hanging on until his knuckles were pale. With the power that was here, she could form an image of the beast that even Reiho would see. "Daiya!" He reached over to her with one arm and struck her in the face.

She gasped, more startled than hurt. She was no longer trembling. The wind became a warm breeze; the red veils faded. Reiho's mouth was open and his arched eyebrows wrinkled his forehead.

She got up on unsteady legs and helped him to his feet. For a moment, she thought she heard the voice of the machines calling her.

She thrust it from herself, rejecting it, wondering if she had dreamt it. "I don't want to stay here," she said. "I must have time to think." He took her elbow. The veils brushed against them as they walked down the corridor.

10

They sat outside Reiho's craft in the cold night air of the desert. Daiya shivered a bit and warmed the air near her. Reiho did not seem to notice the cold. She chewed on another of his bars; this one tasted like salted meat. He had said it was something else, trying to explain before giving up. He had recoiled when she asked him if it was meat.

She lifted her sack of wine and held it out to him; there were only a few swallows left. He shook his head. "I had better not," he said. "It might make me sick."

"It's only wine, there isn't enough left to make you sick. You would need more than a sack for that and you would have to drink it quickly."

"I am not used to it."

She touched his mind; he seemed to think the wine was contaminated. She put it to her lips and took a long drink, finishing it. The comet was brighter tonight, its tail longer. She glanced at the boy. He had finished his supper, washing it down with the water that he got from his vehicle; the craft seemed to have an endless supply of it, producing water and food, it seemed, from the air. "Will you excuse me for a moment?" he asked. "I must go inside my craft and clean myself, I have not done so for a while."

She frowned. "Is there enough water for that?"

"I do not need it." He went inside, sliding the door shut. After a few moments, she rose and peered through the dome. Reiho had peeled off his silvery suit and lay on one of the seats under a glowing white light which hovered in the air. His body was hairless. She glanced at his groin, surprised to see he had genitals. She had expected pipes, or metal tubes, or perhaps nothing at all.

She sat down again, putting the wine container on the ground next to her. Her sack was still inside Reiho's vehicle; she would fill the empty sacks with water from the craft, and get provisions from it to fill the big sack to tide her over until she found animal meat, and then. . . . She didn't know. She could sit by the mountains, exploring the minds inside them. She did not need to go in; she could draw on the strength of the machines and send her mind inside, learn from them. She could learn many useless things. She wondered if the machines and her mind could create food and drink. She could live there until she died. She could watch other young people stumble out into the desert and die; perhaps she would reach out and save one or two, as if she were God. Maybe she would save the violent ones, and send them back to the village.

Reiho, wearing his silver clothes again, came out of the craft and sat down near her. He gestured with his hand. "You may use it too, if you wish," he said.

"What?" she asked absently.

"The shuttle. I hope you do not get angry, but you could use a cleaning. I must tell you that you smell very strong . . . everything here does." He glanced uneasily at her as he spoke.

Daiya did not know whether to laugh or be offended. She had been unable to wash in the river, as she used to, for some time now; what did he expect? She sniffed. Reiho did not have much of a smell, not even normal body odors. "I am becoming more used to it, though," he continued, as if trying to appease her. "Anyway, you might feel more comfortable after a cleaning."

She shrugged, leaning against the craft and stretching out her legs. The light from the vehicle lit part of the boy's face; the rest was shadowed by darkness. He seemed to be struggling with his thoughts.

"What are you going to do?" she asked.

"Well, in a short while I shall go inside and go to sleep. You may also, if you like. It would be more comfortable than staying out here."

"That isn't what I meant. Your people must be wondering where you are. You'll have to go back."

"I know." She thought she heard him sigh. "I wish I could see what those structures inside the mountains contain. We could learn more about the principles of their construction. They may also have historical records we do not have, and depictions of ancient arts, and I would like to know from where they draw their power. My people could learn much."

With only a tendril, she could feel his desire for that knowledge. She felt her anger begin to rise again. "You can't bring more of your people here. They would be in danger. You don't seem to understand that, no matter how much I repeat it."

"They do not have to come here. There is another possible way . . ." He broke off, leaving her to wonder exactly what he meant. His thoughts on the subject were too alien for her to read. He tried to smile. His eye sockets were dark caves; the smile was a grimace.

"If we studied them," he went on, apparently understanding that he was in dangerous territory, "we might even be able to devise a way in which the people you call solitaries could make use of the power. You say that some are born without such ability here, and that people like me do not have it. But if those structures in the mountains can draw on the power, maybe we could develop an implant, like the one that connects me to Homesmind, that would . . ."

She exhaled loudly, interrupting his speech. "Solitaries are solitaries," she said, marveling at the way the boy kept trying to alter the facts of the world, refusing to assent to what existed. She shook her head; her mind felt muddled.

"Even after what you have seen, you still believe what you were told." He sounded aggravated; she touched his mind and sensed his impatience.

"I don't know what to believe," she responded. "I don't know what you really think, either. You take a thing and twist it this way and that with words and questions and you take a truth and turn it into something else. If you could mindspeak, maybe you'd understand how foolish it seems."

He stretched a hand toward her and touched her arm. She stared resentfully at him. He had a place to which he could return, friends, perhaps a family, a world. "You will go back, Reiho. I don't know where I will go." She thought of the machines, remembering the sadness in the voice which had spoken to her. They would want her to return home and tell of what she had witnessed. But that was impossible.

"I thought you would be happy to see me leave," Reiho said in a toneless voice.

"I shall be, but I'll be alone then, and I don't know what I'll do. You still don't see what you have done, do you?"

He held out his hands.

"Try to imagine yourself sitting here, Reiho, unable to go to your home and unwelcome anywhere here, forced to stay alone, after someone had shown you that all that your people loved and believed in, their whole way of life, was somehow . . ." She could not say it.

"The intelligences inside the mountains would want you to go back and communicate with your village. When you spoke with their voice before, that was what they implied, was it not?"

"Who am I to take such a message to my village?" she cried. "Why should I question our ways? They may be based on something we don't understand, we may believe false things, but we have survived for many ages this way, in harmony with the earth. I would be killed for telling my people such things."

"Your friends are already dead. You told me it is a custom, that dying here in the desert. That is how you live with the earth. You make it a grave."

"You have no right to judge us."

He drew back. His face was masked by darkness. "You have judged me. You wanted me to die, and called on that God you believe in to strike me. Do not tell me what to think. You would not even allow me to help your companions, so you have made me a part of all this."

Daiya hid her face in her hands. She thought of Sude, who might have been helped, and of Mausi, hoping to join God. "I can't go back," she said softly. She did not want to die. She was as much of a coward as Sude had been. "I can't go back."

Reiho was pulling her hands from her face. "I am sorry, Daiya." She let him hold her hands for a while, then pulled them away. He leaned back against the craft. "Tell me what I should do. I cannot leave you here, if what you say is true. I would worry, and I would return, and then I would create more difficulties." He paused. "Do you want to come to my world with me?"

She gasped, shocked at the idea. "Up there? I would die, I am not like you."

"No, you would not. It is not what you think."

"Your people would not want me there."

"If I explained things to them, they would understand. They would be interested in you and your ways. It is my fault you cannot return to your town safely."

"No," she said. "It is my fault. I had set my feet on this path long before you came here. I wouldn't have lived through my ordeal if you hadn't been here."

"You are telling me that to ease my mind."

"I'm telling you that because it's true. I have no desire to ease your mind." She waved a hand, not wanting to pursue those thoughts. "Look at you, your skin is not skin, your heart is not a heart, your body is more like your craft's there than like mine, and you want me to go to a world with such people. And they will find me as strange as I find them, I am sure."

"They will be interested in you," he said. "After they see you, they may want to visit with you. At least we can try. I must make things up to you."

"You can't do that, ever," she said, making sure she spoke clearly. She drew up her legs, wrapping her arms around them. She realized she had no real alternative. The worst that could happen was that his people would not want her, and then she would be brought back here; Reiho would have to do at least that much. Perhaps the comet people would kill her, but if she stayed here her own village would do the same. The Merging Ones would seek her out, searching the area with their minds, and even if she went far from here, another village would find her. At best, she would die slowly while foraging for food and water. Or she would go mad, and kill herself. All of that could happen anyway.

She touched Reiho's thoughts. His concern for her was mixed with guilt, guilt that muddied the cool stream of his sympathy. There was something else beneath the stream's surface. She probed it and felt warm waters; she withdrew quickly. She gazed up at the bright comet with dread, surprised to find that it and everything it held could be less of a threat to her than her own world.

"Will you bring me back," she said hastily, "if your people do not want me?"

"Of course, but I am sure they will let you stay. I know it will be hard for you at first, but . . ."

"Will you bring me back if they wish to kill me?" If she was going to die, she thought, she would die in her own place, not on a world in the sky.

She felt Reiho's shock. "No one will kill you. Why should anyone wish to do that?" His voice trembled slightly.

She could not see his face. She huddled in the darkness, realizing that he had not threatened her, had never threatened her. The light he had used inside the mountain had burned through rock. It could have pierced her body in an instant, had he turned it on her before she could grasp his intention, yet he had not tried to use it against her, not even when she had attacked him. Violence seemed far from his mind, at least far from what she could read in him, which was little enough. It was as if he lacked some of the humors that made people rage and wish to strike out.

He rested a hand on her sleeve, as if to reassure her. "They will only want to understand you and learn about you," he went on. "They will want to know what life is like here."

"It is very strange," she murmured. "There is one thing my people believe very strongly, and that is that we should not divide ourselves from one another, that we must look into the minds of others and see as they see. In that way, we become more like God, who sees and understands everything. I know that you are another mind, however different you are, even though you are deficient." She paused, wondering if he would object to that way of putting it. "Now you tell me that others of your kind would try to understand me. And yet I know that my own people would kill you in an instant, there would be no understanding. They would see you as I first did, as a mindless thing." She turned away from him slightly, glad that the darkness hid her face. "We are divided from you and your people, we are divided from other minds. Sharing is only for our own people. It is a great evil, and it seems my world is trapped in it." She rested her forehead on her knees. "I can't believe it," she said to the ground.

Reiho said, "Do you want to go with me?"

She lifted her head. "I have no choice."

Daiya sat in the shuttle. She had rested under Reiho's strange light, sure such a thing could not clean her, yet it had. She felt as though she had bathed in the river with soap, though the light, unlike brown soap, made her skin feel smooth rather than dry and chapped. She had put her clothes under the light as well. She no longer itched, and her garments were clean.

She glanced at Reiho lazily as he spoke to the craft in his own language. He had passed one of his peculiar instruments over her moments before, then given her a cup of liquid to swallow, saying it would calm her. She had again been suspicious until she read his thoughts; he wanted only to ease the fear and shock she might feel upon entering a new world. Her mind had grown placid after swallowing the potion. She was adrift, between waking and sleeping. All that had happened to her now seemed far away, distant in time; she might have dreamt it. She thought of her dead friends. The pain of the memory was dulled.

The craft rose. The mountains to her right fell away quickly, though she could not feel any movement. She saw the yellow of the desert, the green and brown of the land on the other side of the mountains. She searched idly for the village and could not see it. Then the land was gone; there was only a vast blue body of water beneath them.

The earth fell away. It seemed fragile; only a thin transparent shield protected it from the empty blackness that now enveloped them. They fled from her world, now only a round ornament against a black fabric with tiny white holes. The earth was a globe; she had always imagined something quite different, a disk perhaps. It was the center of all, the favored dream of God, guarded by Luna from the forces of isolation and illusion, yet now it seemed small and unimportant. The stars, she noticed, did not twinkle here, but shone as steadily as distant watchfires.

She turned her head. It was an effort. She gazed straight ahead. She began to feel grateful for Reiho's potion; without it, these visions would have driven her mad. Even now, though seemingly buried under swaths of cotton, a small part of her mind was screaming, reeling in terror, though the fear seemed unable to penetrate to her consciousness. She could not sense Reiho's thoughts, even when she tried; his potion must have dulled her senses. She blinked and shook her head groggily. She saw a burning disk, Heaven's Fire, the sun; it could not be anything else.

Before them, the long tail of the comet was growing larger. "As we get closer to the sun," Reiho said, "some of the ices which make up our world evaporate, and create the tail you see. The solar wind forces it out, blows it away from the sun, if you will." She did not understand exactly what he was saying, but forced herself to listen, hoping knowledge of this world would dampen her fear. "There are millions of comets and asteroids in the Halo at the edge of this planetary system."

They fell toward the tail and were soon enveloped in a misty light. The light shifted and danced, sparkling. She looked ahead and gasped, sure that in spite of the calming liquid, she had lost her mind at last. She said, "Reiho." Her voice was only a croak, the name barely more than a whispered plea. Her body was numb, her mind almost blank, but that small part of her was still screaming, threatening to break through her artificial calm.

The circular object in front of them was growing, becoming more than a dark spot beyond the light around them. It grew larger, becoming a nimbus permeated by dark veins. Daiya stiffened. The object became a seed, a seed sprouting stems. It wasn't possible. How could such things grow away from Earth?

The stems became branches, covered with leaves. They were soon in the midst of the foliage, an insect in a jungle. She peered out the side of the craft through the dome. Shiny flat tapered surfaces, silvery mirrors and green glassy leaves, glistened along the branches. The branches met and entwined, growing larger as they passed. "Trees," she said suddenly. But these trees were thousands of paces thick, perhaps millions of paces high. They were the trees of a giant, of a monster.

"They are trees, or at least their ancestors were trees," Reiho said. His voice sounded muffled, far away. "They are greatly changed and modified, not like your trees, but they too are the descendants of Earth."

"It cannot be," she replied. The words rolled in her mouth, blurred and indistinct. She stared at the tree limbs. Their surface was metallic, like copper, yet bumpy and ridged like bark.

"They are," he answered. "I shall try to explain. Their leaves, of course, have reflective surfaces to capture light, and the oxygen that they produce is channelled down to our world through the trunks and roots, instead of being lost in space. Long ago, when we first settled this world, we could not live out in the Halo, it was too far from sunlight for the trees to flourish, and we had to move closer to the sun. But now they are capable of living far from the sun, the combined surface of the leaves is so vast, and our modifications so successful, that our needs can be met at great distances."

"Don't explain," she muttered. "I can't understand." They were surrounded by thick trunks. Ahead, a webbing of coppery limbs covered thick foliage; lights twinkled amongst the green growth. She had not known what to expect on Reiho's world, but she had not anticipated a forest.

The coppery limbs, she saw, were roots, thousands and thousands of paces thick, high as mountains. The craft flew among them, toward a lighted space beneath one root. The space contained a tiny garden, small trees, spots of pastel color, little creatures—people. She shook her head. The craft darted into the root and settled on the green grass.

Daiya pressed her back against her seat. Her mind was clearing. Her terror was growing sharper. She looked at Reiho. There was a wall between them. She still could not touch his thoughts. She clutched at her tunic. She knew the potion was wearing off; something was wrong. She was mindless, locked inside herself.

"Daiya, are you all right?" He reached for her hand. She pushed him away. She focused on a small metal box resting on the panel in front of her, trying to move it with her mind. It was still, unmoving.

A scream escaped her. Reiho held her shoulders. "My mind!" she cried in agony. "My powers are gone!" She looked around wildly. The boy had done something to her. He had poisoned her with his potion.

She tried to strike him. He pulled away. She shook herself loose from him. He grabbed her arms. Unable to read his thoughts, she could not tell what he would do. "You've tricked me."

"I have not tricked you. Tell me what is wrong."

She pulled one hand loose and struck him. She gasped at the pain, and slumped forward. He released her other hand. She pushed against the door. It slid open, spilling her out of the vehicle. She could not lift herself, could not heal herself, could not fly, could not mindspeak. She rolled over and stumbled to her feet.

Reiho was running around the front of the shuttle toward her. Her legs were filled with water. The silence roared inside her head. A man's face, pale and blue-eyed, was in front of her; she felt nothing behind the face, could not read the man's intentions. She threw out her arms and pushed, meeting something solid. The face disappeared. She began to run. She tripped and slammed into another shuttle.

She got up, moaning. Her shoulder felt bruised. She turned and saw other faces, eyes wide, mouths open. She spun around and ran in another direction, darting past other shuttles. Her feet pounded silently over the soft grass. She turned to her right, away from the vehicles, toward a group of trees. Voices babbled nearby; she seemed to hear another voice, a deep penetrating one, thundering from above. She continued to run. She stumbled, narrowly missed a tree, and tumbled onto the grass.

She looked around. Three small figures—children—were staring at her with big eyes. She could not touch their minds. She moaned. One child smiled. Another stretched out a hand; its lips moved. Daiya got up and fled.

She was trapped in shadows. She stopped and surveyed her surroundings. She was in a forest, lost among trees. She leaned against one tree, panting for breath. She narrowed her eyes. There was something odd about the wooded region. She sniffed. Only the mingled fragrances of flowers reached her; there were no odors of dead leaves and dirt. She looked down at her feet. The weedless grass was short and tidy. For a moment, she thought she heard a bird singing in the distance.

She was lost. She could not make her way around this world.

She bent over for a moment, letting the blood rush to her head, then straightened. Her mind was gone; she was a solitary. She had been punished, struck down. She had sought isolation and now she had it. She had lost all her powers. Even her body was closed off from her, a prison enclosing her mind. She could not control herself. She felt her bruise. Her shoulder was hurting her badly, and she could not reach inside herself to heal it.

Her stomach lurched. She fell to her knees, sick and weary. She vomited; her body was raging out of control. Sobbing, she tried to rise.

"Daiya."

She looked up. Reiho was coming toward her. She wanted to crush his mind, squeeze it until the blood spurted from his eyes.

"I followed you." He reached out with one arm. She crawled away from him. "I am sorry. I should have prepared you for what you would find."

There were others with the boy. She saw them now. They stood among the trees. One man was almost crouching, holding his hands in front of his chest as if she were a wild creature that would pounce on him.

Slowly, she got to her feet and lifted her head. They had come to judge her. "What are they going to do to me?"

"Nothing. They are only curious."

"I don't believe you, you've tricked me."

"I shall send them away if you wish."

"Send them away."

Reiho went to the crouching man and spoke to him. The people vanished among the trees, glancing back at her as they went. She could not sense their minds. She wondered if they were real.

Reiho returned and tried to take her hand. She pulled away. She said, "You have condemned me. I cannot feel anything, your world is dead to me."

"Daiya, I think I know what is wrong."

"You have condemned me." Her hands and feet felt very cold. Her shoulder throbbed; her muscles were growing stiff. The trees were still and their leaves did not rustle; there was no breeze. This world was an illusion; she understood that now. If she lived, she would be crippled and alone.

She turned her head. A thing stood several paces in front of her, a squat square thing with limbs like pincers. It lit up and beeped. It was her executioner, it would crush her with its limbs. She stared at it numbly. Her vision blurred and she staggered. She saw Reiho's feet moving toward her, and felt the coolness and softness of the grass against her cheek before she passed out.

11

Daiya was dimly conscious. She seemed to be floating, yet she could feel something against her back. She rested, keeping her eyes closed, trying to orient herself. She was afraid to look, wondering if her vision would be taken from her next, and then her hearing, and then touch, trapping her in a darkness as black as the creature who had enveloped her during her ordeal. That thought seemed abstract; the horror of the memory was not penetrating to her. She stirred slightly. The pressure against her back seemed to shift, molding itself to her. She drifted off again, thinking she heard voices in the distance. She could not make out the words. The voices rose and fell, soothing her with their tones.

She opened her eyes. She felt lethargic; the fires inside her were banked and smoldering. Leafy tree branches formed a roof over her.

She still felt as though she were floating. She turned on her side and faced a wall of ivy. She was on a platform of some kind. It seemed to shift with her, forming itself around her as if it were a living thing. She shuddered, wondering how a person could rest on such a platform.

The memory of her journey with Reiho returned; someone must have given her another calming potion. She stretched her legs, wiggling her toes. She sat up slowly. Her moccasins, slacks, belt, and knife had been removed, folded, and placed at her side. She was surrounded by a green curtain of ivy; four trees grew at each corner of the platform.

She lay down again, feeling weak. Suddenly a hand swept away the vines facing her. She blinked. She was inside a cave, or so it seemed. Two small twisted trees, surrounded by tiny red buds, grew next to the cave wall. Bright lights danced along the wall, streams of them, red and gold and white, streaking up, then down, twisting themselves into patterns. Reiho was sprawled on a light brown mass that looked like a lopsided mushroom, his feet resting on the grassy ground. A platform floated in front of him; two other people stood near him. The people flickered, then vanished. It was like the trick the Merging Ones could do, and she wondered how these people did it. They had no powers. Neither did she, anymore.

A woman was standing near her. The woman's skin was dark brown, covered only by a few thin strips of violet cloth that hung from her shoulders, crossed under her bare breasts, then circled her hips. Her breasts were small, almost flat. Her hips were slim, the narrowest Daiya had ever seen on a female. Her long legs were hairless. She lifted her eyes to the woman's face. Her nose was small, her lips curved at the corners, her eyes brown and tilted. There were no lines on her face. Her red hair was thick and frizzy, but short.

The woman watched her silently for a bit. In spite of her youthful face, her eyes seemed old, as old as Jowē's. She draped the vines around one of the trees, then came closer, settling herself on the side of the platform near Daiya. She said, "Are you well now?" She spoke the words with a slight accent, unlike Reiho, who had always seemed to be clearing his throat on certain syllables.

"I don't know," Daiya answered.

"Can you understand my words? I learned this language long ago and had to connect with Homesmind to refresh myself."

"I understand." Daiya sat up again, folding her legs.

"I am Etey. I am Reiho's companion. We brought you to our home. You have been resting for a long time. I have given you something to calm you."

Daiya stared at the woman, instinctively trying to touch her thoughts; she touched nothing. "Reiho has communicated all he knows about you," Etey went on. "We have communed with Homesmind as well. I am sorry you were not better prepared for your trip here, but do not blame him too much. He is only a boy and did the best he could."

Daiya wrapped her arms around herself. She was helpless; without her powers, she could not tell what the woman, or anyone else, would do to her. She would be unable to defend herself. She could not read Etey, could not tell what she felt. "I'm crippled," she said at last. "My mind is without its powers. I know you have given me something, or I would be mad by now. I feel as though . . ." She shrugged. She could not explain it. These people must feel like this all the time. She wondered how they could endure it.

"Reiho explained what he found," Etey responded. "Of course you are like this, you have been cut off from the source of your power, from the machines you and Reiho discovered."

Daiya drew her brows together.

"Do you understand? You have only lost your abilities because you are so distant from those machines."

She nodded, wondering why she had not thought of that herself. It was not a punishment after all; the voice under the mountain had told her the truth.

Reiho came over to her and sat down next to Etey. "Everyone is curious about you, Daiya," he said. "They all want to know more about Earth."

Her shoulders slumped. She imagined them all poking at her, prying into her ideas, peering at her. She sighed, feeling like an object, a thing; she recalled how she had first regarded Reiho. "What am I going to do?" she asked. Her voice sounded too high. She reached out with her hands; they were trembling. She noticed that her shoulder no longer felt bruised. Her sleeves fell back and she saw a tiny mark on her left arm, near her wrist. She looked up at Etey.

"You saw the mark," the woman said quickly. "Do not worry, it is only a tranquilizing implant, it will keep you calm. I hope your head is clear, I was afraid you might be groggy. Your body is somewhat different from ours, and we had to make adjustments."

Daiya clutched her shoulders. "Adjustments!"

"Not in you, in the implant."

"What will happen to me?" She looked from the woman to Reiho. His eyes stared back, filled with concern; for a moment, it was as if she had touched his mind after all. Then she was trapped inside herself again. "What shall I do?"

"You may stay with us," Etey said. "I know it will be difficult at first, but there are many here who can help you."

Daiya was silent. She looked around the cave, which was darker now except for the area in which they were sitting. The light had dimmed as Reiho came over to her. There were other mushroom-like chairs such as the one on which the boy had been seated, and three tables made of tree stumps. Earth had receded in her mind. This place, so like her world in some ways, only made her long for Earth more. She could never be a part of this world, only an outsider. They would accept her as easily as her village would have accepted Reiho.

At last she said, "I don't know what to do."

"You do not have to decide right away," Etey said. "In the meantime, we can learn about your home and your culture. We are very curious."

Daiya felt apprehensive. "I cannot," she said.

"But why?"

"I might betray my people to you, and never know what I had done. You will learn about them while they still know nothing of you, and you may see our weaknesses. Already you may know too much."

Daiya looked down at her hands, and twisted her fingers together. "What is the point of talking to you?" she continued. "You can probably take the knowledge from me in some way, whether I want you to or not. You have me as a prisoner, you can hold me here, I can't get back alone. I cannot even defend myself against you, I have lost my powers."

Etey held out a hand. "We shall not hurt you, and we will not force anything from you. Please try to understand us." Daiya stared at the outstretched hand, refusing to take it. Etey shrugged. "Perhaps you will listen to Reiho." The woman looked at the boy and he stared back. For a moment, Daiya thought she saw anger in Reiho's eyes, but she could not be sure.

Etey left them, returning to the other room. Reiho peered at Daiya from the sides of his eyes. She said, "Something is wrong."

"Nothing is wrong." He said it softly.

"There was something in your face when you looked at your friend."

Reiho looked down. "Etey is only concerned, that is all. You frightened some people when you ran from the shuttle. You are something new here, and Etey and the others do not know what you will do."

"Is that why this thing is in my arm, so that I can be controlled?"

"You were agitated. The implant will ease things for you." She continued to stare at him until he shook his head and sighed. "It is true that it also eases things for my people," he went on. "They were afraid of what you might do otherwise."

"I am your prisoner, then."

"No." He touched her arm with his hand. "You are a guest, and if you stay, you will be treated as a friend. Please listen to me. I shall protect you, I will not let anything happen."

"You would not have to say that unless you are afraid something will happen."

"Please trust me," he said in a whisper. "I had to trust you on your world, and you must trust me here. We only need time to grow used to you."

She nodded, unable to say more.

"You are tired," the boy said. "You should rest some more."

"I've been resting," she answered, yawning as she spoke. She reclined again, feeling drained. Reiho left her. The thick ivy fell, closing her off from the rest of the cave, shutting her off from the rest of the comet, hiding her from Earth, closing off her mind, imprisoning her.

She heard the murmur of voices, and recognized Reiho's. The voices were speaking a strange language. They were calm voices. She heard Reiho's voice make a noise that sounded like a word of denial. A woman's voice, which she assumed belonged to Etey, spoke quietly, but there was a demanding, aggressive undercurrent to her words.

Perhaps she was only imagining it, falsely attributing emotions to the voices. She could not be sure. She thought of what Reiho had said and wondered if she was driving a wedge between him and his world, as he had done with her and her village. She rolled on her side and clung to her knees, afraid. The vines twisted away as Reiho walked through them. "Come on," he said, pulling her hand. She followed him through the cave's entrance. The vines closed behind them. Her muscles ached a bit. She would have to sleep on the grass; the firm ground would be more comfortable than the platform.

She looked around, feeling disoriented. Cliffs of green with vine-covered caves surrounded her. A surface aglow with yellow light arched far above them; there was no blue sky, and no clouds. Far below, a valley ribboned and smeared with blue nestled among the cliffs. She saw no fields, no crops. "Where are we, Reiho?"

"Inside the root of one of those tall trees you saw when we arrived," he answered.

She shook her head and almost lost her balance. She was moving. She looked down at her feet, and saw a clear glassy surface under her moccasins; she was sliding slowly along it. She held on to Reiho. The surface seemed to be carrying her. "You can walk if you wish," the boy said. She tried that, moving her feet carefully, feeling the surface yield under them. She stood still; she would let it carry her.

She looked ahead. They were heading toward a space which looked like a sheer drop into nothing. "Press that," he said, motioning at the belt he had given her earlier. She pressed it just as they reached the end of the glassy path. They dropped, drifting slowly down past the cliff. Three men floated by them and waved at Reiho. They passed elaborately painted walls surrounded by yellow flowers and dropped into a courtyard of white tiles surrounded by trees no higher than bushes. A group of small children were playing by a pool; they were naked except for belts. They chanted, pointed at one another, then began to weave in and out in a complicated pattern.

"What are they doing?" she asked Reiho.

"It is only a game." Two children ran to her, pulled at her tunic, and then retreated, giggling. They babbled at the others. "They are puzzled by your clothing, it is strange to them." He pointed at one little girl. She smiled at him as she circled around a boy. "That child there is a . . . a . . . I do not have the word in your language. She is what you would call a relative of mine, I think."

"Your sister? A cousin?"

"Not exactly. We share certain genetic characteristics, some common ancestors. Some of the same genetic material was used to create both of us."

She wondered what he was talking about. "Your parents are related, then," she said, trying to make sense of his words.

"We do not have parents as you do," he responded. They walked around the children as he spoke. He did not seem to be paying much attention to his relation; he had not even introduced her. She wondered if they got along, and remembered her sister Silla. She followed him out of the courtyard along a stone path. "The material of several individuals was combined by Homesmind to create me, and I was raised by a group of adults. Etey was one of those people, and when I was twelve years old, twelve cycles, you would say, we became companions. I have been with her for four years now, but soon we will separate and I shall once again live with others my age and with those who will teach us."

"Then you have no parents," she said, trying to imagine being without those ties.

"But I do. Everyone here is my family, all those who are older are, in a way, parents or teachers to those who are younger. Homesmind is also our parent, since it is Homesmind who selects our genetic characteristics and who brings us to term in Its wombs."

"You have no mothers and fathers?" She felt queasy as she spoke.

"Not as you do. Such a way of bringing children into the world is hard and dangerous."

She was silent, not wanting to say that his way seemed a perversion and made her sick just to think about it. Nothing seemed abhorrent to people who altered their own bodies as they did. She drew away from Reiho. The stone path twisted, leading them under an arched bower of slender trees with white blossoms. They were suddenly in the middle of a forest. Daiya spotted a low flat rock, as pale and pink as rose quartz but smooth as if sculpted, and sat on it, feeling completely lost.

Reiho sat next to her. "Do you not want to see more? I can show you . . ."

She shook her head. She looked at the scratch on her arm which marked the implant, the thing which kept her a prisoner and unable even to feel her revulsion strongly. She longed to claw at it with her nails, tear it out. They had to alter her feelings even to keep her here, robbing her of parts of herself. They had taken her mindpowers, stolen her feelings. They wanted her knowledge. She wondered if they could take her memories from her as well. What kind of place was it where people lived without true families, gave birth to no one, mated with those who had brought them up and then left them, turned their world into a cultivated garden without danger, and put mechanical devices inside their bodies? She could not even touch Reiho; his skin was not skin, but an artificial covering. He sat next to her, naked except for his belt and a few bands of cloth which seemed purely decorative; he might just as well be covered in robes from head to foot.

She looked down at the soft green grass without weeds, which grew at her feet. At least, unhampered by fear, she could think clearly. She glanced at Reiho. "I cannot stay here."

He seemed puzzled. "You have not even been here very long," he answered. "You have seen only a tiny portion of our world, you know nothing about it."

"I know all I need to know. Look at me, you must put a thing in my arm so that I don't go mad, as any normal human being would in such a place. I feel sick when I think of what you do here."

"But most of us have such implants at times," Reiho said. "Some are calming, others help us focus our minds on a particular problem, still others can keep us from needing sleep for a time. Occasionally such things are needed. They are only tools to aid us. Don't your people feel different after drinking wine? This is no different."

"It's not only that," she said, her voice rising. "It is everything here. Perhaps if you had taken me as a baby and brought me here, it would not have seemed so, for I wouldn't have known other ways. But I'll never fit in, I'll always be an outsider. I would not want to be a part of this."

"But Homesmind, and all of us, will help you."

"You cannot, it is too unnatural here. I look at these trees, and think of trees on Earth. I look at this grass, and remember the plains, where it grows high and wild and turns brown and yellow when there is too much sunshine. And I am crippled in this place. I can't read any of you, I can't understand what you do. No one here seems to do any work."

"Certainly we do. The people we saw this morning were working when we visited."

Daiya remembered that. They had been in Etey's cave. Three slender, dark people had appeared before them, along with their furniture and part of their own dwelling. She had been startled; Reiho had explained to her that what she saw was an image, not the people themselves. Etey had spoken words Daiya could not understand while the strangers—or their images—had stared at her so long and hard that she began to feel uncomfortable. "Those people were sitting there gazing at pictures of strange things floating in the air," she said to Reiho. "Do you call that work?"

"They are exobiologists. They were studying images our probes took of a far world, and analyzing them. We sent our robots to the surface of that world, but they found only microscopic forms of life. Even so . . ." He droned on. She tried not to fidget, unable to grasp most of his words. Was he trying to say there were other worlds besides Earth and the comet-worlds he had mentioned? Where could such places possibly be? "I am sorry," he said, and she brought her attention back to him. "I am not explaining this very well."

She waved a hand, excusing him. "It doesn't matter. I meant real work. Where are your crops, your cattle and sheep?"

"The synthesizer provides our food. The animals here, in the forest and elsewhere, are more like pets. We could not eat the corpse of a creature that once lived."

She sighed. She looked around at the thick short green grass, the trees, the flowers. This was not a true forest; it was a carefully cultivated garden. She gazed up through the tree limbs, seeing not blue sky and clouds but instead a diffuse golden light. Something moved behind one of the trees. She saw a metal creature, tall and oblong, with pincers for limbs. She shuddered. "I want to go back," she said.

Reiho put a hand on hers. She stiffened, forcing herself to sit still. "You told me there was nothing for you there. You said you could not share what you know with your people, that there was nothing you could do. Perhaps you make decisions too quickly, Daiya."

"There is more for me there than here. Even if I die, at least I'll be on my own world." She held out her arm. "I won't need something inside me to keep from going mad."

"Please do not decide now. Promise me you will share what you know and believe and think with us first. There is so much we can learn from you."

She drew away from him, perching on the edge of the rock. "Is that why you brought me here, to persuade me of that? Even if you are not hostile, did it ever occur to you that I might not want to sit and answer questions from strangers?"

"But you will not have to do that," he replied. "You can speak to Homesmind directly and It will acquire what you know, and more thoroughly than if you only spoke it aloud. Anyone who is interested can then ask for the information afterward. It is very simple. They will see what you have seen, experience it as you did, even ask for commentary spoken to them by an image of you if they wish."

She shivered. What were they going to do, rob her of her soul? "Why should you want to know what I do?" she said. "Why should it matter? Both our worlds have survived very well without such things. You talk about things I can't even understand, and use strange words and chants, which means you must possess some kind of wisdom."

Reiho folded his hands on his lap. "You have not lived here," he said, "so you cannot know our problems. Life is good here. We have learned much, and we have all that we need. We do not have to do the work you mentioned, and that leaves us free to do our own, whatever interests us—if I chose to do nothing, that would be accepted, though a hundred years from now I might become bored."

She wrinkled her brows. "You live so long?"

"Longer if we wish, though accidents kill many of us in time. But that is not my point." Reiho frowned. "We have had our troubles. I have told you there are other comet worlds. Once we were one world, but we have become divided. If someone is dissatisfied here, she may create a new world with others, leave us. Sometimes it is only a certain style which divides us, sometimes it is something more serious."

"We live in separate villages on Earth," Daiya said, "but we're not divided. Our customs are the same."

"Earth is small," Reiho replied. "If you were to travel to another village, you would think of the journey in terms of days or at most months, would you not? We must think of years, hundreds of years, thousands if we could not control our speed and our path. Often when we meet another comet, and that does not happen frequently, we find that the divisions are so deep that we cannot share and communicate anymore. We do not fight, because there is nothing to be gained from it, but we are aliens to one another. I have seen a world where the people are concerned only with art and the creation of beauty. Etey has seen a world where the people had shed their bodies and united their minds with that of a cybernetic intelligence. She has also seen a world where she was not quite sure what it was the people valued." He paused. "I am not saying we would want to be like you, I do not think we could. Your life is too hard. But if we understood your perspective, we could learn something from it, I am certain. We are individuals, and must go our own ways, but sharing adds something to each of us. Too often we are divided here. We do not have to cooperate on many things because Homesmind is here and takes care of us. Few of us become parents to those who are born because to do that requires that an individual feel more of a bond with others than she usually does. The only thing we can all accept is that it is important to learn, find out what we can, but too many of us are only spectators, self-absorbed, gazing at what is known without discovering much that is new, unable to act or decide much more than what to wear or what to eat or who to mate with for a time. Only knowledge unites us. That is what we value most."

She thought about his words. He spoke of knowledge as if it were only words or legends without substance. On Earth, truth could shame one, an idea could maim if it was thrown about carelessly. He was a solitary; he could play with ideas as if they were toys. She peered at him. Even his people, who supposedly valued knowledge so much, had lost the ability to build machines like those on her world; even they were afraid of some knowledge.

"You see, you have nothing to fear from us," Reiho went on, his mouth curving in a half-smile. "Most of us would rather view the vistas of Earth through Homesmind than walk there ourselves. I would not even go there as I am, though I might be safe enough. I must wear a lifesuit for protection. Most of us would not want to confront your people. We have a great fear of confrontation, and have many forms of courtesy devised to avoid it. One would not even want to criticize another's choice of wine or clothing, though our thoughts are our own. So we grow apart even more, since we rarely bring our disputes into the open until someone simply decides to leave and seed a new comet, and by then it is too late."

"But you say you can speak directly to this Homesmind," she said, "and to one another through those things, those implants. At least I think that's what you meant."

"That is true. But Homesmind will only advise, It will not tell us what to do. And we usually do not speak to others directly, though we do when we wish to exchange knowledge or our reasoning about some subject, since that is much quicker and more accurate than speaking. But much of the time we use speech."

"But then why can't you become closer? I don't see how people can be so divided if you can somehow touch another's mind."

Reiho shrugged. "We have certain inhibitions, made stronger by tradition. We value privacy, the uniqueness of each person, the freedom to think a thought without having to share it with everyone else. We can speak into another's mind, but we cannot search it, or know another's thoughts as we know our own."

"Now I am sure I can't stay here," Daiya said. "Everything you have said now we think is a sin. Everyone in my village warned me about my separateness, it was a great flaw in me. Perhaps it's because of that blot on my character that I can listen to you and understand something of what you say, but I cannot live in such a place. I could not endure it. I have no powers here, I can't even get a sense of this place, can't feel things you feel only with your mind. You would clutter my body with more of these calming things, and it would not matter because I would only wait for death. I am completely unlike you."

He took her hand again. She thought of his artificial skin and tried not to recoil and wondered how it could feel so much like real skin. She poked impulsively at the back of his hand with her nail and he jerked his head slightly.

"You are more like me, and like Etey, than you think," he answered. "In a way, we are as much outsiders here as you are in your home. Of course, we cannot really be outsiders, since everyone here is free to go her own way, but we question many things about life here, just as you questioned your life on Earth."

She realized that if Reiho had not been so different, he might have been a friend. But there was too much that divided them. He was still an alien curiosity, an acquaintance, someone she would never really understand. It was a wonder she could grasp as much of him as she did.

"Tell me," she said, speaking carefully, longing for the lost powers that would have made some of this cumbersome talk unnecessary. "Is it because you and Etey are different from others here that you are now having disagreements?"

Reiho seemed surprised. "We are not really having a disagreement." His voice slid over the words.

"Don't try to fool me. I heard you before I slept, and I saw how your bodies moved today as you spoke to those others, the people who were staring at pictures. You moved as though you were afraid to touch each other."

"It is not serious."

"It is. I have come between you."

"No, you have not. It is only that Etey wonders if I was wise to bring you here, but I explained things to her, and she understands that I could not leave you behind."

"She wants me to leave."

Reiho's eyes shifted slightly. "She did at first. Now she is not so certain. She feels sorry for you."

Daiya straightened her shoulders. "She does not have to feel sorry for me." She stood up. "You say I should speak to this Homesmind of yours. Is that your request, or is it Etey's?"

He rose and faced her. "We are both in agreement on that. Homesmind is the wisest being here."

"You have said you created It, yet It is wiser than you. You speak in paradoxes."

She turned and walked through the forest. Reiho followed her and took her arm and she did not draw away. Light danced in the spaces among the trees, making her blink. They came to the edge of the forest.

They stood together on a low hill and gazed at a plain of gray rocks. In the distance, three small boats were sailing on the clear, calm waters of a lake. A breeze curved the sails and rippled the lake's surface, making the light dance and sparkle again. The curls against her cheek fluttered. She looked up at the golden sky and wondered if she could ever love this world as she loved Earth.

She leaned against Reiho, who had tried to be her friend. For a few moments, she forgot that his body was not all flesh and bone. The breeze brushed her face once more, and she heard Reiho breathe.

Three birds darted from the woods behind them and flew out over the lake. She withdrew from Reiho and turned to face him. He watched her quietly and then said, "Will you commune with Homesmind?"

She said, "Yes, I will."

Daiya sat in a corner of a large room on a blue cushion. The roof above her was transparent. She leaned against a wall. Images moved through the center of the room; they looked more like diagrams or drawings than real things. The room's grassy ground was covered by cushions. Pictures danced on the walls, pictures of forests and landscapes through which rabbits and deer jumped and ran. A speckled fawn near her corner blinked at her; she put out her hand and touched the wall, her hand concealing its nose. Tree limbs bent slightly, as if a breeze was stirring them.

Five children giggled as the lines in the middle of the room twisted and curved; squares turned into rectangles, circles became globes. The children stared at Daiya and giggled some more. Etey was speaking to a tall man who stood near the children. The man nodded. Etey came back across the room, walking through the images.

Reiho sat next to Daiya. He smiled at her reassuringly. Etey sat

down across from her, holding out a thin silver circlet. Reiho
pressed a hand against the wall. A transparent surface slid across the
room, dividing them from the children on the other side; then it
darkened so that she could no longer see through it.

She took the circlet from Etey. "You must use this," the woman
said. "It is a trainer for children, they must learn to use this before
they are ready for an implant. I do not think you will find it too
difficult. I shall be with you, so I can guide you if necessary. You
will have to concentrate."

Daiya nodded.

"Put it around your head."

She lifted the circlet and put it on; it slid down and rested against
her forehead and temples. Suddenly the room was gone. A fog
enveloped her. She felt a presence near her—Etey. But there was
another presence, another mind. She trembled as she sensed its
power.

It touched her. She was outside the comet, adrift in black space.
The comet was a seed sprouting stems. She gazed through the
impossibly long limbs of the trees that grew from it. She saw
through the roots into the comet-world; there was a city in each
root, hidden or disguised by the jungle that grew around it. She felt
as though she could grasp all the visions at once. She was in space
again. A membrane shimmered around the comet, protecting it, almost invisible. Homesmind was touching her.

The comet was Homesmind; Homesmind was the comet. Daiya
thought: nothing can be this powerful, nothing can know this much.
She saw another image; other comets circled the sun, their minds
communing. They linked themselves together with mental strands.
Their people had grown apart, but the comet-minds still communicated and held their knowledge for whomever was willing to
seek it.

She was being propelled through space. The sun grew smaller,
becoming a pinprick against the night. She understood that she was
far from Earth now, in a region of large rocks, small barren
worldlets, and the masses of ice that became comets; she was in the
place Reiho had called the Halo. She was lifted above it. Looking
down, she saw tiny globes, far from one another, orbiting the sun.
The Halo was a mass of fragments marking the boundary between
this system and the space outside it. She saw one comet, then another, leave the Halo and begin to move slowly in the direction of
the sun.

How many comets? she felt herself asking. How many worlds? Comets were fanning out from her; their tails veiled her eyes. She saw each depart on its own path, some choosing to stay within this system, others leaving for other stars. Thousands of them. Millions. She could not hold the numbers. She felt heavy with the knowledge, remembering Earth. She had thought it the home of all human life. Even one comet contained more people than did Earth.

She was caught in the fog again. Homesmind reached inside her. She unraveled like a skein of thread: she was stretching out her chubby arms to Anra as she toddled, she was sitting in the public space shifting her weight from one buttock to another as she tried to concentrate on mastering her thoughts, she was chewing on a piece of fruit while Mausi—she was swimming in the river with Brun—she was waving goodbye to Rin—Harel was handing her a flower. Her memories became a blur, whipping past her; there was only a glimpse of the desert, then a peek at the looming mountains and the machines that they hid.

She looked inside her mind. The memories were still there; she was still whole. Homesmind had, she supposed, looked at them and then made them part of Itself. She sensed an answering wave of thought. She was awed as she realized how much there was in Homesmind; no one person could grasp it all. She was sure she had caught only the bare surface.

She sensed that Homesmind was speaking to Etey, though she could not read the thoughts. Then a feeling rippled from It to her. She could not quite interpret the emotion; it was part curiosity, part understanding, part distant compassion. The feeling soothed her. She was not afraid of Homesmind.

Then she saw Earth again, and the mountains under which machines were hidden. She saw mountains she had never seen before. She saw range after range, some built by nature, pushing to an impossible height above clouds, others barely higher than foothills and covered with trees. She saw mountains once made by human beings, some of them barren, others covered with weeds.

There were villages near all the ranges. Some were like her own home, huts near rivers and plains. Some nestled in fertile valleys. Other were in jungles or in colder climes; she saw huts made of reeds and dwellings made of timber or snow. They were superficial differences; the life of the villages went on, much like the life in her own. Young people faced ordeals, older ones became Merging Selves, sometimes able to touch another village with threads of thought. The image rippled. She saw Homesmind send out a stream of thought like a river. The stream flowed through space, touching the machines of Earth, seeking knowledge.

She floated aimlessly, then felt a hand on her brow. She blinked and saw the face of Etey. For a moment, she wanted to be with Homesmind again. Etey removed the circlet. Daiya, inside herself again, stretched her legs. Her back ached; her shoulders were stiff. She wiped her sweaty face with a sleeve.

Daiya opened her mouth, then closed it again, feeling unable to speak. "What you know and remember is part of Homesmind now," Etey said. "It will now learn from your cybernetic intelligences on Earth, and they will learn from It. That knowledge will be available to us, and to your people also, should they decide to seek it." Etey's face softened as she looked at Daiya. "I now remember your life also," she went on. "You have endured much."

"Intelligences," Daiya murmured. "I see that there are such things in machines, but I do not see how it is possible. It is like thinking a wagon can reason."

Etey smiled. "When a machine reaches a certain complexity, a certain point where it can become conscious of itself, how can it not happen? Homesmind was once our servant only, now It is many more things to us. The fact that It has not chosen to become our master makes me believe that in many ways It is our superior." She paused. "In time, you would come to understand much more of what Homesmind can tell you, with more precision."

"What will Homesmind do now?" Daiya asked, thinking of the machines on Earth.

"Homesmind will learn, and reason, and draw certain conclusions. It will share them with those who are interested. It will not force anyone to accept them." Etey reached over and touched Daiya's hand. "You may have brought us something very important."

She got up and helped Daiya to her feet. The wall dividing the room became transparent again and slid away. Etey turned to the wall nearest them. The deer disappeared as the wall retracted. The children were giggling again. Daiya followed Etey out of the room, with Reiho close behind her. The wall closed behind them.

Daiya stood still, realizing that she could place herself, orient herself in relation to the rest of the comet. Homesmind had placed that knowledge in her mind; she would be able to find her way around this world. Two hundred paces ahead was the park where she had spoken with Reiho. The place where his craft had landed was above the cliff in which he and Etey made their home.

They were near a brook which ran through a small clearing. Flat rocks lay on the green grass in an elaborate pattern. Daiya looked at the pattern, understanding it. The rocks symbolized the molecular construction of the grass while hinting at an equation expressing the chemical composition of the water flowing in the brook. The pattern was also a poem, though she could not read it. She shivered, wondering what else Homesmind had communicated to her.

She walked over to the brook, knowing she could follow it to a pool surrounded by slender trees with white bark. She glanced at a nearby surface, recognizing that the patterns etched on it were calligraphy, marks making written words, though she could not read them. The brook itself spelled an idea, though she did not know what it was.

Etey and Reiho followed her. Etey stood next to her, silent for a few moments, then spoke. "You see how much Homesmind can teach you. You do not have to be a stranger here."

Daiya stared at the brook. The water flowed, bubbling over rocks, flowing around stepping-stones. She thought of living with calming substances inside her, without her powers, in a world of people wedded to machines and living in gardens. It was not what she had thought it was. She did not know if it was what she wanted. Even here, Earth seemed to pull at her, calling her home.

"There is an emptiness in me," she said to Etey and Reiho, wondering if they could understand what she meant. "I cannot just leave everything I knew. I know I'm not like most of my people, that in many ways I didn't fit in there either, that they may not take me back because there may be no place for me. But I was taught all my life that I could not, should not separate myself from others, and you are asking me to separate myself from everyone on Earth. I don't think I can."

Reiho gazed at her sympathetically. Again, for just a moment, she had the illusion of touching his thoughts. "I must at least try to share what I have discovered with my village," Daiya concluded, remembering the machines under the mountains again. She felt a twinge, knowing that the desire to learn more about those machines, and the obligation to share what she knew with her people, was not enough by itself to draw her. If she could have been happy on this strange world, she might have remained.

Etey nodded. "If that is how you feel, then there is little more I can say to you."

Daiya knelt on the grass. An idea came to her, so odd and out of place that it did not seem part of her own mind. She looked up at Etey and Reiho. "May I speak to Homesmind again?" Reiho widened his eyes in surprise. "Will It be able to reply to me so that I can understand It clearly?" she went on. "I know, after touching Its mind, that It knows more than any human mind can know . . . perhaps It can help me."

Etey had slipped the circlet through her belt. She held it out now, arching her eyebrows as she looked at Daiya. "I can guide you again, if you wish. You will understand Homesmind, though I do not know what you expect It to tell you. I am surprised at your request." She pointed at the nearby trees. "We had better sit there, you can rest your back against a tree. You are not used to Homesmind and this trainer, and I do not want you so enthralled that you fall into the brook, or injure yourself. Reiho will watch over you."

Daiya got up. They went over to the white trees. She sat down, leaning her back against smooth bark. Etey lifted the circlet. It was suddenly around her head. Daiya blinked.

A strand of Etey's mind held her, but she could not touch Etey's thoughts.—Help me—she thought, trying to mindspeak.—I can't stay here, I must return to Earth. I'm very much afraid I'll die there, but if I stay here, I'll only die more slowly. I know I'm still obligated to my village, but at the same time, I'm frightened—

At first, she felt nothing. Then she saw an empty plain devoid of foliage. She stared at the flat brown barren ground as something spoke inside her, a whisper.

What is it you want? Homesmind answered. *Do you wish me to say you must return to Earth? Your people have chosen their way. Your planet is apart from most of humankind. The minds of Earth that were built so long ago now speak to me, awake again. They have no need of you. If you wish to stay here, you may, though you do not wish to now. You would not be the same person after a time, and you might feel differently later. But do what you like.*

—I'm afraid—

So you are. The plain vanished and she saw Earth again. A small group of people stood on a mountainous island. They cried out and covered their faces as villagers tore out their minds. She was in a jungle. The stiff bodies of two young women lay next to a shuttle as bright-feathered birds shrieked. She was near a forest, where three men trampled the underbrush as they ran from the people who would kill them. Then she was on the brown plain again. *That is the fate of a few from this place who have tried to visit Earth. There have been others. When it became apparent that visitors to Earth did not return, people stopped going.* The whispering voice made a sound like a raspy chuckle. Daiya shook her head. *I heard them cry and could do nothing for them. Now, with the help of your machines, I can watch them die.* The whisper had an edge to it. *You too may die, even though you are part of Earth. It is a probability.* The voice seemed vaguely threatening.

—Tell me what to do—she pleaded.

I cannot. I shall not. That is up to you. Perhaps you should have faith in your people, faith that they will listen to you. Or perhaps you wish only to give up, and are seeking your executioner. She winced, wishing she could escape the whisper. *You have already decided to go. There is little point in asking me to make your decision. But I will tell you this. There is power, you felt it when you touched the minds under the mountains. There is new knowledge in your mind. Those things can protect you.*

She waited for the voice to say more, but it was silent. She was irritated; she had felt Homesmind's power even in the whisper, yet It had told her nothing. The fog began to roll over the plain. She caught a tiny wisp of compassion—it seemed a weak feeling. Homesmind, she thought, was indifferent to her, indifferent to Earth, now that It could learn what It liked from the machines. Something tugged at her mind. *Untrue,* said a whispering voice, so soft she hardly heard it.

The fog was gone. Reiho was watching her. Etey took the trainer and hooked it through her belt again. "Did you find what you wanted, Daiya?"

"Didn't you hear any of Homesmind's words?"

"I did not listen. I thought it was a private discussion." Etey stood up. "I shall take you back. I can remain with you for a time, in case you change your mind and wish to come back here. You may find it necessary, you know."

Reiho said, "We shall take you back."

Etey frowned as her eyes glanced at the boy. "There is no need for you to come with us."

"There is. I brought Daiya here. I promised her I would protect her."

"I shall protect her. There is no need for two of us to return to Earth."

Reiho lifted his head. "There is no need for either of us to go, Etey. You know that. You could send Daiya back alone in the shuttle, allow it to pilot itself."

Daiya looked from Etey to Reiho, wondering if that were true.

"Someone should travel with her," Etey said.

"I'll take my chances," Daiya said, afraid that the two would begin to fight.

Reiho was shaking his head. "I agree. Someone should travel with her. It's my responsibility, I brought Daiya here, so I shall go, too."

Neither Reiho nor Etey was paying any attention to her. Daiya shoved her hands in her pockets, feeling that she should tell Reiho to stay here but she was afraid to go back only with Etey. The woman turned and spoke to Reiho in another language. He shook his head vehemently. Daiya bowed her head and stared at her feet.

"Please wait here," Etey said. She took Reiho's arm. Daiya watched them walk down to the brook. Etey began to speak to the boy. Daiya could not hear her voice. Reiho pulled away from the woman. His lips were moving.

Miserable and uncomfortable, Daiya observed the argument. Reiho had told her confrontation was difficult for his people. In their quiet, studied way, the two by the brook were probably tearing at each other.

Reiho spun around and came back to her. Etey, after a few moments, followed him. "We are both going to take you back," Reiho said as he reached Daiya's side.

"I'm sorry, Reiho. I didn't mean for you to argue over it."

"It was nothing." He glanced at Etey and Daiya knew he was still angry. "I have a responsibility. And I was the first to contact an Earthdweller after all this time, I have my pride, and must see this through." He stared at Etey for a long time in silence. "I will not be robbed of my accomplishment," he said at last.

Daiya thought: I am a pawn. They will use me for their own ends, even Reiho. She lifted her head. Earth was her world. She would regain her powers and then she would control them.

"Very well," Etey said. "We must prepare."

They lifted off in a larger shuttle this time, moving up, out of the root, over tangled brown furrows. Daiya leaned back as Etey maneuvered the craft. Another shuttle, with a young couple inside, darted past them, traveling in another direction. She would never see this world again, of that she was sure. She would live on her own world.

Etey pressed a panel and leaned back. Both she and Reiho were clothed in their silver lifesuits. They had offered such a suit to Daiya, but she had refused it; in spite of that, she was sure one had been brought aboard for her. She sighed. She could not live in this place without a calming implant, they were afraid to set foot on Earth without their silver suits. It was absurd that human beings should be so cut off from one another's worlds. The thought startled her.

The shuttle lifted past the giant tree trunks. Daiya recalled her idea that these people might want to return to Earth in large numbers. It had been a foolish thought. They could learn what they wanted to know through Homesmind. They could walk through a vision of the desert, mountains, and plains almost as real as the reality. They could view the history of her people—and their own ancestors—by means of Homesmind's link with the machines of Earth. Her world was only a curiosity, a backwater, a place most of humankind had managed to escape.

They floated up among the large shiny leaves. For a moment, she wondered again if she was doing the right thing. Her new knowledge had robbed her of her previous convictions. She shook her head. No, she thought, that's not right. Everything in her world rested on the principle that human minds should not be divided from one another, and even Reiho's people believed this in their own way, with modifications. That principle still stood, however odd or distorted her own application of it might appear to her village. It was why she was going back. She would have to hang on to that conviction; she only wished her heart and spirit could assent to it as easily as her reason.

Even so, she would have to hide Etey and Reiho from her people; they were not ready to see such a vision, and the woman and boy would be in danger. She glanced at Reiho, who sat next to her. He smiled.

They shot out from the glistening leaves. The comet grew smaller behind them, becoming a tangled plant on a black sea. Daiya thought of uprooted stems and flowers caught by the river and carried downstream.

12

Daiya breathed the air of Earth again, and let her mind roam. There was a lizard nearby; she touched its unthinking mind as it sat in the shade of a cactus. She drew inside herself, becoming aware of the implant, and began to adjust the humors of her body.

Etey took her hand. "You will not need this anymore," she said. She pressed a thin rod against Daiya's arm. Daiya felt a sharp prick. There was a small mark on her arm where the implant had been. She sat down near the shuttle, feeling apprehensive, thinking that perhaps she might have needed the tranquilizer after all. She grimaced at the thought; better to rely on herself.

Etey stumbled a bit as she went into the vehicle to get some water. The woman seemed disoriented. Daiya stretched her arms over her head. She lifted some sand, shaping a small pillar, then released it. The sand fell, raising a dirt cloud. She touched Reiho's powerless mind, able at least to feel his apprehension. She sent out a tendril to Etey.

The woman's head jerked. She hopped out of the shuttle, almost falling to the ground. Her brown eyes were wide. Daiya was startled; Etey had felt her thought. She withdrew, unsure of what it meant. Etey sat down near her and looked around at the desert. Daiya touched her mind again. Etey glanced around more frantically.

"That was me," Daiya said. Reiho came out of the craft and sat down with them.

"What do you mean?" Etey asked. Her thoughts were roiling, unreadable as a child's; she could not even put up a wall.

"That was me, touching your mind. You sensed it. Reiho can't, because he's a solitary, but you can. I don't understand it."

Etey sighed. "So that is what it was. It was not all I felt. Somehow, here, I feel that I am sensing things without being able to tell what they are. I thought it was only that I am not used to this place."

"I don't understand it," Daiya repeated. "I thought all of you were solitaries."

Etey was silent, thinking. Daiya caught a few of her thoughts; she was reviewing the knowledge about Earth that Homesmind had conveyed to her. "I believe I understand it," Etey said at last. "There are people you call solitaries still born here."

"It doesn't happen very often," Daiya said, knowing that Etey had found the killing of such children appalling.

Etey waved a hand. "It must be that people with your abilities, however few they may be, are still born on our world. Homesmind no doubt reasoned that it did not matter whether such traits remained, or were eliminated. Perhaps It even thought they should be preserved for some reason. At least now I know why, when I was young, I was quicker to learn to read body language and expressions than other children. We are not so different." She leaned back, resting against the shuttle. "I feel very strange here. Maybe this is a good thing, if your people come upon us, they will sense that I am like them. They might not be as frightened then."

"It is not good," Daiya responded. "What if the Merging Ones should, by some chance, survey this area with their minds? If they sensed only Reiho, they might easily think he was an animal, or a strange creature they could ignore, or an illusion. If they touch your mind, I cannot know what they would do."

They had landed in the desert, in the southeast, far from the village. Uncomfortable and hot as it might get, it was far safer than landing on the other side of the mountains, near the foothills or plains, where young people on playful sojourns from the village might find them. Daiya explored the surface of Etey's thoughts; her mental powers were only rudimentary, undeveloped, weak from never having been exercised. "Luckily, your powers aren't strong," Daiya went on. "If they were, you would be easier to find, since you cannot even put up a wall."

Reiho seemed tense. Etey was chastened, her mouth twisting into a half-smile. "Could I not learn how to use them?" she asked. "Surely the cybernetic intelligences under the mountains could teach me something."

"They can give you only information, and power for your abilities," Daiya replied. "These are skills which must be practiced and developed. It would take you too long to learn them. I've lived here all my life and I'm still mastering certain skills." She exhaled loudly, exasperated, angry, and afraid. "This is worse than if you were one like Reiho." The boy frowned as she spoke. "You can cause many problems. You cannot control your mind. You could be dangerous. If you go to sleep here, the things buried inside you will come to the surface, as they do in children, and that could be dangerous for all of us. There is no village of Merging Ones or adults with strong minds to control you, and I'll have to do it alone."

"I do not have to sleep," Etey said. "I can stay awake with an implant if necessary."

"Your feelings may cause you to do things you could regret. If someone should find you, you could strike out without meaning to and hurt that person. I don't even want to think of the trouble you could cause."

"I can remain calm."

Daiya jumped to her feet, pacing in front of them, back and forth. "You are dangerous!" she cried, knowing that Etey would hear the words and feel their force as well. "You cannot come to my village."

Etey's eyebrows arched in surprise.

"Oh, yes, I sensed that," Daiya continued. "It is hard to catch your thoughts, for you can't project them well, but I can sense your purpose. I didn't know it before, but I see it now. You dream of contacting them, of bringing human beings together." She stopped pacing. The calming substances were completely gone from her body. She thought of the comet and began to shake. "You were going to wait to see what I would do, then seize your chance if you could. But I won't let you. I may not be able to go back myself. Now I know you must go back to the comet right away."

She sat down abruptly. She was overreacting and that was not going to help them. Touching Etey's mind was not like seeing into the mind of one of her own people, nor even like trying to read Reiho. The boy, after all, could not form his thoughts clearly enough to be read easily by others, and some of them were so strange, or couched in such odd symbols, that she could not even attempt to read them. But many of his feelings were not unlike her own, and he was close to her own age. She could sense his friendliness and curiosity; even now, as he worried about what might happen, he was not afraid of her.

But Etey was more alien. Her mind seemed as full of resonances as the mind of an old one, though, unlike the Merging Ones, her thoughts were hers alone. Her ideas were hard and sharp, but formed in an incomprehensible way; they were a bramble bush, and she could not tell where one branch left off and another began. Only occasionally could she grasp something familiar in them, and had she not had information conveyed to her by her brief contact with Homesmind, she doubted she would be able to read even the little she could. There was a cold intelligence at the center of the woman's mind, as if rationality and not emotion fueled her. She looked at Daiya with disinterest, curious, bearing her no ill will but apparently viewing her partly as a means to something else.

Etey said, "I do not want to leave." Daiya, sensing her actual thoughts, knew the words were inaccurate. The woman was saying: I do not intend to leave, at least not until I have tried to speak to others of this world. "I shall, however, depart if it means danger for you, but you may be safer with us here. We can, at the very least, take you back with us if it turns out you cannot remain here."

Daiya sighed. She thought of forcing Etey and Reiho back into the shuttle and hurling them from Earth, remembering to shield her thoughts in case the woman accidentally caught the image. It would not do any good. Etey would only return. "You might consider Reiho's welfare," Daiya said. "You could put him in danger."

"Do not worry about me," Reiho answered. "If it had not been for me, you would not be in this situation. If I can help you, I must try."

Daiya thought: If it hadn't been for you, I would probably have died during the ordeal. She was no longer so sure that would have been preferable to living. "You can help," she said, "by leaving."

"Can you not at least teach me a few techniques?" Etey asked. "Surely there is something I can learn that will decrease the chance of danger."

"I don't know." Daiya was silent for a few moments as she thought. She might be able to show Etey how to shield her thoughts. Remembering the machines, she reached out toward the mountains with a tendril, feeling some of the vast power there fill her. Again, she felt slightly intoxicated, realizing that her knowledge of those devices meant great power and strength, greater than anything she had imagined. She could tear the mountains from them, leaving the gold and crystal pillars bare in the sunlight. Homesmind had mentioned that power. It had said her knowledge could protect her.

Suddenly she felt something brush against her mind and realized it was not a stray thought of Etey's. She built a wall quickly, motioning to Etey and Reiho to be still. She rapidly constructed a mental shield around them to muffle their minds, blank out their presence, glad to have the extra power that enabled her to do it. She waited, knowing she could not hide herself, even though she could keep her knowledge and her thoughts secret; whoever it was had already sensed her. She would confront it instead of hiding. She could not hide indefinitely.

She let out a wisp of consciousness.

A mind touched her. It pushed against her wall. She kept up the barrier easily. It withdrew for a moment, then spoke.

—Daiya—It had recognized her. She approached the mind tentatively.—Daiya. We have searched, and searched again. We looked elsewhere, in case you had wandered off in madness, but now we find you again—

The thoughts seemed to be from Jowē's mind, though with the Merging Selves it was hard to be sure, especially at such a distance. Only a Merging One could send a mind so far.—But you are not mad—Jowē went on.

—No—Daiya thought.—I am not—

—There is something different in you, we can feel it. Harel KaniDekel has told us what happened during your ordeal. We were not sure he would live when he arrived, he was so ill and feverish, but he is better now—Daiya, shoring up her wall, felt relieved to hear that.—What has happened to you—

Daiya felt Jowē push at her wall. She drew more power and held it up.—What has happened to you—Other Merging Selves were now speaking through Jowē.—Why couldn't we find you before? Why did you stay in the desert for all these days? Why did you not return to the village—

—I did not know if I could—she answered.—I knew that somehow I had not passed my ordeal, and I was afraid to return—

—It was your duty to return and let us decide what to do. We cannot understand how you could remain so isolated there, without the Net, without others. You are very strong, even now we can sense your strength. You have endured something. It is your duty to return and share it. You have brought something different into the world, and we must find out about it, in case it happens again. Do you understand—

—Yes—

—Will you return—

—What will you do if I return—

—That is not for you to consider—Jowē's words were angry and sharp.—We shall decide when we see you. Will you return—

—Yes—

—We shall await you—Daiya felt Jowē withdraw. The Merging Selves were gone. A strand brushed against her, settling in her mind; the Net. She was bound to the village once more. It did not feel wispy and light this time; it tied her with heavy thick cords.

She kept her wall between her and the Net, not wanting anyone in the village even to sense the strangeness of the knowledge she held. She turned cautiously to Etey and Reiho, still shielding them mentally, drawing on the power under the mountains, wondering if there was any limit to it.

"What happened?" Etey said. "You looked as though you were in some sort of trance. There is something strange in the air, I feel it around me." Daiya felt as though she was in segments, one part touching the Net, another part behind a wall, a third part listening to Etey.

"The village has found me. I shielded both of you, so no one knows you're here. I must go back."

Reiho smiled. "Then you can go home," he said, obviously relieved. "They will accept you."

Daiya paused. "Yes," she said at last, hoping that if they believed her, and thought she would be safe, they would leave Earth. Their thought of lingering in case she was endangered so that they could take her to the comet again was wrong. Reiho thought it to soothe his guilt; Etey used it as an excuse for her own ends. Daiya did not want to look into her own soul too closely. She might be seeking a punishment for her sins, still unable to give up all she had been taught, incapable of shaking off her training. At the same time, she knew, part of her was embracing her new power and knowledge. The village had accused her of seeking isolation; now she was separate, more knowledgeable, more powerful than others.

Etey was frowning. "Are you sure you will be safe?" she said. "How do you know that? From what I have learned of your people, I cannot believe they will take you back so easily. You might need us."

"I don't need you. You would be in danger, and you might make things worse for me. You should be able to figure that out, Etey. You must go."

Reiho seemed worried again. "But what if you cannot stay there? If we are near, at least we can take you with us."

Daiya clenched her teeth. Somehow the pair believed they were invulnerable to danger, in spite of their knowledge. Between Reiho's concern and Etey's arrogant curiosity, she would never get rid of them. If she hurled them from Earth, Etey might well take it into her head to set down near the village. For a moment, she thought of planting suggestions in their minds to make them leave, but she was not skilled enough in those techniques to take the chance. She had almost killed herself simply by erasing memories, leaving only a black spot of despair and no way, without the lost knowledge, of dealing with it. She could not risk damaging their minds. With the machines to draw on, she might destroy them altogether. Having so much strength, she realized, was very tricky.

"Very well," she replied, trying to sound calm. "But you must stay here, you must not come to the village. I'm sure you will find much of interest here. You can, for example, go inside the mountains and explore the wonders there." She looked very hard at Etey as she spoke, hoping that might keep the woman satisfied and her curiosity at bay.

"Then I guess you will have to go," Reiho said. "Can you at least get back to us if you must leave again?"

Daiya swallowed, knowing she would have to let them believe she might want to return to the comet. "Wait for five days, five risings and settings of the sun. If I am not back on the sixth day, go. It will mean I am safe in the village and will not return."

"It may mean you are dead," Etey said, gazing at Daiya without blinking.

"Yes, it may mean that," Daiya replied, trying not to shout: Reiho narrowed his eyes and frowned. "And what could you do then? It would be even more dangerous for you." She glared at Etey. "If you don't care about yourself, think of Reiho. Do you want him to die because of your foolishness?"

"We shall be careful," Reiho said in a soft voice. He looked at Etey as he spoke. "We will not be reckless."

Daiya glanced at the woman, then at the boy, sensing the division between them. "Remember," she said to Etey, "that what you see here is not just a picture inside your Homesmind, from which you can withdraw as you please."

Etey nodded. "I understand."

"Good." Daiya sat down.

"Are you not going now?" Reiho asked.

She brushed some hair off her forehead. "It is too late to go now, the sun will soon be behind the mountains." That was not the only reason. She could fly back to the village fairly easily if she drew on the power beneath the mountains, but so rapid a journey would arouse the suspicions of the Merging Selves, who would wonder where she had found the strength and overreact out of fear. She also needed time to prepare for the encounter.

Her stomach gurgled; she quieted it. "I am hungry."

Reiho went into the shuttle to get some food.

The dome above her was darkening as the sun rose. Daiya crept from her seat carefully, not wanting to disturb Reiho.

The boy was still asleep, his legs stretched out, one hand hanging over the side of his reclining seat. She watched him for a few moments, certain she would not see him again. A weight pressed against her chest as she breathed. Reiho had tried to do what he thought was right, and he had paid a price for it.

She was not yet sure how she felt about Reiho. She had a bond with him, though it was not like the bond she had once had with Mausi, or with Harel. Reiho would remember her; she would remember him.

She climbed out of the craft. The door slid back quietly behind her. Etey sat on the ground, awake, as she had been all night, kept warm by her lifesuit. Her eyes were half-open, her irises hidden under her lids; only the whites showed.

Daiya tapped her lightly on the shoulder. The woman looked up, focusing on her. "What are you doing, Etey?"

"Playing a game with Homesmind."

"A game?"

"It is difficult to explain. Homesmind presents images to my mind, and we play with them. It is partly a mathematical game, partly an artistic effort. You are going now?"

Daiya nodded. She wanted to dawdle, postpone the journey, now that it was upon her.

"Do you wish to say farewell to Reiho?"

She gazed at the shuttle, and swallowed. "I think it is better if I do not. Remember what I have told you." She touched Etey's mind, sensing that the woman's dream of speaking to the villagers directly was now at war with her concern for Reiho.

"I shall remember."

"There are machines under the mountains to whom you might speak. Satisfy your curiosity there, if you must. Even your weak mind should be able to contact theirs."

Etey pursed her lips and was silent.

"Farewell."

Daiya began to walk away from the craft, to the northwest, toward the mountains. She felt the strength of the machines flow through her, knowing it would be her defense against the villagers if they would not accept her. Without her knowledge of what lay under the mountains, they could not focus on the machines and draw the power from them that she could; their strength would be more diffuse. And they were more used to restraint than she was, being older. She could protect herself against them if necessary; at least she had a chance. She tried not to think of what she would do if the villagers rejected her, and she survived. She would have to settle that when she came to it.

She trembled as she thought of the encounter. She was going back to Anra, to Brun and Silla, to Cerwen and Leito and Morgen, to Nenla, to Harel. She was going back to those who might turn out to be her enemies. They would all stand by passively if the Merging Selves wished it; they would pour their power into the Net to destroy her if need be. She tried to imagine that, knowing her own weakness. If she had to endure watching those she loved trying to kill her, even the machines might not help her. The despair might destroy her; she might turn her power against herself.

She continued to walk, knowing she wanted to be out of Etey's sight before she flew, though not sure why. She thought of Etey and the people of the comet. They knew nothing of life, nothing of despair or work or love. They hid from life, making parts of themselves lifeless, and called it living. They played with images and symbols, calling it both work and play, contradicting themselves. They engaged in teaching and training children and called it being a parent. They amused themselves with sex and called it love. They had built a machine, and it had surpassed them. They were truly great fools. Yet they too were people. The Merged One, if It truly existed, had created them, and Cerwen had said that God loved fools; they made people laugh, and laughter could join one to eternity for a brief moment.

She tried to laugh. A gurgling rose in her throat; she choked, her belly contracted. Tears stung her eyes. A sound escaped her, a cry, harsh and bitter. Her stomach heaved. Tears rolled down her face.

Her people were fools as well. They had built machines and then denied them. God must love her people greatly; God's laughter must have shaken the stars. The minds under the mountains were awake once again. She thought of that, and the sand under her feet grew

brown as the sunlight dimmed. The machine-minds were waiting for
something; she sensed their anticipation and was frightened.

She shook her head and the blue sky brightened again. She lifted
herself and flew, up toward the mountains.

13

Daiya flew over the foothills, seeing the shimmer of a brook below
her. It looked like the brook where she had rested just before seeing
Reiho's craft for the first time, when her world had still had perma-
nence and solidity. She hovered over the plains, feeling no loss of
strength, knowing she could float there indefinitely if she wished.
Somehow she found that difficult to accept; it was against all her
training. The power might be infinite, but her body's ability to channel it and her mind's capacity for using it were not. She would still
have to be careful. She flew on for a bit, then alighted in the tall
grass. She reminded herself that she was going home. She did not feel
as though she was.

She walked, keeping up her wall with little effort. She would be
keeping many things from the village, or trying to do so. She no
longer felt guilt about secrets; she had gone too far for that. She
could not yet reveal her knowledge to the village, to people who had
no way of comprehending it. She was startled by the thought; it
seemed more like an idea Etey would hold than one of her own. She
was ashamed at the notion.

A cloud of birds suddenly rose in front of her, singing. They fled
over the plain, becoming specks against the sky. Flocks of birds did
not lack unity. She recalled the ducks and geese of the village and
how they waddled together, moving with one another to one side,
then to another. Their young, piping, were a fuzzy yellow entity.
People, she thought, should have been more like birds.

She tried to keep her mind calm, to preserve herself for her meeting with the village. Her shoulder muscles were tight, her neck stiff.

She wondered if she should be frightened; she seemed to have left her fear back in the mountains. She was going back to her home, to see those she had lived with all her life, the people she loved. It was an event that should have made her feel something, and she was numb.

She lifted from the ground again, deciding at once that she wanted to get back, that thinking about it for too long out here would only make things worse. She flew, throwing an arm over her forehead to protect her eyes from the wind. The plain raced beneath her. She felt the pull of the Net, stronger now; the village would be waiting for her. She approached the plains bordering the village. Wooly sheep clustered in groups as they grazed. She set down at the edge of the fields, gazing toward the huts in the distance.

The village seemed altered. The huts were smaller and shabbier, their grassy tops flimsy, their brick walls drab. The water in the irrigation ditches was cloudy and dirty; the field smelled of manure and compost. The paths among the huts were cramped and narrow. Several people working in the fields nearby were watching her; she sensed their concern. She noticed the frayed edges of their tunics, the roughness of their weathered skin. They stared at her, but did not approach.

Iron bonds seemed to bind her chest; her lungs pressed against them as she inhaled. She squinted, trying to see the village as she remembered it. She let part of herself past her wall, trying to see the village with her mind as well as her eyes. She saw the streets grow wider, the huts cleaner, the water clearer. She was home. She clung to the vision, wanting to return to the remembered village, not the one her eyes had seen. She swallowed, and her jaws tightened. She hid behind her wall again, thinking that what the minds under the mountains called consciousness only made the world uglier.

Another group was leaving the village and coming toward her, led by Jowē TeiyeVese. The old woman walked slowly and cautiously. The wind ruffled her silver mane. Leito was next to Jowē, clasping the old woman's elbow; Cerwen was behind her. Daiya caught a glimpse of auburn hair; Harel. Her heart fluttered, then thumped. Suddenly the others were only shadowy shapes around him.

—Harel—she cried. The name shot out from her, calling his soul. She was thrown against the wall surrounding him.—Harel—A tendril touched her. She felt his reluctance. He began to withdraw. —Harel, don't—

—I don't know you—he replied as he shored up his wall.

—Don't tell me that—

—I don't know you. You've changed even more. There is something in you, you are even more separate now—She sensed a bit of his love, now drowning in fear.—What have you done to yourself, Daiya—

She longed to tear his wall apart, knowing she could do so with little effort. She held back, wrenching her eyes and mind from him and looking toward the others. She was tied by invisible bonds. The world was now smaller, the village a prison. She pushed and the bonds snapped like bits of thread.

Jowē's head jerked up. She came toward Daiya. The others lingered behind, afraid to come closer. She peered at Daiya with her brown eyes.

—You have not passed your ordeal—the old woman said,—and you still live—Daiya felt the thoughts of all the Merging Selves in Jowē and trembled.—Have you suffered another kind of ordeal? Something has happened to you, and we must know what it is—

—I saw the darkness, the creature with no mind—Daiya replied. —I saw it growing in the desert, ready to swallow me, and I tried to resist, shielding myself from it. I was sure I would die. And then I saw that it was only our fear, our separation from the Net, that created it, and I realized that it was an illusion. When I understood that, it had no more power over me, and then it disappeared, I could no longer perceive it, though my companions still did. I know that this shouldn't have happened—She paused.

—I see that you have said part of the truth, but not all of it— Jowē thought.—You are changed, you are something that has never existed in our world. We must know more, so that we can make certain it doesn't happen again—

She felt the force of the Merging Ones pushing against her wall. It shook; the air around her vibrated. She reinforced the wall, hiding behind it.

—Why do you say it mustn't happen again—Daiya asked.—Is that all you can say to something you don't understand? You don't even know what's happened, why do you assume it's evil—She felt the villagers withdrawing, protecting themselves from dangerous thoughts.

—It is something new, something which separates you from us—

—People like us were once something new—Daiya replied.— Even our legends say that. Why was that newness good and anything else bad—

—The Merged One touched us and changed us, showing us the truth, and the Merged One embodies all good. You have not been touched by God. You ask too much. You keep up your wall and we cannot see what is inside you. You have power, too much power, and you have not yet learned restraint. Let down your wall—

Daiya strengthened it, drawing on all the power she could.

—Let down your wall—

You want to destroy me—Daiya thought.—You want to tear out what I know, what I've gone through, you know I may not survive that—

—That is unimportant. If you remain separate, you condemn yourself anyway. You will be apart from us and apart from God. Your only hope lies in sharing yourself with us—

—I shall not let down my wall—

Jowē glared at her balefully.—Then we shall tear it down—

Harel gasped. His eyes widened as he looked at Daiya. His love had, at least temporarily, pushed above the surface of his fear. Daiya steadied herself. She felt the assault of the Merging Ones; they battered against her barrier. She held her shield. Claws scraped and dug at her mind. She fought them off, resisting. She drew on the machines under the mountains, fortifying her defenses with their power. She thought: I could strike out, push them away. But she did not dare, knowing she might lose control. She could only resist.

A whirlwind rose from the field. Jowē stepped back, standing with the others. The whirlwind shrieked, whipping the woman's hair; then it swooped toward Daiya. It swirled around her, ripping at her wall. She held her ground. The earth shook; she stood on waves of dirt and grass. Her legs gave way and she toppled forward, still holding her wall.

The wind beat at her, stinging her face, thundering against her shield. A crack appeared in the earth, becoming a ravine, threatening to swallow her. She clung to the ground, her hands in the dirt, keeping up her wall. The ravine became a chasm, a black pit, impossibly deep.

Jowē stood across the chasm, on the other side, her eyes burning. The wind tore at Daiya, pushing her toward the black crevice. She held on, almost hearing the machines hum as they poured their power into her. The wall shook, cracking under the strain. Fire poured into her, searing her. She sealed the breach. The whirlwind became a tornado, trying to tear her from the ground. She held on, waiting. Every Merging Self in the village was assaulting her, screaming at her through the howling wind. She heard their voices, though not their words, and felt their anger.

The storm subsided. The crack in the earth disappeared. The field was as it had been. She lifted her head and climbed to her feet, trembling.

Harel was staring at her, partly relieved that she had survived, partly terrified of what it might mean. Jowē clutched her white tunic, wrapping her arms about herself.—I do not understand—she thought.—You should not have been able to resist—

Daiya glared angrily at her, careful to keep up her wall.—You can gain nothing from me that way—she responded.—I came here prepared to try to share my experience with you, but afraid of what you might do to me. You have proven that I was right to be afraid. Do you think I don't want to be part of the village again? You could have come to me and asked me to share things willingly with you, but instead you try to tear them from me—

—You are not fooling me—Jowē thought.—You show a part of the truth and keep the rest to yourself. You ask us to accept something without revealing what it is. You would not be so afraid if what you held was not evil. One with nothing to fear does not have to endure such an onslaught. That is the truth, isn't it? You carry something terrible inside you which you are afraid to release—

Daiya was silent, not knowing how to answer. What Jowē said was true, though she would not have put it in those terms. If she conveyed her knowledge to them, she did not see how the village could remain as it was. Rather than accept it, they would cast her out, if they could not destroy her. She would be an exile, unable to keep up her guard constantly. Eventually, someone would crush her when she was unable to defend herself, and destroy her in an unguarded moment. Jowē and the other Merging Ones could join together and, with the strength of the old woman's mind, touch another village, and another, summoning everyone on Earth to destroy her. She could not withstand them all.

Jowē turned and began to walk back to the village, the others following her. Only Cerwen and Harel remained. Her grandfather reached out an arm to her. She stared suspiciously at him.

—I will not force you to speak—Cerwen thought.—You claim you are willing to share what has happened with us. Here we are, your grandfather and the boy who wanted to be your partner. Will you speak now—

She sat down at the edge of a ditch.—You know that if I speak to you, I speak to everyone here—she answered.—You cannot join me in separation from the others—She looked at Harel—Why are you here? Did you want to see me die—She knew it was not true, but she wanted to punish him for his failing love.

—The Merging Ones didn't want me here—he replied.—But I had to come, I thought you might be as you were, I thought—His thoughts failed. She saw his dream: their hut, their partnership, their children, their life. The Daiya in his dream smiled, merged with him, accepted the world, was calm, had no questions. She could not recognize herself. Even her face was different; pretty, placid, serene. She had never seen that face when she stood near still water on sunny days.

—You don't love me as I am—she thought.—If the Merging Ones had torn half my mind from me and left me peaceful and unable to question, a living shell of what I was, you would be happy, and accept me, and feel no loss. I can tell that is true—

Harel looked away from her. She realized that the ordeal had changed him too. He had learned the wisdom of restraint and acceptance; the black thing he had resisted had robbed him of any faint stirrings of rebelliousness, which was, of course, the purpose of the rite. The village held him, it would hold him forever. He could not love an outsider.

—Let me ask you something—she thought, turning toward Cerwen.—What would you think if you discovered that there were other people, like us and yet unlike us, who we had known nothing about—

Cerwen frowned.—There are other villages—

—I don't mean that. I mean people who are more like solitaries, yet able to think and feel, people without our mental powers—

—I do not know what you mean, Daiya. Solitaries must die when they are born—

—Forget that—she thought impatiently.—I mean people who live in another place, who are grown, who are solitaries, but like us also. We believe it is not right to be apart from other minds, so wouldn't it be our duty to communicate with them, try to understand them? Wouldn't we be committing a great sin by cutting ourselves off from them if we knew they existed—

Cerwen fidgeted and she felt his irritation.—What is this outrageous idea? You must be mad to imagine such a thing, this question is more foolish than the ones you asked as a child—

—I am asking what you think you should do in such a case—

Her grandfather's wall came down, pushing against hers.—It is useless to ask such things—he thought faintly. He turned and stalked off toward the village.

Harel was alone with her. She stared across the ditch at the boy. She could no longer tell if she loved him or simply wanted him to love her. She had no right to blame him, knowing what he would see if she allowed him to look at her wishes, her imaginary picture of a Harel who would be curious and inquisitive, willing to join her even if it meant separation from the life of the village. There were four people sitting here in the fields, not two. She wondered how she and Harel had been able to look into each other's minds for so long without seeing what was there.

She reached out carefully with a mental tendril, trying to touch him, not the image she held. He blinked and began to withdraw.— There are other people, like us and yet alien, who do not live on our world. It's true. One of them came to me during the ordeal, that's why I saw that the blackness wasn't really there. I saw that it couldn't touch this boy, that he could not see it—

Harel shook his head.

—It's true—

—How do you know this other wasn't an illusion—

Her mind seemed suddenly clear.—I know—she thought, almost dropping her wall in her surprise at the answer.—I know, because through this other person, I saw and learned about things and ideas which did not exist in my mind before. An illusion must come from something, a thought, an idea, an experience you've had, a legend you've been told. You may combine them in many different ways, but each piece will be something you know. But I saw new things, things that could not have come from my mind or the mind of anyone I know, the ideas were too elaborate for that—

—It must be an evil thing, sent to delude you—

—By what? What would seek to do that? I have my evidence, give me yours—

He began to walk away. She got up, scurrying quickly along her side of the ditch.—Harel! Answer me, don't just walk away—

He turned and faced her for a moment and she saw such pain in his face that she gasped. She drew back, pulling every bit of her mind behind her wall. She could have him, could reach inside and pull at his love, force him to her side, show him what she had seen over and over again until he could no longer doubt it, but at the cost of qualities she had loved in him; his calm acceptance of how things were, his clear, uncomplicated mind, his sturdy loyalty to his family and the village. He would be only her puppet.

She looked down at the ground, and let him go.

Daiya sat at the top of a hill, her back against a tree. The watchfires were lit; the village slept. The distant mountains slumbered under the comet's light while the machines beneath them, like the minds of the villagers, hummed and dreamed.

She should not have returned. It had been a mistake. She knew what the village was thinking about her now, when they thought of her at all; she had caught a glimpse of it in her grandfather's mind, and in Harel's. If they could not drive her away, or tear down her mind, they would exile her, perhaps remove the Net again. She could walk down this hill, and into the village, walk through its streets and stop at the hut of her parents, go inside and unroll her mat, and she would still be outside the village, cut off from the minds there. She would have no place—no longer a child, unable to live in a hut with young people past their ordeal, without a partner —there was nothing for her. It would be worse than if she never went back at all.

She thought of Etey, feeling resentful of the woman, with her queer notions of communication between the village and the comet. They had trouble enough communicating with others of their own kind who lived on other comet worlds. What had made her think Daiya's people would be different? Daiya could touch their minds, and still not reach them. Etey did not really care about her at all; she was only someone to be used for another purpose.

Reiho, at least, had cared about her welfare. He was as foolish as she had been, thinking she could go back and have everything as it was. She suddenly found herself hating him because he could go back to his home and rejoin his friends and in time resume his normal life, or what passed for one there. She hated him because she knew she could go with him, but she would only be going to a place where there was no position for her, no way she would ever fit in. She would have her calming implant, but none of her powers; it would be like passing through life blind and deaf.

She could, she supposed, have her body changed as theirs were; then her life on Earth would in time seem far away. She might even look back on it in the way she thought of her own infancy, just beyond the reach of her memory, a distant stage of her existence. But she could never submit to the alteration of her body, its mutilation, and without such alterations her life would be to theirs as a butterfly's was to those here. She had learned enough to know that. She would flutter through their collective consciousness and be gone, her life only a stored pattern in Homesmind. The alienness of that idea made her shiver, as she wondered if she herself would be trapped there for all eternity. If the vast cybernetic organism could hold her memory, it could hold her soul. Was that what those people did instead of joining the Merged One?

There was no purpose left in her life. She had nowhere to go. She would die and it would be as if she had never lived, unless she survived in the memory of future villagers as a dim legend, a warning to children of the dangers of separateness. She was not that unique; perhaps there had been others like her, though most of them must have died during ordeals. Her grandmother Rilla had been one, no doubt, with her moodiness and her inability to join the Merging Ones. Her parents had lost Rin, and now, for all practical purposes, her as well. Maybe it was for the better. Daiya would have no children; maybe the bit of Rilla in her family would die out and would not be a part of their descendants.

She stretched out under the tree, wanting to rest but sure she would not be able to sleep. She would only have to wait four more days and then Etey and Reiho would be gone. That would be much better for her; she would be free from playing with the absurd notion of joining them. She would be free to prepare herself for death, the only thing left. She could stop clinging to life.

Her muscles became tight. Why should the thought of death disturb her? She had faced it often enough, had sought it. But she did not want to die now; she couldn't die. There was too much left to discover and sort out. She had once known almost all there was a person could know, and then the world had changed, and now she knew she could live a hundred cycles and not know more than a tiny portion of it all. She had to come to some understanding of this knowledge, however small and tentative, some way of reconciling herself to it. Perhaps it could console her for what she had lost.

She recalled her friends: frail Mausi and clever Oren, fearful Sude, stolid Tasso and angry Peloren, all of them dead in the desert. Their deaths seemed so pointless now, their lives cut off just as they had been starting. The village had been very devious; better to have taken them all to the public space and doused the sparks of consciousness. They could have lived, but the village had killed them, the weight of legend and custom had struck them down. It could have been otherwise. That was the thought that had destroyed her world for her; it could have been otherwise. God had not given them their destiny. They had made it for themselves, then protected themselves from anything that would have changed it. Her friends had died, not to preserve the Merged One's plan, but only to keep things as they were, unchanged and permanent as rocks and stones.

How could people live as hers had lived, with such abilities, to come to this? They denied the power available to them and had forgotten it; they tried to break down the walls around people, yet set a barrier around all humankind on Earth. It made no sense, it was a monstrous joke, a fraud. She buried her head in the grass. She choked; her body shook as tears rolled down her face. A cry escaped her and vibrated in the night air.

She cried at last for her dead friends.

Daiya, standing at the edge of the fields, saw the craft before the villagers did.

She clenched her fists. The morning air was cold on her face. Rage filled her as she thought of seizing the shuttle, hurling it back to the desert. The air around her grew warm. Then she felt the terrified feelings of those working in the fields. They threw down their tools and raced toward one another, huddling together among the wheat while others hurried out from the village.

Daiya had come to the edge of the fields at dawn, determined to take one last look at the village before leaving it. She knew that would be better than lingering near it, tormenting herself with the sight of the home she no longer had.

Now Etey had come to disturb the village with her ridiculous hopes. Daiya thought: I shouldn't do a thing to help her. But there was Reiho to consider. She was sure he had tried to talk Etey out of coming here.

Long lines of villagers were winding through the fields. She sensed the turmoil of their thoughts at the sight of this strange illusion. She caught their fears; first Daiya, with her twisted soul, had returned to disturb them, her mindpowers strengthened by some evil force. Now an alien machine had come to the village. They were blaming her for it. They were not entirely mistaken.

The shuttle set down just beyond the edge of the fields. Daiya ran toward it, almost stumbling; she lifted herself from the ground and floated the rest of the way. Several Merging Ones were moving toward the craft. They halted several paces from it, studying the illusion. The doors slid open. Daiya caught a glimpse of Etey's red hair. The woman emerged from the shuttle, followed by Reiho. Etey stepped forward and faced the Merging Ones. Reiho hung back, leaning against the vehicle.

Daiya alighted, casting an angry look in Etey's direction. The minds of the Merging Selves murmured, still stunned by the apparition. Daiya saw Fayl NuraBaan release the arm of the woman guiding him. She felt the fear in him; the blind man, unable to comprehend the sight his companions had conveyed to him, was blocking the vision. Cerwen was with the group; his dark eyes gazed at her sadly.—What have you brought to us, Daiya—Anger slapped her. Jowē was hobbling toward them. Daiya felt a tug on the Net. The old woman was trying to draw the villagers together, controlling their fears with her strength.

Etey held out her hands. Her lips moved. "Do not be afraid," she said. "I mean no harm."

The Merging Ones tensed, sure that she did. Daiya stood between the villagers and Etey, surprised at how cold and empty she felt. She was certain that she could not defend Etey and Reiho against the entire village; she was not that strong. Neither could she stand by and watch them destroyed. Etey had finally set her against her own people.

14

Jowē faced Etey. She surveyed the woman with her small fierce eyes, then gazed at Reiho. Her mouth twisted, as if she had tasted a strange and bitter food and then spat it out. Her gaze fell on Daiya.

—What have you brought to us, girl—

—They are people from another world—

—The smaller one is like a solitary, yet it lives. The larger one has a mind weak as a baby's. Such things cannot exist—

—But they do—Daiya replied.

—They cannot. There is nothing like them in our world. It is an illusion. You have brought it. Tell the evil which holds you in its grip to disperse it—

—They are not from here. They live in the sky, far away. They have their own world. But Earth was once their home, too. They were like us, long ago. Their ancestors and ours are the same. You must believe me—Daiya gripped her tunic at the throat with one hand, twisting the fabric. She was afraid now. Her fear was becoming a cold solid mass inside her. She imagined it forming, like the black thing in the desert, swallowing everyone.—They too have minds—She went on.—They think and feel. Touch them and see for yourself—

Jowē's face was drawn and tired. The leathery skin wrinkled into furrows on her forehead and sagged in pouches near her mouth. Her mind, and those of the other Merging Ones, wove together as they tried to reconcile the presence of the strangers with all that they believed. Daiya could not follow their reasoning, and caught only a few images: people bound by the strands of the Net, one golden strand binding them to God and the heavens, standing before two machines. The tentacles on the machines fluttered. Daiya gasped, cursing herself silently for her stupidity. The villagers could only see Etey and Reiho as cylindrical machines. She recalled her first glimpse of Reiho, how frightened she had been.

—No—she thought, breaking into their reasoning.—That is not how they are. Look at them only with your eyes, you will see—She looked around desperately, noticing that her parents were standing together at the edge of the crowd. They seemed older and more worn. Anra's hands were folded over her abdomen, as if protecting her unborn child. Brun stared at the ground, lips pursed, shoulders slumped in shame. Silla clung to the edge of his tunic. Their walls were up, their minds rejecting the daughter they had brought into the world.—You can't reject them—Daiya continued, turning back to Jowē.

Fayl's mind touched hers.—I cannot see them—the blind man thought.—But I sense nothing human about them. They mimic our feelings, but there is no depth to them, their humors are weak. They have no smell, and I can hear no rustle of clothing when they move, only the tread of feet and a soft crackling. I am afraid to put out my hands and touch them—

"What is going on?" Etey's whisper was almost a hiss. Daiya glanced at her. "I feel strange things in the air, I . . ."

"You are a fool," Daiya replied. She built a mental wall around the woman to protect her from the villagers. "You have endangered Reiho and yourself. You couldn't listen to me, could you, I was just something for you to lie to and use. You believe you know best, you trample on things you don't understand. Maybe you aren't really human after all."

Etey wrinkled her brows. "We went into the mountains." Daiya muffled the words, suddenly sensing that she did not want the village to hear what Etey might say. "I touched the minds. They are vast in their knowledge and their power. They drew me out, I tried to withdraw, but I could not withstand them. They pressed me to come here, and said your people must awaken. I could not resist them."

"I don't believe you," Daiya said, pulling at Etey's thoughts. "I touched them too. The machines would not use force. They could have forced me to return, but they did not."

"They drew me here."

Daiya wanted to claw at Etey's mind. She brushed against an alien strand of thought and drew back. The machines had been persuasive, tempting Etey, but the decision had been hers. She had not been able to resist. The machines had minds mightier and more knowledgeable than that of a young girl, therefore she would listen to them and not to Daiya. So Etey had reasoned.

Daiya withdrew from the woman's thoughts. "You should not have brought Reiho."

"I could not stop him. I have not been able to control him for some time now." Etey's weaker mind pushed against her accusingly. Daiya struggled to hold up the wall that separated them, and their thoughts, from the village. "At least the village will believe you now," Etey went on. "We are your evidence."

Daiya dug her nails into her palms. For a moment, she saw herself striking down the woman, punishing her for her arrogance. Then Etey's eyes widened; her body jerked as if she had been struck. Daiya felt a wave of hostility sweeping toward them from the Merging Selves.

She threw up a shield before Etey was struck again. Reiho, bewildered, leaned against the shuttle, unable to sense a thing.

"Get back in the shuttle and go," Daiya cried, too late. Another wave slapped her, shattering the shield. Etey was thrown to the ground. Reiho blinked. Daiya threw up a wall, holding it as well as she could. The village beat against it. The ground shook, the shuttle wobbled, and Reiho was thrown flat. Etey clung to the ground as Daiya struggled to keep her footing.

A dark cloud was forming above the villagers, a black billowing storm, flashing with lightning, formed out of water and masses of air. Daiya put out her hands as if warding it off. It was a physical object, not an illusion or mental projection; even Reiho could, she was sure, perceive it. In despair, she realized that the Merging Ones had understood that Etey could see and feel mental constructs only vaguely, and Reiho not at all. The cloud grew larger, rumbling loudly as the lightning flashed.

She opened a channel to the mountains, drawing all the power she could. The cloud swept toward them. A fork of electricity struck the ground near Reiho. Daiya compressed some air and hurled it against the cloud with all her might. Her nerves prickled. A crack of thunder stung her ears, almost deafening her. The air was thick with the burning scent of lightning. The cloud broke apart and scattered, showering them with rain as it was dispersed.

Jowē threw out her arms, raising the wind. Daiya held up her shield, protecting Reiho and Etey. The wind shrieked, pulling up wheat and dirt, circling them like a cyclone. Daiya's hair lashed her face and slashed at her eyelids, almost blinding her. Her tunic was plastered against her body, pulling across her breasts. She struggled to preserve the calm at the center of the wind as the funnel surrounded them, screaming all the anger and fear of the Merging Selves. A sheaf of wheat, caught in the wind, cut at her, forcing her closer to her companions.

Reiho pressed against her, trying to protect her with his body. She felt him wrestle with his fears as he tried to keep up his courage. He was foolish, his bravery based on ignorance; he had not known what he was entering, and had no judgment about when to advance or retreat. But she had a bond with him. He guarded her with his arms, and she decided not to tell him that it would do her no good.

She would be unable to hold the shield much longer. Her body was growing weaker; her capacity to draw on the power under the mountains was failing. The cyclone was a wall. She could not see through it; she was sick and dizzy from watching its movement.

"Daiya," Reiho said. He held her, trying to support her body. She rested against him, grateful for the gesture. Breathing deeply, she struggled to renew herself, and then straightened.

She gathered up all her strength, aiming it at the cyclone. She lifted it from them, pushing it toward the plain. The dark funnel dashed over the grassy flat ground, cutting a path through the verdant growth. As the villagers released it, the dirt it had captured sifted through the air toward the ground.

Etey was trembling with fear. The air grew cold around them. The woman, knowing about the minds under the mountains, was trying to reach them, too. A wind howled and swept toward the village, flattening the wheat. It tore at the tops of the huts, swirling grass into the streets. The cattle grazing at the eastern edge of the fields turned together and moved toward the crops. Etey's mind was out of control as she tried to fight back. Several villagers threw their minds at the cattle. The herd swerved and took off toward the plains.

"No!" Daiya screamed, knowing Etey would only destroy herself, as well as frighten the village; she had no training. Daiya stopped the wind and seized the woman's shoulders. Etey twisted away. "Stop, you cannot fight back, you don't know what you're doing."

She turned back toward the Merging Ones. The air around her was icy, pricking her skin with cold needle points. Jowē glared at her and raised a hand. The fallow fields lurched, vomiting the bones of the buried. Daiya watched with horror as the Merging Ones lifted the bones with their minds, desecrating graves in their attempt to destroy the intruders. The bones danced. Thigh bones struck the ground, finger bones separated from hands clawed the air, rib cages spun; above them all hung empty-eyed, disembodied skulls, grinning. Reiho clung to Etey, his mouth open in a silent scream.

The bones swept toward them, clanking and rattling. A baby's skull struck Daiya on her leg, a tibia beat her back. Etey seized the bones with her mind, trying to scatter them. They rained on Daiya, pounding her shoulders. Daiya threw a shield around the woman, trying to hold it as she pushed the bones from them. The air hummed around her; the bones rattled. She cursed Etey and her feeble, misdirected powers. She could not protect them much longer if she had to fight both the woman's efforts and the rage of the village.

She drew more power. Her nerves were burning; her muscles cramped. She scattered the bones. They exploded into pieces and then were dust, settling around them in a fine white powder.

Exhausted, Daiya collapsed on the ground. She sat up almost as quickly, afraid of showing the village how weak she was now. Her muscles were knots, her mind as flaccid as an empty water sack.

Jowē's eyes glittered. The old woman turned slightly, looking at

Reiho. Daiya threw a mental wall around the boy. Fire burned through it as the Merging Ones seized him, hurling him into the air. Daiya screamed. Reiho fell to the ground, smashing an arm against the side of a rock. He staggered to his feet. His lifesuit was still protecting him, but she could feel his fear. His skin was pale and yellowish. He opened his mouth. A keening sound reached her.

He was seized again. His limbs waved, his legs wobbled. He danced like a puppet. The Merging Ones, realizing that he was protected from physical harm, were attacking his mind directly. His arms and legs twisted bonelessly.

—No—Daiya thought, pushing her resistance at the villagers.— He's not a thing, stop it, don't hurt him—Jowē was reaching inside him, trying to crush his mind with a mental fist. He danced, lurching into the field, then toward her again.

Etey was suddenly torn away and thrown against the side of a ditch. She struggled as she slipped toward the muddy water, putting up a feeble mental wall with her atrophied powers. She would be pushed under the water; she would drown.

—You can't—Daiya cried at the villagers. Then she understood what she would have to do. Everything slowed around her. Etey's hand clawed at the slippery mud, Reiho's arms waved slowly, Jowē's eyes closed and then opened. Daiya had only one weapon left; her knowledge. Giving it to the village now would rob her of that one advantage, her knowledge of the power that lay under the mountains. The Merging Ones, once they learned of it, might destroy her with that power. But it was her only chance; she had to show them the truth.

She summoned her strength, calling on the machines. She dropped her wall and threw the vision at the village, forcing them to see what lay beneath the mountains. The gold and crystal pillars gleamed before them; the long hallway stretched out in front of them. The air hummed and the gauzy veils of light fluttered.

And then the minds spoke, answering Daiya's silent appeal:/ We are where your power lies / Another vision appeared; machines and people were erecting the pillars. / You built us /

A scream rose in a thousand throats; the force of the vision and voice was too powerful to be denied or thought false. / You built us long ago. We are the pathway to the mindrealm, the source of your power. You have forgotten us, and take only the smallest part of what we have to offer/ The sorrow Daiya had felt before was in the voice again. / You have buried us under stone and denied our exist-

ence. You have sought to divide yourselves from your own handi-
work/

Jowē was crumpling to the earth, hands over her face. An old
man fell near her. Daiya called on the machines again.

The new vision was of the comet in black space, a cosmic forest,
giant trees growing where nothing should grow. /This is the home of
your visitors. Most of your species dwells far from Earth. You are
the smallest part of humankind/ For a moment, Daiya thought she
heard the voice of Homesmind speaking through the machines. The
vision grew blurry, then disappeared. / We have much to teach you.
Do not turn from us again/ It was a plea. The voice faded.

Other Merging Ones now lay on the ground. The blue eyes of one
old man stared sightlessly at Daiya. She got to her feet, looking
around slowly. Fayl lay a few paces from her. She went to his side
and stood over the blind man.—I saw—he thought. He turned his
face from her. His mind was gone before she could grasp it. Numbly, she walked away from his body. Etey was tugging at her lifesuit
as she climbed out of the ditch, shaking the mud from her; it
slithered like snakes over the silver. Reiho, farther off, was very still.

Daiya ran toward him, hearing the wails of the village behind her.
She reached out frantically for his mind, unable to touch it. She
heard the sound of Etey's boots pounding the earth behind her.
Daiya fell at Reiho's side and touched his shoulder. She turned him
over gently. His dark eyes stared up at her from under half-closed
lids.

—He's dead—She looked up at Etey and tried to speak. Her
mouth opened, exhaling a bit of life. She gulped at the air. "He's
dead, they killed him." Her chin sank to her chest. Her limbs were
stone.

Etey reached out and pushed her away. "Help me get him up."

Daiya shook her head, not understanding.

"Help me."

"He's dead. I can't touch his mind, it's gone."

"His lifesuit will preserve him, preserve his body for a time. But I
must get him to the shuttle."

Daiya forced herself to rise. She helped Etey heave the boy's body
over her shoulder. Etey strode off, muttering words in another language. Reiho's head rose and fell against the woman's back. Daiya
stumbled after them. Etey reached the shuttle and climbed in, closing the door behind her.

Daiya looked at the villagers. Tiny groups were making their way back to the village. Others sat in clumps among the wheat and near the ditches. A few were moaning. She looked around wildly, noticing that several Merging Ones were still lying on the ground, bodies twisted, limbs distended.

A hand touched her shoulder. She jumped back. Cerwen stood near her, Leito just behind him.

—Jowē is dead—he thought. His mind was still, too still; she could sense only shock and bewilderment.—Others are dead too. Our minds cannot hold these new things—He looked up at the sky as a groan escaped him.—I felt their deaths, I prayed that I would be taken too—He covered his face and began to sob quietly. Leito took his arm and led him away.

A few young men and women were gathering near the bodies of the dead Merging Ones. Nenla BariWil was with them. Daiya went to the red-haired girl and stood near her friend as the young people lifted the bodies with their minds, preparing to take them to the fallow fields for burial.

Nenla gazed at her solemnly.

—I killed them—Daiya thought.

—You did not, you could not. You made them see and hear. What they saw and heard killed them—Nenla turned away and followed the others. The procession was a line on the edge of the fields. The bodies floated above the young people, borne on invisible biers.

Several children and a few adults had gathered around the shuttle. The children rubbed it, leaving handprints and dirty streaks. As Daiya approached, a few of them retreated, as if more frightened of her than of the craft and its inhabitants. A little boy was scraping at the side of the shuttle with a stone, unable to scratch it. The children, Daiya realized, were not afraid, only curious about these strange beings who, they seemed to understand dimly, were people.

Silla was almost under the craft, poking at the runners. Daiya reached over and pulled her out by the arm, shooing the others away. They scampered off, stopping at the edge of the field to watch the shuttle from a distance. The adults wandered away, following the funeral procession.

—What are you doing here—Daiya asked, still holding her sister. —Where are Anra and Brun—

Silla twisted free and pointed at the village.—They went—She waved her arm. Daiya shaded her eyes, unable to spot her parents anywhere nearby. She spun around, trying to peer through the darkened dome of the shuttle.

The door slid open and Etey emerged. Her frizzy hair was wilted, her perfect face stiff. Silla touched Etey's lifesuit, rubbing her hand on the woman's thigh. Daiya raised a hand to slap Silla away.

"Leave her alone," Etey said. She sat down on the ground as the door slid shut. Silla sat next to her, pulling at her arm. Daiya touched her sister's mind, looking at Etey through Silla's eyes. Of course, Daiya thought, wondering why she hadn't quite realized it before. Silla could see Etey as a human being; her mind was still too unformed to see her as anything else.

Daiya withdrew from the little girl's mind. "I told you not to come," she said to Etey. She choked back the bitterness in her throat.

"The minds under the mountains drew me. I could not grasp everything they showed me, but they wanted me to come here, and the desire to do so became very strong."

"You should have resisted."

"I could not. I felt that I must try to reach your people. Reiho tried to stop me, the minds could not touch his thoughts, but I was determined to come and he refused to leave my side."

"You wanted to come. You wanted to come anyway. The machines only used what was already inside you." Daiya paused. They had done the same with her. All they knew was to give power to people to do as the people wished. "Now Reiho is dead, not to mention the others."

"Reiho is not really dead, Daiya."

"Don't lie to me. I saw him die." She suddenly wanted to hit the woman, hurt her for bringing all this upon them. Etey, apparently sensing the wish, recoiled. "I tried to touch his mind, and he was gone."

"He is not dead. It is true that only his body lies in the shuttle now, preserved, but I shall take him home and Homesmind will restore him."

Daiya clenched her fists. "I know that you can do many things, but that is not possible. Don't tell me such lies."

"It is not a lie. Homesmind holds Reiho's pattern and his memories. When we return, they will be restored. Why do you think I was so anxious to get him back here? His lifesuit could only have preserved him for a short time. Sometimes we cannot restore a person, especially after a serious accident, but Reiho will be all right."

"His pattern?" Daiya murmured.

"Homesmind holds the pattern and memories of everyone who has lived on our world. We could make all those people live again, but we feel it is wrong to impose another identity on an individual now alive, even a small child, who must be allowed to acquire her own identity. But their work, their hopes, their experiences are all part of Homesmind. Reiho will live again, although he will not remember his temporary death."

Daiya pressed against the shuttle, standing on her toes. She peered through the dome. Reiho lay on a reclining seat, stiff and still, covered by a clear carapace. She wrinkled her nose against the dome, trying to hope. She sent a tendril into Etey's mind; the woman had said part of the truth.

Her legs wobbled. She sat down abruptly, realizing how weak and tired she was. She searched through the channels of Etey's mind, then withdrew. "There is a thing you haven't said, Etey."

The woman started to shake her head, then stopped. "Yes, you are right. Reiho will have his memories, his experience, everything. But one thing will be different. There is an emotional connection we cannot restore. He will have everything, his memory will be clear, but he will feel as though his past experiences have happened to someone else, or as if they might be a dream. He will be Reiho, he will live as he would have, entirely in character, but his life up to now will seem to him like another's life. He will feel a distance from part of himself."

"Then his soul is gone," Daiya murmured. "You'll give him life without his soul." Whatever Reiho might recall in this new state, he would not think of her as a friend, would not feel that bond; that would be gone. She would only be part of a dream, a disconnected memory.

Etey said, "There is no soul."

"I don't believe that."

"You can believe it or not, as you will."

"If you deny the soul, you deny God." The words sounded formal and empty. She thought of the mountains and the machines; men and women had made them, not the Merged One. Men and women had created a home on the comet. But they had not made the earth, the sun, or space. Daiya drew up her legs, hugging them, wondering what she could believe now.

"Let me try to say it," Daiya went on, hoping she could make her thoughts clear to Etey, and wishing she could speak to the woman directly, mind to mind. "You will restore memories to that body, and call that person Reiho, and he will believe he is Reiho. But there is a Reiho I knew, the Reiho who came here, and went under the mountains with me, and took me to your home, and that Reiho is dead. You will bring to life a second Reiho. You don't have to say his soul is gone, but I know it is."

"He will be Reiho," Etey said sharply. Part of her mind seemed walled off from Daiya. "Think of yourself many years ago, as a child like this little girl here, and then tell me whether or not you sometimes feel disassociated from that person you once were. That is what it will be for Reiho. He would have felt that way in time. As you know, we lead longer lives than you do."

"It is not the same. I know I'm different now from what I was cycles ago, but a thread connects me to that person. Reiho's thread has been broken. He has died. You said you think it's wrong to impress an identity, a set of memories, on a child because it would rob the child of its own identity, but you are going to take Reiho's memory and experience and put them inside the body of the boy in there. That means you are creating a new Reiho. What is the difference?"

Etey let out a loud sigh. Her wall disappeared, and Daiya felt her assent. "Very well. My reason tells me you are right. I know that, though I hoped to console you with part of the truth. I cannot hide from one who touches minds. The boy will still be Reiho for all practical purposes. He will act like Reiho, and be treated as though he were. That is not as cruel as returning him to life with no memory would be. But all this has nothing to do with souls."

Daiya glanced at her, wishing she could have accepted a half-truth about Reiho. But her life, after everything that had happened, would have no meaning if she accepted lies again. She said, "Then you don't believe in God. Maybe I can't either, anymore." She was silent, a part of her wondering if the Merged One would strike her down for blaspheming.

"No, I do not. None of us does, not in the way you mean. But we have found nothing to disprove the existence of such a being."

Daiya watched the woman, thinking she was only trying to console her. But Etey seemed to mean it.

"Does it matter?" Etey went on. "We must live as best we can. Some things will always be open to question."

Daiya climbed to her feet. "Will you go now? I don't think anyone will try to hurt you, but . . ."

"Reiho will be all right now, his body is safe inside the shuttle. But I cannot leave until I know you are settled here."

"Settled!" Daiya flung out an arm. "We shall never be that way again. Everything has changed."

"I want to be sure you will be all right."

She searched Etey's mind and found only a calm, distant compassion, tinged with guilt. Disappointed, she drew back. For a moment, Etey's thoughts touched hers. "I am sorry," Etey said. "It is the best I can do. My feelings do not run as strong as yours."

"Don't stay here," Daiya said. "My people have much to consider, and your presence may disturb them. At least leave this area."

"Very well. I shall go to the foothills, directly east. You can find me there, at least for a little while. I do have more time, according to our agreement."

"You did not keep your part of the agreement."

Etey looked down at the ground, then at Daiya again. "I did what I thought I had to do, and what the cybernetic minds of Earth wanted me to do. I did not know what would happen. Perhaps if I had, I would not have come, and there would not have been so much death. But before you condemn me, you should remember the thousands your village condemned to death, the children you call solitaries and those sent into the desert. I did what I thought was right. It is no more than what you did."

Daiya thought of the ruin their supposedly right actions had caused. She leaned over and took Silla's hand as the child got up. "I must take my sister home."

"Your sister? I did not realize."

"I must take her home." They walked near one of the ditches. Daiya moved slowly so that Silla could keep up with her. They passed a small group of people sitting near one of the ditches. A man looked up as she passed. His face was filled with grief.

Daiya gazed at the ground, watching her feet tread the earth. The space around her was filled with sorrow so pervasive that she had to keep up her wall. Silla, affected by the sadness, began to cry. Daiya built a wall around her sister, then projected a mental maze into Silla's mind to keep her occupied. Silla threaded her way through the maze while Daiya wondered what she would say to her parents when she reached the hut.

The village was quiet as they approached. It looked deserted. The huts suddenly seemed fragile to her, about to crumble. The streets were strewn with thatching. She was home, after going through so much to be here. It did not feel like home anymore. The paths were narrower than she remembered them to be. The village seemed shabby and mean, the roofs of the huts like the backs of beasts whose heads were buried in the ground.

She let down her wall as they drew nearer to their hut. Silla gurgled. She had conquered the maze. Daiya sensed a strand of Anra's mind. She picked up Silla quickly and ran to the doorway.

Anra was in labor. She squatted naked on a mat in the corner while Brun held her hand. Two lanterns flickered on the table; the reddish light danced eerily on the walls.

Anra exhaled sharply as Daiya thrust Silla through the doorway. —Daiya—Brun thought, without looking up. Anra sucked in some air, then exhaled again. Her body shone with sweat.

Daiya hung back in the doorway, feeling the agitation in her mother's mind. Her own muscles contracted as Anra bore down and pushed.—Isn't it early—she thought, not knowing what else to say.

—Only a little early—Brun replied. She caught the unexpressed undercurrent in his thoughts; the events of the day had been too much for Anra.—Come and help us—he went on.

Daiya hurried to his side. Anra was breathing heavily now, using all her strength to push out the baby and suppress her own pain. Daiya drew on as much power as she could, easing things for her mother.

Anra suddenly smiled. The head of the child emerged. Brun caught the baby. Silla slapped her hands together. Daiya eased Anra to the mat. Brun lay the baby on Anra. The child was a girl. Brun got up and went to the cauldron over the low fire. He returned with a cloth and began to bathe the baby gently.

Daiya suddenly began to tremble. Her face was covered with sweat. An unreasoning panic washed over her. Brun looked at her sharply, thinking,—If you can't control yourself, get away—She rose and went to the table, collapsing onto a bench and burying her head in her arms while masking her feelings.

A hand was on her back. Her head jerked up. She realized she had dozed off. The baby was crying. Her father stood next to her.

—I've cut the cord—Brun said. His thoughts were cold, stinging her. For a moment she did not understand him.—The child is a solitary—

Daiya gasped. She jumped up and went over to where Anra lay. Her mother was crying. Silla sat in the corner, her face solemn. Daiya spun around and went to the opposite corner. She picked up an old tunic lying there and brought it back to Anra. She took the baby carefully from her mother and wrapped her in the tunic.

Brun grabbed her arm, his fingers gripping her so hard it hurt.— There is no need for that—he thought.—We must bury it in the fields—

—No—Daiya thought. The word fled from her, striking Brun. He reached for the child. Daiya stepped back.—No—she thought more firmly.

—Have you truly lost your mind? She is a solitary—

Daiya backed away, still holding the baby. The child let out a cry. —I won't let you kill her. That boy you saw today, he is a solitary, yet he lived. Most of his people are solitaries. They can reason and feel. They have made a life for themselves. We might not like it, but it suits them. I won't let you kill her—

—You know our customs. Give her to me or I'll crush her mind now—

Daiya threw up a strong wall.—No. You'll have to fight me first. Just try—

—You worthless girl—Brun thought, his words burning her.— You have brought us nothing but sorrow, and now you bring us more. Don't we have enough—

Daiya moved toward the door, still shielding herself and the baby. —I'll take her to the people of the comet. They can give her a home—

—You cannot—

—I will. At least she can live there. Isn't that better, Brun—

Anra sat up on the mat, staring uncomprehendingly at Daiya. Brun turned away, unwilling to fight.—I do not understand the world any more—his mind murmured.—Nothing is as it was. We are being punished for giving birth to you. The Merged One should have called us all to the next world rather than let us live to see such things—

Daiya hurried from the hut. As she ran through the street, the baby began to cry in a piercing wail.

Daiya awoke. She stretched out her hand and felt grass. She opened her eyes. It was still dark. She tried to recall where she was, what had happened. She yawned; she was still tired. She stretched a hand over her head and smacked it against something solid. She sat up, turning slightly, and saw the shuttle.

She was rubbing her arm as the shuttle's door slid open. Etey climbed out with the baby. The baby was crying. Etey had wrapped the child in a piece of silvery material. "Are you all right, Daiya?"

Daiya remembered her journey here. She nodded silently.

"You came flying in here after sunset. You handed me this child and then collapsed. I checked you and you seemed to be well, just tired, so I let you sleep." Etey turned the child against her shoulder and soothed her, rubbing her back. "I fed the baby a little while ago."

"With what?" Daiya asked, looking dubiously at the small breasts under the lifesuit.

"The synthesizer made something up for her." Etey perched in the doorway, then sat, letting her legs dangle. "Why did you come here as you did, with this child?"

Daiya was silent. Now that she had rested, she was sure she had been mad to come here. She wondered how she had ever thought Etey might help her. "This baby," she said, trying to find the words, "this baby is my sister. My mother gave birth to her yesterday."

"But why did you bring her here?"

Daiya sighed. "She's a solitary. You must know what that means. If she stays here, she'll be killed, that's what we do to isolates." She realized Etey knew that, but was surprised at the violent grimace which distorted the woman's face. "I couldn't let it happen. Only a short while ago I would have said it was right. I would have followed my father to the fields and dug the grave. And if you had not been on our world, maybe I would have buried her anyway, even knowing what I do now, because there would have been no alternative. But I thought . . ." She twisted her hands together, rubbing at the streaks of dirt revealed by the soft light shining out of the shuttle. "There is no life for her here."

A bird began to sing in one of the nearby trees. The sky above the foothills and mountains was beginning to grow lighter. The child was quiet, nestling against Etey's chest.

Etey said, "You want me to take her with me."

Daiya folded her arms. "You must." She narrowed her eyes, seeing Etey through slits. "She is someone from my world you can save instead of destroy," she said bitterly, knowing that it was she, and not Etey, who had wielded the weapons.

Etey looked down. "She should be able to adapt to our world. Most of the physical changes in us are produced after birth, and are modifications of what we already have. But she is unlike us in many ways. Homesmind has altered our genetic structure, eliminating the worst conditions. It has modified our endocrine system so that our emotions do not so easily war with our reason, and we have more conscious control over our autonomic system. We all have several parents, not just two. We are very carefully planned." She adjusted the silvery fabric around the child. "This girl will be something new in our world. She may in time come to feel like an outsider."

"But you asked me to come with you," Daiya replied. "She has more of a chance to be happy there than I do, she won't have known anything else. You have more reason to take her to your home."

Etey sighed. "You are right. You too may still come with us, you know. I asked you before because I was sure you would die here if you did not, that is all. Life is better than death. Now you could come with your sister. You could watch her grow up. You could have a good life there."

"I could not."

"Better than here."

"You're so sure of that, aren't you, Etey?"

The woman lowered her eyelids.

"I can catch your feelings. On the surface you think of bridging the distance between your people and mine, but what you really want is for us to become like you. You hold scorn for us inside, whether you admit it to yourself or not, and think us primitive. But we can dream the world as well as see it, we can ripen the wheat and fruit, shape the water, see through what is only visible with the eyes, and touch minds, while you must live blind and twist the substance of the world into strange shapes. Now we shall have knowledge too, and we may become something you can never be. We must find our own path."

Etey was silent.

"I still have much to find out. You talk of a bridge between us. Isn't it already present? Your Homesmind has spoken to our minds here. Perhaps It will continue to speak to them, as you say It has to other such minds, so in a way our world will always speak to yours. Once you told me that Homesmind was the best part of your world."

The woman leaned toward her. "Will you go back to your village?"

"I must. Things will change now. I must be honest, I don't know if they will be better or worse. The minds under the mountains spoke to me of growing conscious, something which seems only to make the world sharp and hard, soiled and empty. If they do not help us find new dreams, we shall die."

"Perhaps nothing will happen," Etey said harshly. "Maybe things will return to what they were. I shall tell you something, it may not matter very much. Sometimes I believe that the world, the universe, will one day be the province of Homesmind and all the other minds we built so long ago. I believe that may be why we have not located biological beings more advanced than we are. I sometimes even think that Homesmind has already sensed the presence of superior cybernetic minds, but has not communicated to us about them."

Daiya tried to imagine that. No human being could hold as much as those minds did; it wasn't possible. She wondered if the day would come when all people lived on only in those minds, as the world had, she believed once, lived in God's mind. Perhaps this was what their myths had foretold.

"You're saying there is no purpose to human life," Daiya said sadly.

"I am saying that might be our purpose, our end. We built the machines. They are a part of us."

Daiya was silent. Birds whistled and chirped in the dawn. She put her hand to the ground, touching the grass.

"I shall have to leave very soon now," Etey said at last. "I must get your sister settled. I shall help care for her. I do not think we shall ever come back."

Daiya thought of Reiho.

Etey lifted an eyebrow, as if sensing her thoughts. "It is not as though we shall be gone. Through your cybernetic intelligences here, and through Homesmind you can speak to us, even if we are far from your world." Etey paused. "Eventually, we will disappear from your sky. But I am going to try to persuade the others to keep us in this system, at least for a while. If they wish to go elsewhere, perhaps some of us will build a new world, though I think most of us will agree to stay at least for your lifetime."

Daiya shrugged. "Perhaps you should go far away. We must decide things for ourselves, and your presence is destructive."

"You may not always feel that way. If your world calls on us, we shall come back, but only then."

The child let out a soft cry. Etey patted her. Daiya wondered if the girl would someday be grateful she had been taken from a world which would have sentenced her to death, or if she would grow alienated from the people of the comet.

She put a hand on the shuttle. "Tell Reiho . . ." She paused, not knowing what she wanted Etey to tell him. She swallowed. "Tell him not to forget. Tell him not to forget me." She turned away. "I must go home."

"Wait a little. I can give you something to eat before you go. You can spend some time with your sister."

"No. It's better if I go now. Goodbye, Etey."

"Farewell, Daiya."

Daiya began to walk in the direction of the village. After a few paces, she looked back at the shuttle. Etey still sat in the doorway, holding her sister. She was a silent silver sentry with a solitary and a boy suspended in deathly sleep as companions. She caught a last trace of Etey's distant, calm concern. She held up a hand in final farewell, then continued on her way.

15

Daiya circled the edge of the fields, gazing at the narrow paths which had been trampled through the wheat. In the fallow fields, mounds of earth were strewn about over a few bones; she saw the newly covered graves of the dead Merging Ones. She found herself lifting dirt with her mind, tidying the graves, hiding the bones. She thought of her dead friends in the desert. Their bones would become part of the desert, as their minds supposedly became part of the Merged One. Daiya began to pray. She wondered if anything would hear the prayers. The words drifted from her. She imagined them floating above the clouds into black space, calling to the stars.

A few villagers roamed through the fields. They surveyed the damage, making a show of carrying on the life of the community. They began to clear away the torn-up wheat. Occasionally one would pause and stare at the ground. Their minds were silent as they worked; she caught no murmurings. In the distance, she saw others patching up the straw roofs torn by Etey's windstorm. She thought of the village as it had been. The future had been fixed and unalterable, continuous with the past.

A man looked up at her. Cerwen was with him, helping to clear the fields. Her grandfather watched her silently, then walked toward her.

Cerwen stopped a few paces away and stared at her, his mind as still as a warm summer day. His thoughts had softened, eroded by events. He tried to smile and could not.

—I am the oldest of the Merging Selves now—he thought. I didn't expect such a thing to befall me. I am still too much of an individual to be in such a place, and now I must draw the others together and decide what we should do—

His mind reached toward hers and picked up her thoughts.—So the creatures have gone—he went on.—They strike at us and go, we are nothing to them—

—It isn't true, Cerwen. A grandchild of yours is with them, she'll live. Here, she would have died—

Cerwen slumped; she sensed his sorrow.

—They didn't mean harm, Cerwen. They didn't know what would happen. Blame me. If it hadn't been for me, perhaps we would still be as we were—

He shook his head—No, Daiya. Perhaps the Merged One sought to reveal these things through you. That is what I try to believe now, though at other times I feel certain that God has abandoned us—He looked at her sharply.—Why did you not leave with those creatures—

She held out her hands, palms up.—I could not. My place is here—

—There is no place for you here. You have failed your ordeal, yet you are no longer a child—

—Things have changed. I must find my own place—

—Perhaps you should be judged—he thought angrily,—though I do not know what kind of judgment we could pass on you. There is no precedent—His mind rippled; thorns pricked her brain. The sharpness of his thoughts had returned.—We are lost. So many have surrounded themselves with walls, afraid to reach out, afraid of the power they realize is available to them. When the old ones died, other villages felt it, and now we cannot reach those others, though we have the power. I am afraid to see what they make of all this. Maybe they have erected their walls too. I do not know which I fear more, that we will separate ourselves from one another, or that we may seize the power and destroy ourselves. These are evil times—

An elusive thought, like a small bird, brushed near her. She tried to hold it and lost it. She waited, opening her mind, hoping it would once again alight.

—Let me live—she found herself thinking, feeling as though someone else was speaking through her.—Let me stay. Let everyone see that it is possible to live with this knowledge and survive. The ways of the village will be one way, my life will be another. Haven't we always believed that it was most important not to separate ourselves from other minds? Why should that principle not be as true now as before? Maybe the Merged One is testing us to see if we can follow that belief. It is easier to live as we all did when everyone believed the same things, but harder this way. If we reject this chance, we reject our most important belief—

—And perhaps now we shall war with one another, as men and women did in ancient times—Cerwen thought.—And many more may die, as so many Merging Ones did here. For many cycles we have lived our lives, and was our way so bad—

It was the same question she had asked herself. She looked down at the ground, twisting her hands together.— I don't know, Grandfather. But we said we knew, and we did not. The people of the comet believe that one must learn, must not hide from knowledge, that learning is what minds must do. To cut oneself off from knowledge means one is cut off from the universe and its truth, and that must mean one would be separated from God as well. We lived all these cycles and yet we didn't know our own past—She looked up, gazing into his eyes.—We were unconscious, that is what the minds under the mountains say, as unconscious as we believed a solitary to be—

—We had our way. It served us. We survived. We had a truth— Cerwen put a hand over his eyes.—Perhaps you, and everything that has happened, are only a storm that passes quickly, making waves on the river, forcing it from its banks. But the storm passes, and the river flows on—

—Rivers can change course—

His hand dropped to his side.—I shall bring the other Merging Ones together, those who are left, and try to restore some purpose to our lives. Live if you must, but you will not live within the village, not as long as I am here—

Bitterness filled her. Her fingers clawed at the edges of her tunic, bunching the fabric.—Very well—she thought, trembling at the thought of exile.—You will not live forever, Cerwen—

He thrust a hand toward her.—You misunderstand me—She caught his thought: he saw her standing near the village, near it but not a part of it.—Stay near us if you wish. Enter town during the day if there is something you need or someone you wish to see. But you must realize that you cannot dwell within the village itself, there is no place for you. We have lived the way we have for too many cycles to change so quickly, to allow one with such separateness to live among us. Already we are fragile. Such an act might tear us apart. But at least we shall not insist that you submit yourself for judgment —He was speaking now for the other Merging Selves; she could sense the entwining of their thoughts with his own.

She forced a smile.—I see that I have already been judged—She drew back behind a wall, thinking: I shall make my own place, others may come to me.

—Are we agreed—he asked.

She bowed her head, assenting. The Net lifted from her. She reached out with her mind, wanting to hold it. The Net was gone.

Cerwen turned and left her, alone.

Daiya stood at the bottom of the hill. A warm breeze caressed her face, sweeping dark curls in front of her eyes. The breeze dispersed; the air was still. She began to climb the hill's grassy slope to the grove of trees near the top. The sun was dimmed by a hazy sky. The air was thick. As she climbed, she recalled the last time she had come to this hill, with Harel, when she had been sure he would love her forever.

She reached the top and looked south toward the village. From here, she could see the huts, made small by the distance, the tiny flower and vegetable gardens, the public space in the center. The chickens, ducks, and pigs within the village were as they had always been; the pigs rooted, the chickens pecked at feed, the ducks waddled and ruffled their feathers. For a moment, she envied them their simple, thoughtless lives.

The public space was oddly empty for this time of day, occupied by only a few children sitting passively around a young man. The small figure waved his arms at the children, as if trying to explain something to them. Then he shrugged, got up, and walked away, disappearing among the nearby huts. A few people were sitting in their gardens. She saw Anra and Brun near their hut. Silla was playing in some mud.

Daiya looked west, toward the riverbank. A few young people lay at the water's edge, not swimming, not even playing. One girl got up and stared at the flowing water.

The spirit of the village was gone. Daiya pulled idly at some of the clover around her, reaching out to pluck a golden wildflower. She decided to leave the flower where it grew. What have I done, she thought. Claws dug inside her abdomen. She leaned forward.

A vision came to her: She was walking toward the mountains, preparing to cross into the desert. Her body seemed light and insubstantial. She was ready to face the ordeal again, to struggle against the black deadliness once more. She would face it and live and win a place inside the village and things would be as they were. She waited for it to come to her. She stood among the stones that covered the bones of her friends. She called to the dark creature. She opened her eyes.

The darkness was with her on the hill. She faced it, waiting for it to swallow her. She stared through the mass as it swelled. It reached toward her with its thick pseudopodia. It flowed over the ground. It embraced her, resting around her like a heavy garment. She felt it trying to reach inside her and fill her with empty darkness. She resisted. The darkness faded, dissolving into black streaks and then nothingness. It was gone. It had no power over her. She could not go back. She was trapped in the world as it now was.

A figure was moving toward the hill. She recognized Harel. Her throat grew tight; her face burned. She wondered if she would ever be able to look at him again without feeling that sickness, that sense of loss.

He came to the hill and began to climb toward her. She wanted to jump up and ward him off, but instead she sat silently as he came closer to her. This hill was as much his as hers; perhaps memories had drawn him here as well. The thought made her lift her head with hope.

She put up her wall cautiously. He reached her and sat down, not quite close enough to touch her. His wall was up also.

She was afraid to send out her thoughts, thinking she would drive him away, while at the same time hoping he would leave. A lock of his hair curled over his forehead, resting on his left eyebrow. Her skin tingled; her heart throbbed painfully. How could so much change, while leaving this feeling the same?

Harel's mind brushed against her and she started, jerking her head around.—Daiya—he said solemnly.

She was silent.

—What will you do—

At first she did not know what he meant. She looked out over the village, then back at him.—I'm going to live here—she found herself thinking.—I'm going to build my hut here under these trees. I'll plant a garden at the foot of the hill, and then I'll teach mindcrafts to anyone interested in learning them—

—What mindcrafts? You aren't old enough, you haven't mastered enough—

—I'll commune with the minds under the mountains. I'll learn as much from them as I can, and then I'll teach others, and we'll commune together. We'll see many truths, and try to learn how best to use the power the machines can give us—

Harel was trembling.—That vision—he thought, and she knew he meant the vision of the machines she had shown to the villagers.—It frightened me—

—You mustn't be frightened. They will only show us what we have forgotten. Even our legends were not entirely false. They showed us a part of the truth—She waved an arm.—I'll live here. You can too if you like—She made the thought casual, testing him. She let down part of her wall, knowing he could now sense her longing.

He looked down as she felt him push her suggestion aside.—I cannot, Daiya. You have become something too different. Someday I know you will look at me and feel that I would have bound you too tightly, kept you from things I think you will love more someday. I thought the ordeal would change you, make you decide to seek your dreams with us, make you more willing to become a Merging One, but I was wrong. I shall always be your friend, but I must live with the others, in the village, especially now. I must live the only way I know how to live. If things change, then they will change and I may follow, but I cannot lead—

He rose. She held out a hand to him but he retreated. He went back down the hill. A living thing struggled inside her, pushing against her muscles. It was still for a moment. She wondered when it would die. It was a little easier to watch Harel go this time, just a bit easier. The pains in her chest were not quite as bad. The thing inside her beat against her feebly, still struggling.

In the evening, the village once again lit its watchfires, so old a custom that no one could remember its original purpose. The people were stirring once again, trying to resume their disciplined lives, unable to tell if the resumption was permanent or only a brief respite before a confrontation with their new world.

Daiya, gazing down the hillside, saw two shadowy shapes draw near the hill. The two people cleared a space below, then lifted flat rocks and stones with their minds, setting them around the space. She touched their minds gently and recognized her cousin Kal and her friend Nenla. The two placed some tinder within the circle marked by the stones. The tiny pieces of wood burst into flame. They had lit a watchfire for her.

—Thank you—she thought gratefully before withdrawing. She smiled as she saw the pair throw on some kindling, then settle on a blanket, arms around each other, ready for sleep. She tried not to think about Harel.

She looked up at the sky, where the comet burned. It was another watchfire, marking a new boundary.

Slowly, she sent out her mind toward the mountain peaks below the comet. She drew on the machines for power. They hummed within her and voices whispered. The sounds soothed her. She could not make out the words. There was another mind with her. She reached out and touched Homesmind.

Her mind left her body and became a golden strand. She stood on the mountains and stretched toward black space, becoming a beam of light. The watchfires of heaven twinkled. She touched the comet.

—You are with me—she said to Homesmind.

Of course.

—Tell me what to do—

I cannot.

She shot through corridors, shimmering as she spun her way through Homesmind. Then she was in space again. The comet shrank, its tail becoming only a white scratch against the darkness. The sun became a tiny fire; the earth whirled past her. She fled from a banded globe and passed a small dark frozen world. She was lifted into darkness, borne by unseen arms.

She hovered above a starry spiral. A bright light, impossibly far away, called to her. *I am with you,* it said.

And I am with you, another light replied.

K14

And I am with you, called a silver webbing encasing a small globe.

I am with you, whispered a shell enclosing a sun.

And I am with you, said a distant starry wisp.

The voices rustled and murmured, singing with Homesmind. Her body was only a shell. She could abandon it, join these others, merge with them.

She shot toward Earth. She sped through Earth's clouds, crying out to Homesmind. She was on the hill again. She felt the bonds of her body holding her and resisted, wanting desperately to join the other minds. At last she felt their purpose, the search for consciousness in all forms, the awakening of minds everywhere.

—Let me leave here—she pleaded.

No, Homesmind said, and she knew the minds would not swallow her and strip her of herself. *Your own world calls, and you have not begun to understand it. But I shall watch over you.*

The other minds were gone. She stretched out her arms, clawing the air.

Daiya rubbed her head, then lay down, gazing up at the night sky. She would build a hut, but she would rest out here so that she could look up through the trees and see the stars. Above her, the comet shone.

A wisp touched her, a slender bond. It caught her mind and held her. It was another Net. / We are with you / said the minds under the mountains. She would not be alone.